McTeague

A Story of San Francisco

by

Frank Norris

McTeague
A Story of San Francisco
by Frank Norris

Copyright © 2024

All Rights reserved.

No part of this publication may be reproduced, stored in a retrieval system, or transmitted in any form or by any means, electronic, mechanical, photocopying or Otherwise, without the written permission of the publisher.
The author/editor asserts the moral right to be identified as the author/editor of this work.

ISBN: 978-93-63057-37-1

Published by
DOUBLE 9 BOOKS
2/13-B, Ansari Road
Daryaganj, New Delhi – 110002
info@double9books.com
www.double9books.com
Tel. 011-40042856

This book is under public domain

ABOUT THE AUTHOR

Frank Norris (1870-1902) was an American novelist and journalist known for his realistic and naturalistic writing style. He was born in Chicago, Illinois, and raised in a family with a strong literary background. Norris studied at the University of California, Berkeley, and later attended Harvard University. Norris is best remembered for his novels that depicted the social issues and struggles of his time. His most notable work is "The Octopus: A Story of California" (1901), a sprawling epic that explores the conflicts between wheat farmers and the powerful railroad monopolies in California. The novel is considered a classic of American literature and is often associated with the naturalist literary movement. Tragically, Norris's writing career was cut short when he died at the age of 32 due to complications from appendicitis. Despite his short life, he left a lasting impact on American literature, influencing later writers such as Upton Sinclair and Theodore Dreiser. His works continue to be celebrated for their realism, vivid portrayals of the human condition, and insightful social commentary.

CONTENTS

CHAPTER 1	7
CHAPTER 2	15
CHAPTER 3	27
CHAPTER 4	36
CHAPTER 5	44
CHAPTER 6	60
CHAPTER 7	74
CHAPTER 8	87
CHAPTER 9	100
CHAPTER 10	119
CHAPTER 11	137
CHAPTER 12	154
CHAPTER 13	165
CHAPTER 14	174
CHAPTER 15	183
CHAPTER 16	195
CHAPTER 17	207
CHAPTER 18	212
CHAPTER 19	225
CHAPTER 20	242
CHAPTER 21	250
CHAPTER 22	274

CHAPTER 1

It was Sunday, and, according to his custom on that day, McTeague took his dinner at two in the afternoon at the car conductors' coffee-joint on Polk Street. He had a thick gray soup; heavy, underdone meat, very hot, on a cold plate; two kinds of vegetables; and a sort of suet pudding, full of strong butter and sugar. On his way back to his office, one block above, he stopped at Joe Frenna's saloon and bought a pitcher of steam beer. It was his habit to leave the pitcher there on his way to dinner.

Once in his office, or, as he called it on his signboard, "Dental Parlors," he took off his coat and shoes, unbuttoned his vest, and, having crammed his little stove full of coke, lay back in his operating chair at the bay window, reading the paper, drinking his beer, and smoking his huge porcelain pipe while his food digested; crop-full, stupid, and warm. By and by, gorged with steam beer, and overcome by the heat of the room, the cheap tobacco, and the effects of his heavy meal, he dropped off to sleep. Late in the afternoon his canary bird, in its gilt cage just over his head, began to sing. He woke slowly, finished the rest of his beer—very flat and stale by this time—and taking down his concertina from the bookcase, where in week days it kept the company of seven volumes of "Allen's Practical Dentist," played upon it some half-dozen very mournful airs.

McTeague looked forward to these Sunday afternoons as a period of relaxation and enjoyment. He invariably spent them in the same fashion. These were his only pleasures—to eat, to smoke, to sleep, and to play upon his concertina.

The six lugubrious airs that he knew, always carried him back to the time when he was a car-boy at the Big Dipper Mine in Placer County, ten years before. He remembered the years he had spent there trundling the heavy cars of ore in and out of the tunnel under the direction of his father. For thirteen days of each fortnight his father was a steady, hard-working shift-boss of the mine. Every other Sunday he became an irresponsible animal, a beast, a brute, crazy with alcohol.

McTeague remembered his mother, too, who, with the help of the Chinaman, cooked for forty miners. She was an overworked drudge, fiery and energetic for all that, filled with the one idea of having her son rise in life and enter a profession. The chance had come at last when the father died, corroded with alcohol, collapsing in a few hours. Two or three years later a travelling dentist visited the mine and put up his tent near the bunk-house. He was more or less of a charlatan, but he fired Mrs. McTeague's ambition, and young McTeague went away with him to learn his profession. He had learnt it after a fashion, mostly by watching the charlatan operate. He had read many of the necessary books, but he was too hopelessly stupid to get much benefit from them.

Then one day at San Francisco had come the news of his mother's death; she had left him some money—not much, but enough to set him up in business; so he had cut loose from the charlatan and had opened his "Dental Parlors" on Polk Street, an "accommodation street" of small shops in the residence quarter of the town. Here he had slowly collected a clientele of butcher boys, shop girls, drug clerks, and car conductors. He made but few acquaintances. Polk Street called him the "Doctor" and spoke of his enormous strength. For McTeague was a young giant, carrying his huge shock of blond hair six feet three inches from the ground; moving his immense limbs, heavy with ropes of muscle, slowly, ponderously. His hands were enormous, red, and covered with a fell of stiff yellow hair; they were hard as wooden mallets, strong as vises, the hands of the old-time car-boy. Often he dispensed with forceps and extracted a refractory tooth with his thumb and finger. His head was square-cut, angular; the jaw salient, like that of the carnivora.

McTeague's mind was as his body, heavy, slow to act, sluggish. Yet there was nothing vicious about the man. Altogether he suggested the draught horse, immensely strong, stupid, docile, obedient.

When he opened his "Dental Parlors," he felt that his life was a success, that he could hope for nothing better. In spite of the name, there was but one room. It was a corner room on the second floor over the branch post-office, and faced the street. McTeague made it do for a bedroom as well, sleeping on the big bed-lounge against the wall opposite the window. There was a washstand behind the screen in the corner where he manufactured his moulds. In the round bay window were his operating chair, his dental engine, and the movable rack on which he laid out his instruments. Three chairs, a bargain at the second-hand store, ranged themselves against the wall with military precision underneath a steel engraving of the court of Lorenzo de' Medici, which he had bought because there were a great many figures in it for the money. Over the bed-lounge hung a rifle manufacturer's advertisement calendar which he never used. The other ornaments were a small marble-topped centre table covered with back numbers of "The

American System of Dentistry," a stone pug dog sitting before the little stove, and a thermometer. A stand of shelves occupied one corner, filled with the seven volumes of "Allen's Practical Dentist." On the top shelf McTeague kept his concertina and a bag of bird seed for the canary. The whole place exhaled a mingled odor of bedding, creosote, and ether.

But for one thing, McTeague would have been perfectly contented. Just outside his window was his signboard—a modest affair—that read: "Doctor McTeague. Dental Parlors. Gas Given"; but that was all. It was his ambition, his dream, to have projecting from that corner window a huge gilded tooth, a molar with enormous prongs, something gorgeous and attractive. He would have it some day, on that he was resolved; but as yet such a thing was far beyond his means.

When he had finished the last of his beer, McTeague slowly wiped his lips and huge yellow mustache with the side of his hand. Bull-like, he heaved himself laboriously up, and, going to the window, stood looking down into the street.

The street never failed to interest him. It was one of those cross streets peculiar to Western cities, situated in the heart of the residence quarter, but occupied by small tradespeople who lived in the rooms above their shops. There were corner drug stores with huge jars of red, yellow, and green liquids in their windows, very brave and gay; stationers' stores, where illustrated weeklies were tacked upon bulletin boards; barber shops with cigar stands in their vestibules; sad-looking plumbers' offices; cheap restaurants, in whose windows one saw piles of unopened oysters weighted down by cubes of ice, and china pigs and cows knee deep in layers of white beans. At one end of the street McTeague could see the huge power-house of the cable line. Immediately opposite him was a great market; while farther on, over the chimney stacks of the intervening houses, the glass roof of some huge public baths glittered like crystal in the afternoon sun. Underneath him the branch post-office was opening its doors, as was its custom between two and three o'clock on Sunday afternoons. An acrid odor of ink rose upward to him. Occasionally a cable car passed, trundling heavily, with a strident whirring of jostled glass windows.

On week days the street was very lively. It woke to its work about seven o'clock, at the time when the newsboys made their appearance together with the day laborers. The laborers went trudging past in a straggling file— plumbers' apprentices, their pockets stuffed with sections of lead pipe, tweezers, and pliers; carpenters, carrying nothing but their little pasteboard lunch baskets painted to imitate leather; gangs of street workers, their overalls soiled with yellow clay, their picks and long-handled shovels over their shoulders; plasterers, spotted with lime from head to foot. This little army of workers, tramping steadily in one direction, met and mingled with other toilers of a different description—conductors and "swing men" of the cable company going on duty; heavy-eyed night clerks from the drug stores on their way home to sleep; roundsmen returning to the precinct police station to make their night report, and Chinese market gardeners teetering past under their heavy baskets. The cable cars began to fill up; all along the street could be seen the shopkeepers taking down their shutters.

Between seven and eight the street breakfasted. Now and then a waiter from one of the cheap restaurants crossed from one sidewalk to the other, balancing on one palm a tray covered with a napkin. Everywhere was the smell of coffee and of frying steaks. A little later, following in the path of the day laborers, came the clerks and shop girls, dressed with a certain cheap smartness, always in a hurry, glancing apprehensively at the power-house clock. Their employers followed an hour or so later—on the cable cars for the most part whiskered gentlemen with huge stomachs, reading the morning papers with great gravity; bank cashiers and insurance clerks with flowers in their buttonholes.

At the same time the school children invaded the street, filling the air with a clamor of shrill voices, stopping at the stationers' shops, or idling a moment in the doorways of the candy stores. For over half an hour they held possession of the sidewalks, then suddenly disappeared, leaving behind one or two stragglers who hurried along with great strides of their little thin legs, very anxious and preoccupied.

Towards eleven o'clock the ladies from the great avenue a block above Polk Street made their appearance, promenading the sidewalks leisurely, deliberately. They were at their morning's marketing. They were handsome women, beautifully dressed. They knew by name their butchers and grocers and vegetable men. From his window McTeague saw them in front of the stalls, gloved and veiled and daintily shod, the subservient provision men at their elbows, scribbling hastily in the order books. They all seemed to know one another, these grand ladies from the fashionable avenue. Meetings took place here and there; a conversation was begun; others arrived; groups were formed; little impromptu receptions were held before the chopping blocks of butchers' stalls, or on the sidewalk, around boxes of berries and fruit.

From noon to evening the population of the street was of a mixed character. The street was busiest at that time; a vast and prolonged murmur arose—the mingled shuffling of feet, the rattle of wheels, the heavy trundling of cable cars. At four o'clock the school children once more swarmed the sidewalks, again disappearing with surprising suddenness. At six the great homeward march commenced; the cars were crowded, the laborers thronged the sidewalks, the newsboys chanted the evening papers. Then all at once the street fell quiet; hardly a soul was in sight; the sidewalks were deserted. It was supper hour. Evening began; and one by one a multitude of lights, from the demoniac glare of the druggists' windows to the dazzling blue whiteness of the electric globes, grew thick from street corner to street corner. Once more the street was crowded. Now there was no thought but for amusement. The cable cars were loaded with theatregoers—men in high hats and young girls in furred opera cloaks. On the sidewalks were groups and couples—the plumbers' apprentices, the girls of the ribbon counters, the little families that lived on the second stories over their shops, the dressmakers, the small doctors, the harness-makers—all the various inhabitants of the street were abroad, strolling idly from shop window to shop window, taking the air after the day's work. Groups of girls collected on the corners, talking and laughing very loud, making remarks upon the young men that passed them. The tamale men appeared. A band of Salvationists began to sing before a saloon.

Then, little by little, Polk Street dropped back to solitude. Eleven o'clock struck from the power-house clock. Lights were extinguished. At one o'clock the cable stopped, leaving an abrupt silence in the air. All at once it seemed very still. The ugly noises were the occasional footfalls of a policeman and the persistent calling of ducks and geese in the closed market. The street was asleep.

Day after day, McTeague saw the same panorama unroll itself. The bay window of his "Dental Parlors" was for him a point of vantage from which he watched the world go past.

On Sundays, however, all was changed. As he stood in the bay window, after finishing his beer, wiping his lips, and looking out into the street, McTeague was conscious of the difference. Nearly all the stores were closed. No wagons passed. A few people hurried up and down the sidewalks, dressed in cheap Sunday finery. A cable car went by; on the outside seats were a party of returning picnickers. The mother, the father, a young man, and a young girl, and three children. The two older people held empty lunch baskets in their laps, while the bands of the children's hats were stuck full of oak leaves. The girl carried a huge bunch of wilting poppies and wild flowers.

As the car approached McTeague's window the young man got up and swung himself off the platform, waving goodby to the party. Suddenly McTeague recognized him.

"There's Marcus Schouler," he muttered behind his mustache.

Marcus Schouler was the dentist's one intimate friend. The acquaintance had begun at the car conductors' coffee-joint, where the two occupied the same table and met at every meal. Then they made the discovery that they both lived in the same flat, Marcus occupying a room on the floor above McTeague. On different occasions McTeague had treated Marcus for an ulcerated tooth and had refused to accept payment. Soon it came to be an understood thing between them. They were "pals."

McTeague, listening, heard Marcus go up-stairs to his room above. In a few minutes his door opened again. McTeague knew that he had come out into the hall and was leaning over the banisters.

"Oh, Mac!" he called. McTeague came to his door.

"Hullo! 'sthat you, Mark?"

"Sure," answered Marcus. "Come on up."

"You come on down."

"No, come on up."

"Oh, you come on down."

"Oh, you lazy duck!" retorted Marcus, coming down the stairs.

"Been out to the Cliff House on a picnic," he explained as he sat down on the bed-lounge, "with my uncle and his people—the Sieppes, you know. By damn! it was hot," he suddenly vociferated. "Just look at that! Just look at that!" he cried, dragging at his limp collar. "That's the third one since morning; it is—it is, for a fact—and you got your stove going." He began to tell about the picnic, talking very loud and fast, gesturing furiously, very excited over trivial details. Marcus could not talk without getting excited.

"You ought t'have seen, y'ought t'have seen. I tell you, it was outa sight. It was; it was, for a fact."

"Yes, yes," answered McTeague, bewildered, trying to follow. "Yes, that's so."

In recounting a certain dispute with an awkward bicyclist, in which it appeared he had become involved, Marcus quivered with rage. "'Say that again,' says I to um. 'Just say that once more, and'"—here a rolling explosion of oaths—"'you'll go back to the city in the Morgue wagon. Ain't I got a right to cross a street even, I'd like to know, without being run down—what?' I say it's outrageous. I'd a knifed him in another minute. It was an outrage. I say it was an OUTRAGE."

"Sure it was," McTeague hastened to reply. "Sure, sure."

"Oh, and we had an accident," shouted the other, suddenly off on another tack. "It was awful. Trina was in the swing there—that's my cousin Trina, you know who I mean—and she fell out. By damn! I thought she'd killed herself; struck her face on a rock and knocked out a front tooth. It's a wonder she didn't kill herself. It IS a wonder; it is, for a fact. Ain't it, now? Huh? Ain't it? Y'ought t'have seen."

McTeague had a vague idea that Marcus Schouler was stuck on his cousin Trina. They "kept company" a good deal; Marcus took dinner with the Sieppes every Saturday evening at their home at B Street station, across the bay, and Sunday afternoons he and the family usually made little excursions into the suburbs. McTeague began to wonder dimly how it was that on this occasion Marcus had not gone home with his cousin. As sometimes happens, Marcus furnished the explanation upon the instant.

"I promised a duck up here on the avenue I'd call for his dog at four this afternoon."

Marcus was Old Grannis's assistant in a little dog hospital that the latter had opened in a sort of alley just off Polk Street, some four blocks above Old Grannis lived in one of the back rooms of McTeague's flat. He was an Englishman and an expert dog surgeon, but Marcus Schouler was a bungler in the profession. His father had been a veterinary surgeon who had kept a livery stable near by, on California Street, and Marcus's knowledge of the diseases of domestic animals had been picked up in a haphazard way, much after the manner of McTeague's education. Somehow he managed to impress Old Grannis, a gentle, simple-minded old man, with a sense of his fitness, bewildering him with a torrent of empty phrases that he delivered with fierce gestures and with a manner of the greatest conviction.

"You'd better come along with me, Mac," observed Marcus. "We'll get the duck's dog, and then we'll take a little walk, huh? You got nothun to do. Come along."

McTeague went out with him, and the two friends proceeded up to the avenue to the house where the dog was to be found. It was a huge mansion-like place, set in an enormous garden that occupied a whole third of the block; and while Marcus tramped up the front steps and rang the doorbell boldly, to show his independence, McTeague remained below on the sidewalk, gazing stupidly at the curtained windows, the marble steps, and the bronze griffins, troubled and a little confused by all this massive luxury.

After they had taken the dog to the hospital and had left him to whimper behind the wire netting, they returned to Polk Street and had a glass of beer in the back room of Joe Frenna's corner grocery.

Ever since they had left the huge mansion on the avenue, Marcus had been attacking the capitalists, a class which he pretended to execrate. It was a pose which he often assumed, certain of impressing the dentist. Marcus had picked up a few half-truths of political economy—it was impossible to say where—and as soon as the two had settled themselves to their beer in Frenna's back room he took up the theme of the labor question. He discussed it at the top of his voice, vociferating, shaking his fists, exciting himself with his own noise. He was continually making use of the stock phrases of the professional politician—phrases he had caught at some of the ward "rallies" and "ratification meetings." These rolled off his tongue with incredible emphasis, appearing at every turn of his conversation—"Outraged constituencies," "cause of labor," "wage earners," "opinions biased by personal interests," "eyes blinded by party prejudice." McTeague listened to him, awestruck.

"There's where the evil lies," Marcus would cry. "The masses must learn self-control; it stands to reason. Look at the figures, look at the figures. Decrease the number of wage earners and you increase wages, don't you? don't you?"

Absolutely stupid, and understanding never a word, McTeague would answer:

"Yes, yes, that's it—self-control—that's the word."

"It's the capitalists that's ruining the cause of labor," shouted Marcus, banging the table with his fist till the beer glasses danced; "white-livered drones, traitors, with their livers white as snow, eatun the bread of widows and orphuns; there's where the evil lies."

Stupefied with his clamor, McTeague answered, wagging his head:

"Yes, that's it; I think it's their livers."

Suddenly Marcus fell calm again, forgetting his pose all in an instant.

"Say, Mac, I told my cousin Trina to come round and see you about that tooth of her's. She'll be in to-morrow, I guess."

CHAPTER 2

After his breakfast the following Monday morning, McTeague looked over the appointments he had written down in the book-slate that hung against the screen. His writing was immense, very clumsy, and very round, with huge, full-bellied l's and h's. He saw that he had made an appointment at one o'clock for Miss Baker, the retired dressmaker, a little old maid who had a tiny room a few doors down the hall. It adjoined that of Old Grannis.

Quite an affair had arisen from this circumstance. Miss Baker and Old Grannis were both over sixty, and yet it was current talk amongst the lodgers of the flat that the two were in love with each other. Singularly enough, they were not even acquaintances; never a word had passed between them. At intervals they met on the stairway; he on his way to his little dog hospital, she returning from a bit of marketing in the street. At such times they passed each other with averted eyes, pretending a certain preoccupation, suddenly seized with a great embarrassment, the timidity of a second childhood. He went on about his business, disturbed and thoughtful. She hurried up to her tiny room, her curious little false curls shaking with her agitation, the faintest suggestion of a flush coming and going in her withered cheeks. The emotion of one of these chance meetings remained with them during all the rest of the day.

Was it the first romance in the lives of each? Did Old Grannis ever remember a certain face amongst those that he had known when he was young Grannis—the face of some pale-haired girl, such as one sees in the old cathedral towns of England? Did Miss Baker still treasure up in a seldom opened drawer or box some faded daguerreotype, some strange old-fashioned likeness, with its curling hair and high stock? It was impossible to say.

Maria Macapa, the Mexican woman who took care of the lodgers' rooms, had been the first to call the flat's attention to the affair, spreading the news of it from room to room, from floor to floor. Of late she had made a great discovery; all the women folk of the flat were yet vibrant with it. Old Grannis came home from his work at four o'clock, and between that time and six Miss Baker would sit in her room, her hands idle in her lap, doing nothing, listening, waiting. Old Grannis did the same, drawing his armchair near to the wall, knowing that Miss Baker was upon the other side, conscious, perhaps, that she was thinking of him; and there the two would sit through the hours of the afternoon, listening and waiting, they did not know exactly for what, but near to each other, separated only by the thin partition of their rooms. They had come to know each other's habits. Old Grannis knew that at quarter of five precisely Miss Baker made a cup of tea over the oil stove on the stand between the bureau and the window. Miss Baker felt instinctively the exact moment when Old Grannis took down his little binding apparatus from the second shelf of his clothes closet and began his favorite occupation of binding pamphlets—pamphlets that he never read, for all that.

In his "Parlors" McTeague began his week's work. He glanced in the glass saucer in which he kept his sponge-gold, and noticing that he had used up all his pellets, set about making some more. In examining Miss Baker's teeth at the preliminary sitting he had found a cavity in one of the incisors. Miss Baker had decided to have it filled with gold. McTeague remembered now that it was what is called a "proximate case," where there is not sufficient room to fill with large pieces of gold. He told himself that he should have to use "mats" in the filling. He made some dozen of these "mats" from his tape of non-cohesive gold, cutting it transversely into small pieces that could be inserted edgewise between the teeth and consolidated by packing. After he had made his "mats" he continued with the other kind of gold fillings, such as he would have occasion to use during the week; "blocks" to be used in large proximal cavities, made by folding the tape on itself a number of times and then shaping it with the soldering pliers; "cylinders" for commencing fillings, which he formed by rolling the tape around a needle called a "broach," cutting it afterwards into different lengths. He worked slowly, mechanically, turning the foil between his fingers with the manual dexterity that one sometimes sees in stupid persons. His head was quite empty of all thought, and he did not whistle over his work as another man might have done. The canary made up for his silence, trilling and chittering continually, splashing about in its morning bath, keeping up an incessant noise and movement that would have been maddening to any one but McTeague, who seemed to have no nerves at all.

After he had finished his fillings, he made a hook broach from a bit of piano wire to replace an old one that he had lost. It was time for his dinner then, and when he returned from the car conductors' coffee-joint, he found Miss Baker waiting for him.

The ancient little dressmaker was at all times willing to talk of Old Grannis to anybody that would listen, quite unconscious of the gossip of the flat. McTeague found her all a-flutter with excitement. Something extraordinary had happened. She had found out that the wall-paper in Old Grannis's room was the same as that in hers.

"It has led me to thinking, Doctor McTeague," she exclaimed, shaking her little false curls at him. "You know my room is so small, anyhow, and the wall-paper being the same—the pattern from my room continues right into his—I declare, I believe at one time that was all one room. Think of it, do you suppose it was? It almost amounts to our occupying the same room. I don't know—why, really—do you think I should speak to the landlady about it? He bound pamphlets last night until half-past nine. They say that he's the younger son of a baronet; that there are reasons for his not coming to the title; his stepfather wronged him cruelly."

No one had ever said such a thing. It was preposterous to imagine any mystery connected with Old Grannis. Miss Baker had chosen to invent the little fiction, had created the title and the unjust stepfather from some dim memories of the novels of her girlhood.

She took her place in the operating chair. McTeague began the filling. There was a long silence. It was impossible for McTeague to work and talk at the same time.

He was just burnishing the last "mat" in Miss Baker's tooth, when the door of the "Parlors" opened, jangling the bell which he had hung over it, and which was absolutely unnecessary. McTeague turned, one foot on the pedal of his dental engine, the corundum disk whirling between his fingers.

It was Marcus Schouler who came in, ushering a young girl of about twenty.

"Hello, Mac," exclaimed Marcus; "busy? Brought my cousin round about that broken tooth."

McTeague nodded his head gravely.

"In a minute," he answered.

Marcus and his cousin Trina sat down in the rigid chairs underneath the steel engraving of the Court of Lorenzo de' Medici. They began talking in low tones. The girl looked about the room, noticing the stone pug dog, the rifle manufacturer's calendar, the canary in its little gilt prison, and the tumbled blankets on the unmade bed-lounge against the wall. Marcus began telling her about McTeague. "We're pals," he explained, just above a whisper. "Ah, Mac's all right, you bet. Say, Trina, he's the strongest duck you ever saw. What do you suppose? He can pull out your teeth with his fingers; yes, he can. What do you think of that? With his fingers, mind you; he can, for a fact. Get on to the size of him, anyhow. Ah, Mac's all right!"

Maria Macapa had come into the room while he had been speaking. She was making up McTeague's bed. Suddenly Marcus exclaimed under his breath: "Now we'll have some fun. It's the girl that takes care of the rooms. She's a greaser, and she's queer in the head. She ain't regularly crazy, but I don't know, she's queer. Y'ought to hear her go on about a gold dinner service she says her folks used to own. Ask her what her name is and see what she'll say." Trina shrank back, a little frightened.

"No, you ask," she whispered.

"Ah, go on; what you 'fraid of?" urged Marcus. Trina shook her head energetically, shutting her lips together.

"Well, listen here," answered Marcus, nudging her; then raising his voice, he said:

"How do, Maria?" Maria nodded to him over her shoulder as she bent over the lounge.

"Workun hard nowadays, Maria?"

"Pretty hard."

"Didunt always have to work for your living, though, did you, when you ate offa gold dishes?" Maria didn't answer, except by putting her chin in the air and shutting her eyes, as though to say she knew a long story about that if she had a mind to talk. All Marcus's efforts to draw her out on the subject were unavailing. She only responded by movements of her head.

"Can't always start her going," Marcus told his cousin.

"What does she do, though, when you ask her about her name?"

"Oh, sure," said Marcus, who had forgotten. "Say, Maria, what's your name?"

"Huh?" asked Maria, straightening up, her hands on he hips.

"Tell us your name," repeated Marcus.

"Name is Maria—Miranda—Macapa." Then, after a pause, she added, as though she had but that moment thought of it, "Had a flying squirrel an' let him go."

Invariably Maria Macapa made this answer. It was not always she would talk about the famous service of gold plate, but a question as to her name never failed to elicit the same strange answer, delivered in a rapid undertone: "Name is Maria—Miranda—Macapa." Then, as if struck with an after thought, "Had a flying squirrel an' let him go."

Why Maria should associate the release of the mythical squirrel with her name could not be said. About Maria the flat knew absolutely nothing further than that she was Spanish-American. Miss Baker was the oldest lodger in the flat, and Maria was a fixture there as maid of all work when she had come. There was a legend to the effect that Maria's people had been at one time immensely wealthy in Central America.

Maria turned again to her work. Trina and Marcus watched her curiously. There was a silence. The corundum burr in McTeague's engine hummed in a prolonged monotone. The canary bird chittered occasionally. The room was warm, and the breathing of the five people in the narrow space made the air close and thick. At long intervals an acrid odor of ink floated up from the branch post-office immediately below.

Maria Macapa finished her work and started to leave. As she passed near Marcus and his cousin she stopped, and drew a bunch of blue tickets furtively from her pocket. "Buy a ticket in the lottery?" she inquired, looking at the girl. "Just a dollar."

"Go along with you, Maria," said Marcus, who had but thirty cents in his pocket. "Go along; it's against the law."

"Buy a ticket," urged Maria, thrusting the bundle toward Trina. "Try your luck. The butcher on the next block won twenty dollars the last drawing."

Very uneasy, Trina bought a ticket for the sake of being rid of her. Maria disappeared.

"Ain't she a queer bird?" muttered Marcus. He was much embarrassed and disturbed because he had not bought the ticket for Trina.

But there was a sudden movement. McTeague had just finished with Miss Baker.

"You should notice," the dressmaker said to the dentist, in a low voice, "he always leaves the door a little ajar in the afternoon." When she had gone out, Marcus Schouler brought Trina forward.

"Say, Mac, this is my cousin, Trina Sieppe." The two shook hands dumbly, McTeague slowly nodding his huge head with its great shock of yellow hair. Trina was very small and prettily made. Her face was round and rather pale; her eyes long and narrow and blue, like the half-open eyes of a little baby; her lips and the lobes of her tiny ears were pale, a little suggestive of anaemia; while across the bridge of her nose ran an adorable little line of freckles. But it was to her hair that one's attention was most attracted. Heaps and heaps of blue-black coils and braids, a royal crown of swarthy bands, a veritable sable tiara, heavy, abundant, odorous. All the vitality that should have given color to her face seemed to have been absorbed by this marvellous hair. It was the coiffure of a queen that shadowed the pale temples of this little bourgeoise. So heavy was it that it tipped her head backward, and the position thrust her chin out a little. It was a charming poise, innocent, confiding, almost infantile.

She was dressed all in black, very modest and plain. The effect of her pale face in all this contrasting black was almost monastic.

"Well," exclaimed Marcus suddenly, "I got to go. Must get back to work. Don't hurt her too much, Mac. S'long, Trina."

McTeague and Trina were left alone. He was embarrassed, troubled. These young girls disturbed and perplexed him. He did not like them, obstinately cherishing that intuitive suspicion of all things feminine—the perverse dislike of an overgrown boy. On the other hand, she was perfectly at her ease; doubtless the woman in her was not yet awakened; she was yet, as one might say, without sex. She was almost like a boy, frank, candid, unreserved.

She took her place in the operating chair and told him what was the matter, looking squarely into his face. She had fallen out of a swing the afternoon of the preceding day; one of her teeth had been knocked loose and the other altogether broken out.

McTeague listened to her with apparent stolidity, nodding his head from time to time as she spoke. The keenness of his dislike of her as a woman began to be blunted. He thought she was rather pretty, that he even liked her because she was so small, so prettily made, so good natured and straightforward.

"Let's have a look at your teeth," he said, picking up his mirror. "You better take your hat off." She leaned back in her chair and opened her mouth, showing the rows of little round teeth, as white and even as the kernels on an ear of green corn, except where an ugly gap came at the side.

McTeague put the mirror into her mouth, touching one and another of her teeth with the handle of an excavator. By and by he straightened up, wiping the moisture from the mirror on his coat-sleeve.

"Well, Doctor," said the girl, anxiously, "it's a dreadful disfigurement, isn't it?" adding, "What can you do about it?"

"Well," answered McTeague, slowly, looking vaguely about on the floor of the room, "the roots of the broken tooth are still in the gum; they'll have to come out, and I guess I'll have to pull that other bicuspid. Let me look again. Yes," he went on in a moment, peering into her mouth with the mirror, "I guess that'll have to come out, too." The tooth was loose, discolored, and evidently dead. "It's a curious case," McTeague went on. "I don't know as I ever had a tooth like that before. It's what's called necrosis. It don't often happen. It'll have to come out sure."

Then a discussion was opened on the subject, Trina sitting up in the chair, holding her hat in her lap; McTeague leaning against the window frame his hands in his pockets, his eyes wandering about on the floor. Trina did not want the other tooth removed; one hole like that was bad enough; but two—ah, no, it was not to be thought of.

But McTeague reasoned with her, tried in vain to make her understand that there was no vascular connection between the root and the gum. Trina was blindly persistent, with the persistency of a girl who has made up her mind.

McTeague began to like her better and better, and after a while commenced himself to feel that it would be a pity to disfigure such a pretty mouth. He became interested; perhaps he could do something, something in the way of a crown or bridge. "Let's look at that again," he said, picking up his mirror. He began to study the situation very carefully, really desiring to remedy the blemish.

It was the first bicuspid that was missing, and though part of the root of the second (the loose one) would remain after its extraction, he was sure it would not be strong enough to sustain a crown. All at once he grew obstinate, resolving, with all the strength of a crude and primitive man, to conquer the difficulty in spite of everything. He turned over in his mind the technicalities of the case. No, evidently the root was not strong enough to sustain a crown; besides that, it was placed a little irregularly in the arch. But, fortunately, there were cavities in the two teeth on either side of the gap—one in the first molar and one in the palatine surface of the cuspid; might he not drill a socket in the remaining root and sockets in the molar and cuspid, and, partly by bridging, partly by crowning, fill in the gap? He made up his mind to do it.

Why he should pledge himself to this hazardous case McTeague was puzzled to know. With most of his clients he would have contented himself with the extraction of the loose tooth and the roots of the broken one. Why should he risk his reputation in this case? He could not say why.

It was the most difficult operation he had ever performed. He bungled it considerably, but in the end he succeeded passably well. He extracted the loose tooth with his bayonet forceps and prepared the roots of the broken one as if for filling, fitting into them a flattened piece of platinum wire to serve as a dowel. But this was only the beginning; altogether it was a fortnight's work. Trina came nearly every other day, and passed two, and even three, hours in the chair.

By degrees McTeague's first awkwardness and suspicion vanished entirely. The two became good friends. McTeague even arrived at that point where he could work and talk to her at the same time—a thing that had never before been possible for him.

Never until then had McTeague become so well acquainted with a girl of Trina's age. The younger women of Polk Street—the shop girls, the young women of the soda fountains, the waitresses in the cheap restaurants—preferred another dentist, a young fellow just graduated from the college, a poser, a rider of bicycles, a man about town, who wore astonishing waistcoats and bet money on greyhound coursing. Trina was McTeague's first experience. With her the feminine element suddenly entered his little world. It was not only her that he saw and felt, it was the woman, the whole sex, an entire new humanity, strange and alluring, that he seemed to have discovered. How had he ignored it so long? It was dazzling, delicious, charming beyond all words. His narrow point of view was at once enlarged and confused, and all at once he saw that there was something else in life besides concertinas and steam beer. Everything had to be made over again. His whole rude idea of life had to be changed. The male virile desire in him tardily awakened, aroused itself, strong and brutal. It was resistless, untrained, a thing not to be held in leash an instant.

Little by little, by gradual, almost imperceptible degrees, the thought of Trina Sieppe occupied his mind from day to day, from hour to hour. He found himself thinking of her constantly; at every instant he saw her round, pale face; her narrow, milk-blue eyes; her little out-thrust chin; her heavy, huge tiara of black hair. At night he lay awake for hours under the thick blankets of the bed-lounge, staring upward into the darkness, tormented with the idea of her, exasperated at the delicate, subtle mesh in which he found himself entangled. During the forenoons, while he went about his work, he thought of her. As he made his plaster-of-paris moulds at the washstand in the corner behind the screen he turned over in his mind all that had happened, all that had been said at the previous sitting. Her little tooth that he had extracted he kept wrapped in a bit of newspaper in his vest pocket. Often he took it out and held it in the palm of his immense, horny hand, seized with some strange elephantine sentiment, wagging his head at it, heaving tremendous sighs. What a folly!

At two o'clock on Tuesdays, Thursdays, and Saturdays Trina arrived and took her place in the operating chair. While at his work McTeague was every minute obliged to bend closely over her; his hands touched her face, her cheeks, her adorable little chin; her lips pressed against his fingers. She breathed warmly on his forehead and on his eyelids, while the odor of her hair, a charming feminine perfume, sweet, heavy, enervating, came to his nostrils, so penetrating, so delicious, that his flesh pricked and tingled with it; a veritable sensation of faintness passed over this huge, callous fellow, with his enormous bones and corded muscles. He drew a short breath through his nose; his jaws suddenly gripped together vise-like.

But this was only at times—a strange, vexing spasm, that subsided almost immediately. For the most part, McTeague enjoyed the pleasure of these sittings with Trina with a certain strong calmness, blindly happy that she was there. This poor crude dentist of Polk Street, stupid, ignorant, vulgar, with his sham education and plebeian tastes, whose only relaxations were to eat, to drink steam beer, and to play upon his concertina, was living through his first romance, his first idyl. It was delightful. The long hours he passed alone with Trina in the "Dental Parlors," silent, only for the scraping of the instruments and the pouring of bud-burrs in the engine, in the foul atmosphere, overheated by the little stove and heavy with the smell of ether, creosote, and stale bedding, had all the charm of secret appointments and stolen meetings under the moon.

By degrees the operation progressed. One day, just after McTeague had put in the temporary gutta-percha fillings and nothing more could be done at that sitting, Trina asked him to examine the rest of her teeth. They were perfect, with one exception—a spot of white caries on the lateral surface of an incisor. McTeague filled it with gold, enlarging the cavity with hard-bits and hoe-excavators, and burring in afterward with half-cone burrs. The cavity was deep, and Trina began to wince and moan. To hurt Trina was a positive anguish for McTeague, yet an anguish which he was obliged to endure at every hour of the sitting. It was harrowing—he sweated under it—to be forced to torture her, of all women in the world; could anything be worse than that?

"Hurt?" he inquired, anxiously.

She answered by frowning, with a sharp intake of breath, putting her fingers over her closed lips and nodding her head. McTeague sprayed the tooth with glycerite of tannin, but without effect. Rather than hurt her he found himself forced to the use of anaesthesia, which he hated. He had a notion that the nitrous oxide gas was dangerous, so on this occasion, as on all others, used ether.

He put the sponge a half dozen times to Trina's face, more nervous than he had ever been before, watching the symptoms closely. Her breathing became short and irregular; there was a slight twitching of the muscles. When her thumbs turned inward toward the palms, he took the sponge away. She passed off very quickly, and, with a long sigh, sank back into the chair.

McTeague straightened up, putting the sponge upon the rack behind him, his eyes fixed upon Trina's face. For some time he stood watching her as she lay there, unconscious and helpless, and very pretty. He was alone with her, and she was absolutely without defense.

Suddenly the animal in the man stirred and woke; the evil instincts that in him were so close to the surface leaped to life, shouting and clamoring.

It was a crisis—a crisis that had arisen all in an instant; a crisis for which he was totally unprepared. Blindly, and without knowing why, McTeague fought against it, moved by an unreasoned instinct of resistance. Within him, a certain second self, another better McTeague rose with the brute; both were strong, with the huge crude strength of the man himself. The two were at grapples. There in that cheap and shabby "Dental Parlor" a dreaded struggle began. It was the old battle, old as the world, wide as the world—the sudden panther leap of the animal, lips drawn, fangs aflash, hideous, monstrous, not to be resisted, and the simultaneous arousing of the other man, the better self that cries, "Down, down," without knowing why; that grips the monster; that fights to strangle it, to thrust it down and back.

Dizzied and bewildered with the shock, the like of which he had never known before, McTeague turned from Trina, gazing bewilderedly about the room. The struggle was bitter; his teeth ground themselves together with a little rasping sound; the blood sang in his ears; his face flushed scarlet; his hands twisted themselves together like the knotting of cables. The fury in him was as the fury of a young bull in the heat of high summer. But for all that he shook his huge head from time to time, muttering:

"No, by God! No, by God!"

Dimly he seemed to realize that should he yield now he would never be able to care for Trina again. She would never be the same to him, never so radiant, so sweet, so adorable; her charm for him would vanish in an instant. Across her forehead, her little pale forehead, under the shadow of her royal hair, he would surely see the smudge of a foul ordure, the footprint of the monster. It would be a sacrilege, an abomination. He recoiled from it, banding all his strength to the issue.

"No, by God! No, by God!"

He turned to his work, as if seeking a refuge in it. But as he drew near to her again, the charm of her innocence and helplessness came over him afresh. It was a final protest against his resolution. Suddenly he leaned over and kissed her, grossly, full on the mouth. The thing was done before he knew it. Terrified at his weakness at the very moment he believed himself strong, he threw himself once more into his work with desperate energy. By the time he was fastening the sheet of rubber upon the tooth, he had himself once more in hand. He was disturbed, still trembling, still vibrating with the throes of the crisis, but he was the master; the animal was downed, was cowed for this time, at least.

But for all that, the brute was there. Long dormant, it was now at last alive, awake. From now on he would feel its presence continually; would feel it tugging at its chain, watching its opportunity. Ah, the pity of it! Why could he not always love her purely, cleanly? What was this perverse, vicious thing that lived within him, knitted to his flesh?

Below the fine fabric of all that was good in him ran the foul stream of hereditary evil, like a sewer. The vices and sins of his father and of his father's father, to the third and fourth and five hundredth generation, tainted him. The evil of an entire race flowed in his veins. Why should it be? He did not desire it. Was he to blame?

But McTeague could not understand this thing. It had faced him, as sooner or later it faces every child of man; but its significance was not for him. To reason with it was beyond him. He could only oppose to it an instinctive stubborn resistance, blind, inert.

McTeague went on with his work. As he was rapping in the little blocks and cylinders with the mallet, Trina slowly came back to herself with a long sigh. She still felt a little confused, and lay quiet in the chair. There was a long silence, broken only by the uneven tapping of the hardwood mallet. By and by she said, "I never felt a thing," and then she smiled at him very prettily beneath the rubber dam. McTeague turned to her suddenly, his mallet in one hand, his pliers holding a pellet of sponge-gold in the other. All at once he said, with the unreasoned simplicity and directness of a child: "Listen here, Miss Trina, I like you better than any one else; what's the matter with us getting married?"

Trina sat up in the chair quickly, and then drew back from him, frightened and bewildered.

"Will you? Will you?" said McTeague. "Say, Miss Trina, will you?"

"What is it? What do you mean?" she cried, confusedly, her words muffled beneath the rubber.

"Will you?" repeated McTeague.

"No, no," she exclaimed, refusing without knowing why, suddenly seized with a fear of him, the intuitive feminine fear of the male. McTeague could only repeat the same thing over and over again. Trina, more and more frightened at his huge hands—the hands of the old-time car-boy—his immense square-cut head and his enormous brute strength, cried out: "No, no," behind the rubber dam, shaking her head violently, holding out her hands, and shrinking down before him in the operating chair. McTeague came nearer to her, repeating the same question. "No, no," she cried, terrified. Then, as she exclaimed, "Oh, I am sick," was suddenly taken with a fit of vomiting. It was the not unusual after effect of the ether, aided now by her excitement and nervousness. McTeague was checked. He poured some bromide of potassium into a graduated glass and held it to her lips.

"Here, swallow this," he said.

CHAPTER 3

Once every two months Maria Macapa set the entire flat in commotion. She roamed the building from garret to cellar, searching each corner, ferreting through every old box and trunk and barrel, groping about on the top shelves of closets, peering into rag-bags, exasperating the lodgers with her persistence and importunity. She was collecting junks, bits of iron, stone jugs, glass bottles, old sacks, and cast-off garments. It was one of her perquisites. She sold the junk to Zerkow, the rags-bottles-sacks man, who lived in a filthy den in the alley just back of the flat, and who sometimes paid her as much as three cents a pound. The stone jugs, however, were worth a nickel. The money that Zerkow paid her, Maria spent on shirt waists and dotted blue neckties, trying to dress like the girls who tended the soda-water fountain in the candy store on the corner. She was sick with envy of these young women. They were in the world, they were elegant, they were debonair, they had their "young men."

On this occasion she presented herself at the door of Old Grannis's room late in the afternoon. His door stood a little open. That of Miss Baker was ajar a few inches. The two old people were "keeping company" after their fashion.

"Got any junk, Mister Grannis?" inquired Maria, standing in the door, a very dirty, half-filled pillowcase over one arm.

"No, nothing—nothing that I can think of, Maria," replied Old Grannis, terribly vexed at the interruption, yet not wishing to be unkind. "Nothing I think of. Yet, however—perhaps—if you wish to look."

He sat in the middle of the room before a small pine table. His little binding apparatus was before him. In his fingers was a huge upholsterer's needle threaded with twine, a brad-awl lay at his elbow, on the floor beside him was a great pile of pamphlets, the pages uncut. Old Grannis bought the "Nation" and the "Breeder and Sportsman." In the latter he occasionally found articles on dogs which interested him. The former he seldom read. He could not afford to subscribe regularly to either of the publications, but purchased their back numbers by the score, almost solely for the pleasure he took in binding them.

"What you alus sewing up them books for, Mister Grannis?" asked Maria, as she began rummaging about in Old Grannis's closet shelves. "There's just hundreds of 'em in here on yer shelves; they ain't no good to you."

"Well, well," answered Old Grannis, timidly, rubbing his chin, "I—I'm sure I can't quite say; a little habit, you know; a diversion, a—a—it occupies one, you know. I don't smoke; it takes the place of a pipe, perhaps."

"Here's this old yellow pitcher," said Maria, coming out of the closet with it in her hand. "The handle's cracked; you don't want it; better give me it."

Old Grannis did want the pitcher; true, he never used it now, but he had kept it a long time, and somehow he held to it as old people hold to trivial, worthless things that they have had for many years.

"Oh, that pitcher—well, Maria, I—I don't know. I'm afraid—you see, that pitcher——"

"Ah, go 'long," interrupted Maria Macapa, "what's the good of it?"

"If you insist, Maria, but I would much rather—" he rubbed his chin, perplexed and annoyed, hating to refuse, and wishing that Maria were gone.

"Why, what's the good of it?" persisted Maria. He could give no sufficient answer. "That's all right," she asserted, carrying the pitcher out.

"Ah—Maria—I say, you—you might leave the door—ah, don't quite shut it—it's a bit close in here at times." Maria grinned, and swung the door wide. Old Grannis was horribly embarrassed; positively, Maria was becoming unbearable.

"Got any junk?" cried Maria at Miss Baker's door. The little old lady was sitting close to the wall in her rocking-chair; her hands resting idly in her lap.

"Now, Maria," she said plaintively, "you are always after junk; you know I never have anything laying 'round like that."

It was true. The retired dressmaker's tiny room was a marvel of neatness, from the little red table, with its three Gorham spoons laid in exact parallels, to the decorous geraniums and mignonettes growing in the starch box at the window, underneath the fish globe with its one venerable gold fish. That day Miss Baker had been doing a bit of washing; two pocket handkerchiefs, still moist, adhered to the window panes, drying in the sun.

"Oh, I guess you got something you don't want," Maria went on, peering into the corners of the room. "Look-a-here what Mister Grannis gi' me," and she held out the yellow pitcher. Instantly Miss Baker was in a quiver of confusion. Every word spoken aloud could be perfectly heard in the next room. What a stupid drab was this Maria! Could anything be more trying than this position?

"Ain't that right, Mister Grannis?" called Maria; "didn't you gi' me this pitcher?" Old Grannis affected not to hear; perspiration stood on his forehead; his timidity overcame him as if he were a ten-year-old schoolboy. He half rose from his chair, his fingers dancing nervously upon his chin.

Maria opened Miss Baker's closet unconcernedly. "What's the matter with these old shoes?" she exclaimed, turning about with a pair of half-worn silk gaiters in her hand. They were by no means old enough to throw away, but Miss Baker was almost beside herself. There was no telling what might happen next. Her only thought was to be rid of Maria.

"Yes, yes, anything. You can have them; but go, go. There's nothing else, not a thing."

Maria went out into the hall, leaving Miss Baker's door wide open, as if maliciously. She had left the dirty pillow-case on the floor in the hall, and she stood outside, between the two open doors, stowing away the old pitcher and the half-worn silk shoes. She made remarks at the top of her voice, calling now to Miss Baker, now to Old Grannis. In a way she brought the two old people face to face. Each time they were forced to answer her questions it was as if they were talking directly to each other.

"These here are first-rate shoes, Miss Baker. Look here, Mister Grannis, get on to the shoes Miss Baker gi' me. You ain't got a pair you don't want, have you? You two people have less junk than any one else in the flat. How do you manage, Mister Grannis? You old bachelors are just like old maids, just as neat as pins. You two are just alike—you and Mister Grannis—ain't you, Miss Baker?"

Nothing could have been more horribly constrained, more awkward. The two old people suffered veritable torture. When Maria had gone, each heaved a sigh of unspeakable relief. Softly they pushed to their doors, leaving open a space of half a dozen inches. Old Grannis went back to his binding. Miss Baker brewed a cup of tea to quiet her nerves. Each tried to regain their composure, but in vain. Old Grannis's fingers trembled so that he pricked them with his needle. Miss Baker dropped her spoon twice. Their nervousness would not wear off. They were perturbed, upset. In a word, the afternoon was spoiled.

Maria went on about the flat from room to room. She had already paid Marcus Schouler a visit early that morning before he had gone out. Marcus had sworn at her, excitedly vociferating; "No, by damn! No, he hadn't a thing for her; he hadn't, for a fact. It was a positive persecution. Every day his privacy was invaded. He would complain to the landlady, he would. He'd move out of the place." In the end he had given Maria seven empty whiskey flasks, an iron grate, and ten cents—the latter because he said she wore her hair like a girl he used to know.

After coming from Miss Baker's room Maria knocked at McTeague's door. The dentist was lying on the bed-lounge in his stocking feet, doing nothing apparently, gazing up at the ceiling, lost in thought.

Since he had spoken to Trina Sieppe, asking her so abruptly to marry him, McTeague had passed a week of torment. For him there was no going back. It was Trina now, and none other. It was all one with him that his best friend, Marcus, might be in love with the same girl. He must have Trina in spite of everything; he would have her even in spite of herself. He did not stop to reflect about the matter; he followed his desire blindly, recklessly, furious and raging at every obstacle. And she had cried "No, no!" back at him; he could not forget that. She, so small and pale and delicate, had held him at bay, who was so huge, so immensely strong.

Besides that, all the charm of their intimacy was gone. After that unhappy sitting, Trina was no longer frank and straight-forward. Now she was circumspect, reserved, distant. He could no longer open his mouth; words failed him. At one sitting in particular they had said but good-day and good-by to each other. He felt that he was clumsy and ungainly. He told himself that she despised him.

But the memory of her was with him constantly. Night after night he lay broad awake thinking of Trina, wondering about her, racked with the infinite desire of her. His head burnt and throbbed. The palms of his hands were dry. He dozed and woke, and walked aimlessly about the dark room, bruising himself against the three chairs drawn up "at attention" under the steel engraving, and stumbling over the stone pug dog that sat in front of the little stove.

Besides this, the jealousy of Marcus Schouler harassed him. Maria Macapa, coming into his "Parlor" to ask for junk, found him flung at length upon the bed-lounge, gnawing at his fingers in an excess of silent fury. At lunch that day Marcus had told him of an excursion that was planned for the next Sunday afternoon. Mr. Sieppe, Trina's father, belonged to a rifle club that was to hold a meet at Schuetzen Park across the bay. All the Sieppes were going; there was to be a basket picnic. Marcus, as usual, was invited to be one of the party. McTeague was in agony. It was his first experience, and he suffered all the worse for it because he was totally unprepared. What miserable complication was this in which he found himself involved? It seemed so simple to him since he loved Trina to take her straight to himself, stopping at nothing, asking no questions, to have her, and by main strength to carry her far away somewhere, he did not know exactly where, to some vague country, some undiscovered place where every day was Sunday.

"Got any junk?"

"Huh? What? What is it?" exclaimed McTeague, suddenly rousing up from the lounge. Often Maria did very well in the "Dental Parlors." McTeague was continually breaking things which he was too stupid to have mended; for him anything that was broken was lost. Now it was a cuspidor, now a fire-shovel for the little stove, now a China shaving mug.

"Got any junk?"

"I don't know—I don't remember," muttered McTeague. Maria roamed about the room, McTeague following her in his huge stockinged feet. All at once she pounced upon a sheaf of old hand instruments in a coverless cigar-box, pluggers, hard bits, and excavators. Maria had long coveted such a find in McTeague's "Parlor," knowing it should be somewhere about. The instruments were of the finest tempered steel and really valuable.

"Say, Doctor, I can have these, can't I?" exclaimed Maria. "You got no more use for them." McTeague was not at all sure of this. There were many in the sheaf that might be repaired, reshaped.

"No, no," he said, wagging his head. But Maria Macapa, knowing with whom she had to deal, at once let loose a torrent of words. She made the dentist believe that he had no right to withhold them, that he had promised to save them for her. She affected a great indignation, pursing her lips and putting her chin in the air as though wounded in some finer sense, changing so rapidly from one mood to another, filling the room with such shrill clamor, that McTeague was dazed and benumbed.

"Yes, all right, all right," he said, trying to make himself heard. "It WOULD be mean. I don't want 'em." As he turned from her to pick up the box, Maria took advantage of the moment to steal three "mats" of sponge-gold out of the glass saucer. Often she stole McTeague's gold, almost under his very eyes; indeed, it was so easy to do so that there was but little pleasure in the theft. Then Maria took herself off. McTeague returned to the sofa and flung himself upon it face downward.

A little before supper time Maria completed her search. The flat was cleaned of its junk from top to bottom. The dirty pillow-case was full to bursting. She took advantage of the supper hour to carry her bundle around the corner and up into the alley where Zerkow lived.

When Maria entered his shop, Zerkow had just come in from his daily rounds. His decrepit wagon stood in front of his door like a stranded wreck; the miserable horse, with its lamentable swollen joints, fed greedily upon an armful of spoiled hay in a shed at the back.

The interior of the junk shop was dark and damp, and foul with all manner of choking odors. On the walls, on the floor, and hanging from the rafters was a world of debris, dust-blackened, rust-corroded. Everything was there, every trade was represented, every class of society; things of iron and cloth and wood; all the detritus that a great city sloughs off in its daily life. Zerkow's junk shop was the last abiding-place, the almshouse, of such articles as had outlived their usefulness.

Maria found Zerkow himself in the back room, cooking some sort of a meal over an alcohol stove. Zerkow was a Polish Jew—curiously enough his hair was fiery red. He was a dry, shrivelled old man of sixty odd. He had the thin, eager, cat-like lips of the covetous; eyes that had grown keen as those of a lynx from long searching amidst muck and debris; and claw-like, prehensile fingers—the fingers of a man who accumulates, but never disburses. It was impossible to look at Zerkow and not know instantly that greed—inordinate, insatiable greed—was the dominant passion of the man. He was the Man with the Rake, groping hourly in the muck-heap of the city for gold, for gold, for gold. It was his dream, his passion; at every instant he seemed to feel the generous solid weight of the crude fat metal in his palms. The glint of it was constantly in his eyes; the jangle of it sang forever in his ears as the jangling of cymbals.

"Who is it? Who is it?" exclaimed Zerkow, as he heard Maria's footsteps in the outer room. His voice was faint, husky, reduced almost to a whisper by his prolonged habit of street crying.

"Oh, it's you again, is it?" he added, peering through the gloom of the shop. "Let's see; you've been here before, ain't you? You're the Mexican woman from Polk Street. Macapa's your name, hey?"

Maria nodded. "Had a flying squirrel an' let him go," she muttered, absently. Zerkow was puzzled; he looked at her sharply for a moment, then dismissed the matter with a movement of his head.

"Well, what you got for me?" he said. He left his supper to grow cold, absorbed at once in the affair.

Then a long wrangle began. Every bit of junk in Maria's pillow-case was discussed and weighed and disputed. They clamored into each other's faces over Old Grannis's cracked pitcher, over Miss Baker's silk gaiters, over Marcus Schouler's whiskey flasks, reaching the climax of disagreement when it came to McTeague's instruments.

"Ah, no, no!" shouted Maria. "Fifteen cents for the lot! I might as well make you a Christmas present! Besides, I got some gold fillings off him; look at um."

Zerkow drew a quick breath as the three pellets suddenly flashed in Maria's palm. There it was, the virgin metal, the pure, unalloyed ore, his dream, his consuming desire. His fingers twitched and hooked themselves into his palms, his thin lips drew tight across his teeth.

"Ah, you got some gold," he muttered, reaching for it.

Maria shut her fist over the pellets. "The gold goes with the others," she declared. "You'll gi' me a fair price for the lot, or I'll take um back."

In the end a bargain was struck that satisfied Maria. Zerkow was not one who would let gold go out of his house. He counted out to her the price of all her junk, grudging each piece of money as if it had been the blood of his veins. The affair was concluded.

But Zerkow still had something to say. As Maria folded up the pillow-case and rose to go, the old Jew said:

"Well, see here a minute, we'll—you'll have a drink before you go, won't you? Just to show that it's all right between us." Maria sat down again.

"Yes, I guess I'll have a drink," she answered.

Zerkow took down a whiskey bottle and a red glass tumbler with a broken base from a cupboard on the wall. The two drank together, Zerkow from the bottle, Maria from the broken tumbler. They wiped their lips slowly, drawing breath again. There was a moment's silence.

"Say," said Zerkow at last, "how about those gold dishes you told me about the last time you were here?"

"What gold dishes?" inquired Maria, puzzled.

"Ah, you know," returned the other. "The plate your father owned in Central America a long time ago. Don't you know, it rang like so many bells? Red gold, you know, like oranges?"

"Ah," said Maria, putting her chin in the air as if she knew a long story about that if she had a mind to tell it. "Ah, yes, that gold service."

"Tell us about it again," said Zerkow, his bloodless lower lip moving against the upper, his claw-like fingers feeling about his mouth and chin. "Tell us about it; go on."

He was breathing short, his limbs trembled a little. It was as if some hungry beast of prey had scented a quarry. Maria still refused, putting up her head, insisting that she had to be going.

"Let's have it," insisted the Jew. "Take another drink." Maria took another swallow of the whiskey. "Now, go on," repeated Zerkow; "let's have the story." Maria squared her elbows on the deal table, looking straight in front of her with eyes that saw nothing.

"Well, it was this way," she began. "It was when I was little. My folks must have been rich, oh, rich into the millions—coffee, I guess—and there was a large house, but I can only remember the plate. Oh, that service of plate! It was wonderful. There were more than a hundred pieces, and every one of them gold. You should have seen the sight when the leather trunk was opened. It fair dazzled your eyes. It was a yellow blaze like a fire, like a sunset; such a glory, all piled up together, one piece over the other. Why, if the room was dark you'd think you could see just the same with all that glitter there. There wa'n't a piece that was so much as scratched; every one was like a mirror, smooth and bright, just like a little pool when the sun shines into it. There was dinner dishes and soup tureens and pitchers; and great, big platters as long as that and wide too; and cream-jugs and bowls with carved handles, all vines and things; and drinking mugs, every one a different shape; and dishes for gravy and sauces; and then a great, big punch-bowl with a ladle, and the bowl was all carved out with figures and bunches of grapes. Why, just only that punch-bowl was worth a fortune, I guess. When all that plate was set out on a table, it was a sight for a king to look at. Such a service as that was! Each piece was heavy, oh, so heavy! and thick, you know; thick, fat gold, nothing but gold—red, shining, pure gold, orange red—and when you struck it with your knuckle, ah, you should have heard! No church bell ever rang sweeter or clearer. It was soft gold, too; you could bite into it, and leave the dent of your teeth. Oh, that gold plate! I can see it just as plain—solid, solid, heavy, rich, pure gold; nothing but gold, gold, heaps and heaps of it. What a service that was!"

Maria paused, shaking her head, thinking over the vanished splendor. Illiterate enough, unimaginative enough on all other subjects, her distorted wits called up this picture with marvellous distinctness. It was plain she saw the plate clearly. Her description was accurate, was almost eloquent.

Did that wonderful service of gold plate ever exist outside of her diseased imagination? Was Maria actually remembering some reality of a childhood of barbaric luxury? Were her parents at one time possessed of an incalculable fortune derived from some Central American coffee plantation, a fortune long since confiscated by armies of insurrectionists, or squandered in the support of revolutionary governments?

It was not impossible. Of Maria Macapa's past prior to the time of her appearance at the "flat" absolutely nothing could be learned. She suddenly appeared from the unknown, a strange woman of a mixed race, sane on all subjects but that of the famous service of gold plate; but unusual, complex, mysterious, even at her best.

But what misery Zerkow endured as he listened to her tale! For he chose to believe it, forced himself to believe it, lashed and harassed by a pitiless greed that checked at no tale of treasure, however preposterous. The story ravished him with delight. He was near someone who had possessed this wealth. He saw someone who had seen this pile of gold. He seemed near it; it was there, somewhere close by, under his eyes, under his fingers; it was red, gleaming, ponderous. He gazed about him wildly; nothing, nothing but the sordid junk shop and the rust-corroded tins. What exasperation, what positive misery, to be so near to it and yet to know that it was irrevocably, irretrievably lost! A spasm of anguish passed through him. He gnawed at his bloodless lips, at the hopelessness of it, the rage, the fury of it.

"Go on, go on," he whispered; "let's have it all over again. Polished like a mirror, hey, and heavy? Yes, I know, I know. A punch-bowl worth a fortune. Ah! and you saw it, you had it all!"

Maria rose to go. Zerkow accompanied her to the door, urging another drink upon her.

"Come again, come again," he croaked. "Don't wait till you've got junk; come any time you feel like it, and tell me more about the plate."

He followed her a step down the alley.

"How much do you think it was worth?" he inquired, anxiously.

"Oh, a million dollars," answered Maria, vaguely.

When Maria had gone, Zerkow returned to the back room of the shop, and stood in front of the alcohol stove, looking down into his cold dinner, preoccupied, thoughtful.

"A million dollars," he muttered in his rasping, guttural whisper, his finger-tips wandering over his thin, cat-like lips. "A golden service worth a million dollars; a punchbowl worth a fortune; red gold plates, heaps and piles. God!"

CHAPTER 4

The days passed. McTeague had finished the operation on Trina's teeth. She did not come any more to the "Parlors." Matters had readjusted themselves a little between the two during the last sittings. Trina yet stood upon her reserve, and McTeague still felt himself shambling and ungainly in her presence; but that constraint and embarrassment that had followed upon McTeague's blundering declaration broke up little by little. In spite of themselves they were gradually resuming the same relative positions they had occupied when they had first met.

But McTeague suffered miserably for all that. He never would have Trina, he saw that clearly. She was too good for him; too delicate, too refined, too prettily made for him, who was so coarse, so enormous, so stupid. She was for someone else—Marcus, no doubt—or at least for some finer-grained man. She should have gone to some other dentist; the young fellow on the corner, for instance, the poser, the rider of bicycles, the courser of greyhounds. McTeague began to loathe and to envy this fellow. He spied upon him going in and out of his office, and noted his salmon-pink neckties and his astonishing waistcoats.

One Sunday, a few days after Trina's last sitting, McTeague met Marcus Schouler at his table in the car conductors' coffee-joint, next to the harness shop.

"What you got to do this afternoon, Mac?" inquired the other, as they ate their suet pudding.

"Nothing, nothing," replied McTeague, shaking his head. His mouth was full of pudding. It made him warm to eat, and little beads of perspiration stood across the bridge of his nose. He looked forward to an afternoon passed in his operating chair as usual. On leaving his "Parlors" he had put ten cents into his pitcher and had left it at Frenna's to be filled.

"What do you say we take a walk, huh?" said Marcus. "Ah, that's the thing—a walk, a long walk, by damn! It'll be outa sight. I got to take three or four of the dogs out for exercise, anyhow. Old Grannis thinks they need ut. We'll walk out to the Presidio."

Of late it had become the custom of the two friends to take long walks from time to time. On holidays and on those Sunday afternoons when Marcus was not absent with the Sieppes they went out together, sometimes to the park, sometimes to the Presidio, sometimes even across the bay. They took a great pleasure in each other's company, but silently and with reservation, having the masculine horror of any demonstration of friendship.

They walked for upwards of five hours that afternoon, out the length of California Street, and across the Presidio Reservation to the Golden Gate. Then they turned, and, following the line of the shore, brought up at the Cliff House. Here they halted for beer, Marcus swearing that his mouth was as dry as a hay-bin. Before starting on their walk they had gone around to the little dog hospital, and Marcus had let out four of the convalescents, crazed with joy at the release.

"Look at that dog," he cried to McTeague, showing him a finely-bred Irish setter. "That's the dog that belonged to the duck on the avenue, the dog we called for that day. I've bought 'um. The duck thought he had the distemper, and just threw 'um away. Nothun wrong with 'um but a little catarrh. Ain't he a bird? Say, ain't he a bird? Look at his flag; it's perfect; and see how he carries his tail on a line with his back. See how stiff and white his whiskers are. Oh, by damn! you can't fool me on a dog. That dog's a winner."

At the Cliff House the two sat down to their beer in a quiet corner of the billiard-room. There were but two players. Somewhere in another part of the building a mammoth music-box was jangling out a quickstep. From outside came the long, rhythmical rush of the surf and the sonorous barking of the seals upon the seal rocks. The four dogs curled themselves down upon the sanded floor.

"Here's how," said Marcus, half emptying his glass. "Ah-h!" he added, with a long breath, "that's good; it is, for a fact."

For the last hour of their walk Marcus had done nearly all the talking. McTeague merely answering him by uncertain movements of the head. For that matter, the dentist had been silent and preoccupied throughout the whole afternoon. At length Marcus noticed it. As he set down his glass with a bang he suddenly exclaimed:

"What's the matter with you these days, Mac? You got a bean about somethun, hey? Spit ut out."

"No, no," replied McTeague, looking about on the floor, rolling his eyes; "nothing, no, no."

"Ah, rats!" returned the other. McTeague kept silence. The two billiard players departed. The huge music-box struck into a fresh tune.

"Huh!" exclaimed Marcus, with a short laugh, "guess you're in love."

McTeague gasped, and shuffled his enormous feet under the table.

"Well, somethun's bitun you, anyhow," pursued Marcus. "Maybe I can help you. We're pals, you know. Better tell me what's up; guess we can straighten ut out. Ah, go on; spit ut out."

The situation was abominable. McTeague could not rise to it. Marcus was his best friend, his only friend. They were "pals" and McTeague was very fond of him. Yet they were both in love, presumably, with the same girl, and now Marcus would try and force the secret out of him; would rush blindly at the rock upon which the two must split, stirred by the very best of motives, wishing only to be of service. Besides this, there was nobody to whom McTeague would have better preferred to tell his troubles than to Marcus, and yet about this trouble, the greatest trouble of his life, he must keep silent; must refrain from speaking of it to Marcus above everybody.

McTeague began dimly to feel that life was too much for him. How had it all come about? A month ago he was perfectly content; he was calm and peaceful, taking his little pleasures as he found them. His life had shaped itself; was, no doubt, to continue always along these same lines. A woman had entered his small world and instantly there was discord. The disturbing element had appeared. Wherever the woman had put her foot a score of distressing complications had sprung up, like the sudden growth of strange and puzzling flowers.

"Say, Mac, go on; let's have ut straight," urged Marcus, leaning toward him. "Has any duck been doing you dirt?" he cried, his face crimson on the instant.

"No," said McTeague, helplessly.

"Come along, old man," persisted Marcus; "let's have ut. What is the row? I'll do all I can to help you."

It was more than McTeague could bear. The situation had got beyond him. Stupidly he spoke, his hands deep in his pockets, his head rolled forward.

"It's—it's Miss Sieppe," he said.

"Trina, my cousin? How do you mean?" inquired Marcus sharply.

"I—I—I don' know," stammered McTeague, hopelessly confounded.

"You mean," cried Marcus, suddenly enlightened, "that you are—that you, too."

McTeague stirred in his chair, looking at the walls of the room, avoiding the other's glance. He nodded his head, then suddenly broke out:

"I can't help it. It ain't my fault, is it?"

Marcus was struck dumb; he dropped back in his chair breathless. Suddenly McTeague found his tongue.

"I tell you, Mark, I can't help it. I don't know how it happened. It came on so slow that I was, that—that—that it was done before I knew it, before I could help myself. I know we're pals, us two, and I knew how—how you and Miss Sieppe were. I know now, I knew then; but that wouldn't have made any difference. Before I knew it—it—it—there I was. I can't help it. I wouldn't 'a' had ut happen for anything, if I could 'a' stopped it, but I don' know, it's something that's just stronger than you are, that's all. She came there—Miss Sieppe came to the parlors there three or four times a week, and she was the first girl I had ever known,—and you don' know! Why, I was so close to her I touched her face every minute, and her mouth, and smelt her hair and her breath—oh, you don't know anything about it. I can't give you any idea. I don' know exactly myself; I only know how I'm fixed. I—I—it's been done; it's too late, there's no going back. Why, I can't think of anything else night and day. It's everything. It's—it's—oh, it's everything! I—I—why, Mark, it's everything—I can't explain." He made a helpless movement with both hands.

Never had McTeague been so excited; never had he made so long a speech. His arms moved in fierce, uncertain gestures, his face flushed, his enormous jaws shut together with a sharp click at every pause. It was like some colossal brute trapped in a delicate, invisible mesh, raging, exasperated, powerless to extricate himself.

Marcus Schouler said nothing. There was a long silence. Marcus got up and walked to the window and stood looking out, but seeing nothing. "Well, who would have thought of this?" he muttered under his breath. Here was a fix. Marcus cared for Trina. There was no doubt in his mind about that. He looked forward eagerly to the Sunday afternoon excursions. He liked to be with Trina. He, too, felt the charm of the little girl—the charm of the small, pale forehead; the little chin thrust out as if in confidence and innocence; the heavy, odorous crown of black hair. He liked her immensely. Some day he would speak; he would ask her to marry him. Marcus put off this matter of marriage to some future period; it would be some time—a year, perhaps, or two. The thing did not take definite shape in his mind. Marcus "kept company" with his cousin Trina, but he knew plenty of other girls. For the matter of that, he liked all girls pretty well. Just now the singleness and strength of McTeague's passion startled him. McTeague would marry Trina that very afternoon if she would have him; but would he—Marcus? No, he would not; if it came to that, no, he would not. Yet he knew he liked Trina. He could say—yes, he could say—he loved her. She was his "girl." The Sieppes acknowledged him as Trina's "young man." Marcus came back to the table and sat down sideways upon it.

"Well, what are we going to do about it, Mac?" he said.

"I don' know," answered McTeague, in great distress. "I don' want anything to—to come between us, Mark."

"Well, nothun will, you bet!" vociferated the other. "No, sir; you bet not, Mac."

Marcus was thinking hard. He could see very clearly that McTeague loved Trina more than he did; that in some strange way this huge, brutal fellow was capable of a greater passion than himself, who was twice as clever. Suddenly Marcus jumped impetuously to a resolution.

"Well, say, Mac," he cried, striking the table with his fist, "go ahead. I guess you—you want her pretty bad. I'll pull out; yes, I will. I'll give her up to you, old man."

The sense of his own magnanimity all at once overcame Marcus. He saw himself as another man, very noble, self-sacrificing; he stood apart and watched this second self with boundless admiration and with infinite pity. He was so good, so magnificent, so heroic, that he almost sobbed. Marcus made a sweeping gesture of resignation, throwing out both his arms, crying:

"Mac, I'll give her up to you. I won't stand between you." There were actually tears in Marcus's eyes as he spoke. There was no doubt he thought himself sincere. At that moment he almost believed he loved Trina conscientiously, that he was sacrificing himself for the sake of his friend. The two stood up and faced each other, gripping hands. It was a great moment; even McTeague felt the drama of it. What a fine thing was this friendship between men! the dentist treats his friend for an ulcerated tooth and refuses payment; the friend reciprocates by giving up his girl. This was nobility. Their mutual affection and esteem suddenly increased enormously. It was Damon and Pythias; it was David and Jonathan; nothing could ever estrange them. Now it was for life or death.

"I'm much obliged," murmured McTeague. He could think of nothing better to say. "I'm much obliged," he repeated; "much obliged, Mark."

"That's all right, that's all right," returned Marcus Schouler, bravely, and it occurred to him to add, "You'll be happy together. Tell her for me—tell her—-tell her——" Marcus could not go on. He wrung the dentist's hand silently.

It had not appeared to either of them that Trina might refuse McTeague. McTeague's spirits rose at once. In Marcus's withdrawal he fancied he saw an end to all his difficulties. Everything would come right, after all. The strained, exalted state of Marcus's nerves ended by putting him into fine humor as well. His grief suddenly changed to an excess of gaiety. The afternoon was a success. They slapped each other on the back with great blows of the open palms, and they drank each other's health in a third round of beer.

Ten minutes after his renunciation of Trina Sieppe, Marcus astounded McTeague with a tremendous feat.

"Looka here, Mac. I know somethun you can't do. I'll bet you two bits I'll stump you." They each put a quarter on the table. "Now watch me," cried Marcus. He caught up a billiard ball from the rack, poised it a moment in front of his face, then with a sudden, horrifying distension of his jaws crammed it into his mouth, and shut his lips over it.

For an instant McTeague was stupefied, his eyes bulging. Then an enormous laugh shook him. He roared and shouted, swaying in his chair, slapping his knee. What a josher was this Marcus! Sure, you never could tell what he would do next. Marcus slipped the ball out, wiped it on the tablecloth, and passed it to McTeague.

"Now let's see you do it."

McTeague fell suddenly grave. The matter was serious. He parted his thick mustaches and opened his enormous jaws like an anaconda. The ball disappeared inside his mouth. Marcus applauded vociferously, shouting, "Good work!" McTeague reached for the money and put it in his vest pocket, nodding his head with a knowing air.

Then suddenly his face grew purple, his jaws moved convulsively, he pawed at his cheeks with both hands. The billiard ball had slipped into his mouth easily enough; now, however, he could not get it out again.

It was terrible. The dentist rose to his feet, stumbling about among the dogs, his face working, his eyes starting. Try as he would, he could not stretch his jaws wide enough to slip the ball out. Marcus lost his wits, swearing at the top of his voice. McTeague sweated with terror; inarticulate sounds came from his crammed mouth; he waved his arms wildly; all the four dogs caught the excitement and began to bark. A waiter rushed in, the two billiard players returned, a little crowd formed. There was a veritable scene.

All at once the ball slipped out of McTeague's jaws as easily as it had gone in. What a relief! He dropped into a chair, wiping his forehead, gasping for breath.

On the strength of the occasion Marcus Schouler invited the entire group to drink with him.

By the time the affair was over and the group dispersed it was after five. Marcus and McTeague decided they would ride home on the cars. But they soon found this impossible. The dogs would not follow. Only Alexander, Marcus's new setter, kept his place at the rear of the car. The other three lost their senses immediately, running wildly about the streets with their heads in the air, or suddenly starting off at a furious gallop directly away from the car. Marcus whistled and shouted and lathered with rage in vain. The two friends were obliged to walk. When they finally reached Polk Street, Marcus shut up the three dogs in the hospital. Alexander he brought back to the flat with him.

There was a minute back yard in the rear, where Marcus had made a kennel for Alexander out of an old water barrel. Before he thought of his own supper Marcus put Alexander to bed and fed him a couple of dog biscuits. McTeague had followed him to the yard to keep him company. Alexander settled to his supper at once, chewing vigorously at the biscuit, his head on one side.

"What you going to do about this—about that—about—about my cousin now, Mac?" inquired Marcus.

McTeague shook his head helplessly. It was dark by now and cold. The little back yard was grimy and full of odors. McTeague was tired with their long walk. All his uneasiness about his affair with Trina had returned. No, surely she was not for him. Marcus or some other man would win her in the end. What could she ever see to desire in him—in him, a clumsy giant, with hands like wooden mallets? She had told him once that she would not marry him. Was that not final?

"I don' know what to do, Mark," he said.

"Well, you must make up to her now," answered Marcus. "Go and call on her."

McTeague started. He had not thought of calling on her. The idea frightened him a little.

"Of course," persisted Marcus, "that's the proper caper. What did you expect? Did you think you was never going to see her again?"

"I don' know, I don' know," responded the dentist, looking stupidly at the dog.

"You know where they live," continued Marcus Schouler. "Over at B Street station, across the bay. I'll take you over there whenever you want to go. I tell you what, we'll go over there Washington's Birthday. That's this next Wednesday; sure, they'll be glad to see you." It was good of Marcus. All at once McTeague rose to an appreciation of what his friend was doing for him. He stammered:

"Say, Mark—you're—you're all right, anyhow."

"Why, pshaw!" said Marcus. "That's all right, old man. I'd like to see you two fixed, that's all. We'll go over Wednesday, sure."

They turned back to the house. Alexander left off eating and watched them go away, first with one eye, then with the other. But he was too self-respecting to whimper. However, by the time the two friends had reached the second landing on the back stairs a terrible commotion was under way in the little yard. They rushed to an open window at the end of the hall and looked down.

A thin board fence separated the flat's back yard from that used by the branch post-office. In the latter place lived a collie dog. He and Alexander had smelt each other out, blowing through the cracks of the fence at each other. Suddenly the quarrel had exploded on either side of the fence. The dogs raged at each other, snarling and barking, frantic with hate. Their teeth gleamed. They tore at the fence with their front paws. They filled the whole night with their clamor.

"By damn!" cried Marcus, "they don't love each other. Just listen; wouldn't that make a fight if the two got together? Have to try it some day."

CHAPTER 5

Wednesday morning, Washington's Birthday, McTeague rose very early and shaved himself. Besides the six mournful concertina airs, the dentist knew one song. Whenever he shaved, he sung this song; never at any other time. His voice was a bellowing roar, enough to make the window sashes rattle. Just now he woke up all the lodgers in his hall with it. It was a lamentable wail:

"No one to love, none to caress,
Left all alone in this world's wilderness."

As he paused to strop his razor, Marcus came into his room, half-dressed, a startling phantom in red flannels.

Marcus often ran back and forth between his room and the dentist's "Parlors" in all sorts of undress. Old Miss Baker had seen him thus several times through her half-open door, as she sat in her room listening and waiting. The old dressmaker was shocked out of all expression. She was outraged, offended, pursing her lips, putting up her head. She talked of complaining to the landlady. "And Mr. Grannis right next door, too. You can understand how trying it is for both of us." She would come out in the hall after one of these apparitions, her little false curls shaking, talking loud and shrill to any one in reach of her voice.

"Well," Marcus would shout, "shut your door, then, if you don't want to see. Look out, now, here I come again. Not even a porous plaster on me this time."

On this Wednesday morning Marcus called McTeague out into the hall, to the head of the stairs that led down to the street door.

"Come and listen to Maria, Mac," said he.

Maria sat on the next to the lowest step, her chin propped by her two fists. The red-headed Polish Jew, the ragman Zerkow, stood in the doorway. He was talking eagerly.

"Now, just once more, Maria," he was saying. "Tell it to us just once more." Maria's voice came up the stairway in a monotone. Marcus and McTeague caught a phrase from time to time.

"There were more than a hundred pieces, and every one of them gold—just that punch-bowl was worth a fortune-thick, fat, red gold."

"Get onto to that, will you?" observed Marcus. "The old skin has got her started on the plate. Ain't they a pair for you?"

"And it rang like bells, didn't it?" prompted Zerkow.

"Sweeter'n church bells, and clearer."

"Ah, sweeter'n bells. Wasn't that punch-bowl awful heavy?"

"All you could do to lift it."

"I know. Oh, I know," answered Zerkow, clawing at his lips. "Where did it all go to? Where did it go?"

Maria shook her head.

"It's gone, anyhow."

"Ah, gone, gone! Think of it! The punch-bowl gone, and the engraved ladle, and the plates and goblets. What a sight it must have been all heaped together!"

"It was a wonderful sight."

"Yes, wonderful; it must have been."

On the lower steps of that cheap flat, the Mexican woman and the red-haired Polish Jew mused long over that vanished, half-mythical gold plate.

Marcus and the dentist spent Washington's Birthday across the bay. The journey over was one long agony to McTeague. He shook with a formless, uncertain dread; a dozen times he would have turned back had not Marcus been with him. The stolid giant was as nervous as a schoolboy. He fancied that his call upon Miss Sieppe was an outrageous affront. She would freeze him with a stare; he would be shown the door, would be ejected, disgraced.

As they got off the local train at B Street station they suddenly collided with the whole tribe of Sieppes—the mother, father, three children, and Trina—equipped for one of their eternal picnics. They were to go to Schuetzen Park, within walking distance of the station. They were grouped about four lunch baskets. One of the children, a little boy, held a black greyhound by a rope around its neck. Trina wore a blue cloth skirt, a striped shirt waist, and a white sailor; about her round waist was a belt of imitation alligator skin.

At once Mrs. Sieppe began to talk to Marcus. He had written of their coming, but the picnic had been decided upon after the arrival of his letter. Mrs. Sieppe explained this to him. She was an immense old lady with a pink face and wonderful hair, absolutely white. The Sieppes were a German-Swiss family.

"We go to der park, Schuetzen Park, mit alle dem childern, a little eggs-kursion, eh not soh? We breathe der freshes air, a celubration, a pignic bei der seashore on. Ach, dot wull be soh gay, ah?"

"You bet it will. It'll be outa sight," cried Marcus, enthusiastic in an instant. "This is m' friend Doctor McTeague I wrote you about, Mrs. Sieppe."

"Ach, der doktor," cried Mrs. Sieppe.

McTeague was presented, shaking hands gravely as Marcus shouldered him from one to the other.

Mr. Sieppe was a little man of a military aspect, full of importance, taking himself very seriously. He was a member of a rifle team. Over his shoulder was slung a Springfield rifle, while his breast was decorated by five bronze medals.

Trina was delighted. McTeague was dumfounded. She appeared positively glad to see him.

"How do you do, Doctor McTeague," she said, smiling at him and shaking his hand. "It's nice to see you again. Look, see how fine my filling is." She lifted a corner of her lip and showed him the clumsy gold bridge.

Meanwhile, Mr. Sieppe toiled and perspired. Upon him devolved the responsibility of the excursion. He seemed to consider it a matter of vast importance, a veritable expedition.

"Owgooste!" he shouted to the little boy with the black greyhound, "you will der hound und basket number three carry. Der tervins," he added, calling to the two smallest boys, who were dressed exactly alike, "will releef one unudder mit der camp-stuhl und basket number four. Dat is comprehend, hay? When we make der start, you childern will in der advance march. Dat is your orders. But we do not start," he exclaimed, excitedly; "we remain. Ach Gott, Selina, who does not arrive."

Selina, it appeared, was a niece of Mrs. Sieppe's. They were on the point of starting without her, when she suddenly arrived, very much out of breath. She was a slender, unhealthy looking girl, who overworked herself giving lessons in hand-painting at twenty-five cents an hour. McTeague was presented. They all began to talk at once, filling the little station-house with a confusion of tongues.

"Attention!" cried Mr. Sieppe, his gold-headed cane in one hand, his Springfield in the other. "Attention! We depart." The four little boys moved off ahead; the greyhound suddenly began to bark, and tug at his leash. The others picked up their bundles.

"Vorwarts!" shouted Mr. Sieppe, waving his rifle and assuming the attitude of a lieutenant of infantry leading a charge. The party set off down the railroad track.

Mrs. Sieppe walked with her husband, who constantly left her side to shout an order up and down the line. Marcus followed with Selina. McTeague found himself with Trina at the end of the procession.

"We go off on these picnics almost every week," said Trina, by way of a beginning, "and almost every holiday, too. It is a custom."

"Yes, yes, a custom," answered McTeague, nodding; "a custom—that's the word."

"Don't you think picnics are fine fun, Doctor McTeague?" she continued. "You take your lunch; you leave the dirty city all day; you race about in the open air, and when lunchtime comes, oh, aren't you hungry? And the woods and the grass smell so fine!"

"I don' know, Miss Sieppe," he answered, keeping his eyes fixed on the ground between the rails. "I never went on a picnic."

"Never went on a picnic?" she cried, astonished. "Oh, you'll see what fun we'll have. In the morning father and the children dig clams in the mud by the shore, an' we bake them, and—oh, there's thousands of things to do."

"Once I went sailing on the bay," said McTeague. "It was in a tugboat; we fished off the heads. I caught three codfishes."

"I'm afraid to go out on the bay," answered Trina, shaking her head, "sailboats tip over so easy. A cousin of mine, Selina's brother, was drowned one Decoration Day. They never found his body. Can you swim, Doctor McTeague?"

"I used to at the mine."

"At the mine? Oh, yes, I remember, Marcus told me you were a miner once."

"I was a car-boy; all the car-boys used to swim in the reservoir by the ditch every Thursday evening. One of them was bit by a rattlesnake once while he was dressing. He was a Frenchman, named Andrew. He swelled up and began to twitch."

"Oh, how I hate snakes! They're so crawly and graceful—but, just the same, I like to watch them. You know that drug store over in town that has a showcase full of live ones?"

"We killed the rattler with a cart whip."

"How far do you think you could swim? Did you ever try? D'you think you could swim a mile?"

"A mile? I don't know. I never tried. I guess I could."

"I can swim a little. Sometimes we all go out to the Crystal Baths."

"The Crystal Baths, huh? Can you swim across the tank?"

"Oh, I can swim all right as long as papa holds my chin up. Soon as he takes his hand away, down I go. Don't you hate to get water in your ears?"

"Bathing's good for you."

"If the water's too warm, it isn't. It weakens you."

Mr. Sieppe came running down the tracks, waving his cane.

"To one side," he shouted, motioning them off the track; "der drain gomes." A local passenger train was just passing B Street station, some quarter of a mile behind them. The party stood to one side to let it pass. Marcus put a nickel and two crossed pins upon the rail, and waved his hat to the passengers as the train roared past. The children shouted shrilly. When the train was gone, they all rushed to see the nickel and the crossed pins. The nickel had been jolted off, but the pins had been flattened out so that they bore a faint resemblance to opened scissors. A great contention arose among the children for the possession of these "scissors." Mr. Sieppe was obliged to intervene. He reflected gravely. It was a matter of tremendous moment. The whole party halted, awaiting his decision.

"Attend now," he suddenly exclaimed. "It will not be soh soon. At der end of der day, ven we shall have home gecommen, den wull it pe adjudge, eh? A REward of merit to him who der bes' pehaves. It is an order. Vorwarts!"

"That was a Sacramento train," said Marcus to Selina as they started off; "it was, for a fact."

"I know a girl in Sacramento," Trina told McTeague. "She's forewoman in a glove store, and she's got consumption."

"I was in Sacramento once," observed McTeague, "nearly eight years ago."

"Is it a nice place—as nice as San Francisco?"

"It's hot. I practised there for a while."

"I like San Francisco," said Trina, looking across the bay to where the city piled itself upon its hills.

"So do I," answered McTeague. "Do you like it better than living over here?"

"Oh, sure, I wish we lived in the city. If you want to go across for anything it takes up the whole day."

"Yes, yes, the whole day—almost."

"Do you know many people in the city? Do you know anybody named Oelbermann? That's my uncle. He has a wholesale toy store in the Mission. They say he's awful rich."

"No, I don' know him."

"His stepdaughter wants to be a nun. Just fancy! And Mr. Oelbermann won't have it. He says it would be just like burying his child. Yes, she wants to enter the convent of the Sacred Heart. Are you a Catholic, Doctor McTeague?"

"No. No, I—"

"Papa is a Catholic. He goes to Mass on the feast days once in a while. But mamma's Lutheran."

"The Catholics are trying to get control of the schools," observed McTeague, suddenly remembering one of Marcus's political tirades.

"That's what cousin Mark says. We are going to send the twins to the kindergarten next month."

"What's the kindergarten?"

"Oh, they teach them to make things out of straw and toothpicks—kind of a play place to keep them off the street."

"There's one up on Sacramento Street, not far from Polk Street. I saw the sign."

"I know where. Why, Selina used to play the piano there."

"Does she play the piano?"

"Oh, you ought to hear her. She plays fine. Selina's very accomplished. She paints, too."

"I can play on the concertina."

"Oh, can you? I wish you'd brought it along. Next time you will. I hope you'll come often on our picnics. You'll see what fun we'll have."

"Fine day for a picnic, ain't it? There ain't a cloud."

"That's so," exclaimed Trina, looking up, "not a single cloud. Oh, yes; there is one, just over Telegraph Hill."

"That's smoke."

"No, it's a cloud. Smoke isn't white that way."

"'Tis a cloud."

"I knew I was right. I never say a thing unless I'm pretty sure."

"It looks like a dog's head."

"Don't it? Isn't Marcus fond of dogs?"

"He got a new dog last week—a setter."

"Did he?"

"Yes. He and I took a lot of dogs from his hospital out for a walk to the Cliff House last Sunday, but we had to walk all the way home, because they wouldn't follow. You've been out to the Cliff House?"

"Not for a long time. We had a picnic there one Fourth of July, but it rained. Don't you love the ocean?"

"Yes—yes, I like it pretty well."

"Oh, I'd like to go off in one of those big sailing ships. Just away, and away, and away, anywhere. They're different from a little yacht. I'd love to travel."

"Sure; so would I."

"Papa and mamma came over in a sailing ship. They were twenty-one days. Mamma's uncle used to be a sailor. He was captain of a steamer on Lake Geneva, in Switzerland."

"Halt!" shouted Mr. Sieppe, brandishing his rifle. They had arrived at the gates of the park. All at once McTeague turned cold. He had only a quarter in his pocket. What was he expected to do—pay for the whole party, or for Trina and himself, or merely buy his own ticket? And even in this latter case would a quarter be enough? He lost his wits, rolling his eyes helplessly. Then it occurred to him to feign a great abstraction, pretending not to know that the time was come to pay. He looked intently up and down the tracks; perhaps a train was coming. "Here we are," cried Trina, as they came up to the rest of the party, crowded about the entrance. "Yes, yes," observed McTeague, his head in the air.

"Gi' me four bits, Mac," said Marcus, coming up. "Here's where we shell out."

"I—I—I only got a quarter," mumbled the dentist, miserably. He felt that he had ruined himself forever with Trina. What was the use of trying to win her? Destiny was against him. "I only got a quarter," he stammered. He was on the point of adding that he would not go in the park. That seemed to be the only alternative.

"Oh, all right!" said Marcus, easily. "I'll pay for you, and you can square with me when we go home."

They filed into the park, Mr. Sieppe counting them off as they entered.

"Ah," said Trina, with a long breath, as she and McTeague pushed through the wicket, "here we are once more, Doctor." She had not appeared to notice McTeague's embarrassment. The difficulty had been tided over somehow. Once more McTeague felt himself saved.

"To der beach!" shouted Mr. Sieppe. They had checked their baskets at the peanut stand. The whole party trooped down to the seashore. The greyhound was turned loose. The children raced on ahead.

From one of the larger parcels Mrs. Sieppe had drawn forth a small tin steamboat—August's birthday present—a gaudy little toy which could be steamed up and navigated by means of an alcohol lamp. Her trial trip was to be made this morning.

"Gi' me it, gi' me it," shouted August, dancing around his father.

"Not soh, not soh," cried Mr. Sieppe, bearing it aloft. "I must first der eggsperimunt make."

"No, no!" wailed August. "I want to play with ut."

"Obey!" thundered Mr. Sieppe. August subsided. A little jetty ran part of the way into the water. Here, after a careful study of the directions printed on the cover of the box, Mr. Sieppe began to fire the little boat.

"I want to put ut in the wa-ater," cried August.

"Stand back!" shouted his parent. "You do not know so well as me; dere is dandger. Mitout attention he will eggsplode."

"I want to play with ut," protested August, beginning to cry.

"Ach, soh; you cry, bube!" vociferated Mr. Sieppe. "Mommer," addressing Mrs. Sieppe, "he will soh soon be ge-whipt, eh?"

"I want my boa-wut," screamed August, dancing.

"Silence!" roared Mr. Sieppe. The little boat began to hiss and smoke.

"Soh," observed the father, "he gommence. Attention! I put him in der water." He was very excited. The perspiration dripped from the back of his neck. The little boat was launched. It hissed more furiously than ever. Clouds of steam rolled from it, but it refused to move.

"You don't know how she wo-rks," sobbed August.

"I know more soh mudge as der grossest liddle fool as you," cried Mr. Sieppe, fiercely, his face purple.

"You must give it sh—shove!" exclaimed the boy.

"Den he eggsplode, idiot!" shouted his father. All at once the boiler of the steamer blew up with a sharp crack. The little tin toy turned over and sank out of sight before any one could interfere.

"Ah—h! Yah! Yah!" yelled August. "It's go-one!"

Instantly Mr. Sieppe boxed his ears. There was a lamentable scene. August rent the air with his outcries; his father shook him till his boots danced on the jetty, shouting into his face:

"Ach, idiot! Ach, imbecile! Ach, miserable! I tol' you he eggsplode. Stop your cry. Stop! It is an order. Do you wish I drow you in der water, eh? Speak. Silence, bube! Mommer, where ist mein stick? He will der grossest whippun ever of his life receive."

Little by little the boy subsided, swallowing his sobs, knuckling his eyes, gazing ruefully at the spot where the boat had sunk. "Dot is better soh," commented Mr. Sieppe, finally releasing him. "Next dime berhaps you will your fat'er better pelief. Now, no more. We will der glams ge-dig, Mommer, a fire. Ach, himmel! we have der pfeffer forgotten."

The work of clam digging began at once, the little boys taking off their shoes and stockings. At first August refused to be comforted, and it was not until his father drove him into the water with his gold-headed cane that he consented to join the others.

What a day that was for McTeague! What a never-to-be-forgotten day! He was with Trina constantly. They laughed together—she demurely, her lips closed tight, her little chin thrust out, her small pale nose, with its adorable little freckles, wrinkling; he roared with all the force of his lungs, his enormous mouth distended, striking sledge-hammer blows upon his knee with his clenched fist.

The lunch was delicious. Trina and her mother made a clam chowder that melted in one's mouth. The lunch baskets were emptied. The party were fully two hours eating. There were huge loaves of rye bread full of grains of chickweed. There were weiner-wurst and frankfurter sausages. There was unsalted butter. There were pretzels. There was cold underdone chicken, which one ate in slices, plastered with a wonderful kind of mustard that did not sting. There were dried apples, that gave Mr. Sieppe the hiccoughs. There were a dozen bottles of beer, and, last of all, a crowning achievement, a marvellous Gotha truffle. After lunch came tobacco. Stuffed to the eyes, McTeague drowsed over his pipe, prone on his back in the sun, while Trina, Mrs. Sieppe, and Selina washed the dishes. In the afternoon Mr. Sieppe disappeared. They heard the reports of his rifle on the range. The others swarmed over the park, now around the swings, now in the Casino, now in the museum, now invading the merry-go-round.

At half-past five o'clock Mr. Sieppe marshalled the party together. It was time to return home.

The family insisted that Marcus and McTeague should take supper with them at their home and should stay over night. Mrs. Sieppe argued they could get no decent supper if they went back to the city at that hour; that they could catch an early morning boat and reach their business in good time. The two friends accepted.

The Sieppes lived in a little box of a house at the foot of B Street, the first house to the right as one went up from the station. It was two stories high, with a funny red mansard roof of oval slates. The interior was cut up into innumerable tiny rooms, some of them so small as to be hardly better than sleeping closets. In the back yard was a contrivance for pumping water from the cistern that interested McTeague at once. It was a dog-wheel, a huge revolving box in which the unhappy black greyhound spent most of his waking hours. It was his kennel; he slept in it. From time to time during the day Mrs. Sieppe appeared on the back doorstep, crying shrilly, "Hoop, hoop!" She threw lumps of coal at him, waking him to his work.

They were all very tired, and went to bed early. After great discussion it was decided that Marcus would sleep upon the lounge in the front parlor. Trina would sleep with August, giving up her room to McTeague. Selina went to her home, a block or so above the Sieppes's. At nine o'clock Mr. Sieppe showed McTeague to his room and left him to himself with a newly lighted candle.

For a long time after Mr. Sieppe had gone McTeague stood motionless in the middle of the room, his elbows pressed close to his sides, looking obliquely from the corners of his eyes. He hardly dared to move. He was in Trina's room.

It was an ordinary little room. A clean white matting was on the floor; gray paper, spotted with pink and green flowers, covered the walls. In one corner, under a white netting, was a little bed, the woodwork gayly painted with knots of bright flowers. Near it, against the wall, was a black walnut bureau. A work-table with spiral legs stood by the window, which was hung with a green and gold window curtain. Opposite the window the closet door stood ajar, while in the corner across from the bed was a tiny washstand with two clean towels.

And that was all. But it was Trina's room. McTeague was in his lady's bower; it seemed to him a little nest, intimate, discreet. He felt hideously out of place. He was an intruder; he, with his enormous feet, his colossal bones, his crude, brutal gestures. The mere weight of his limbs, he was sure, would crush the little bed-stead like an eggshell.

Then, as this first sensation wore off, he began to feel the charm of the little chamber. It was as though Trina were close by, but invisible. McTeague felt all the delight of her presence without the embarrassment that usually accompanied it. He was near to her—nearer than he had ever been before. He saw into her daily life, her little ways and manners, her habits, her very thoughts. And was there not in the air of that room a certain faint perfume that he knew, that recalled her to his mind with marvellous vividness?

As he put the candle down upon the bureau he saw her hairbrush lying there. Instantly he picked it up, and, without knowing why, held it to his face. With what a delicious odor was it redolent! That heavy, enervating odor of her hair—her wonderful, royal hair! The smell of that little hairbrush was talismanic. He had but to close his eyes to see her as distinctly as in a mirror. He saw her tiny, round figure, dressed all in black—for, curiously enough, it was his very first impression of Trina that came back to him now—not the Trina of the later occasions, not the Trina of the blue cloth skirt and white sailor. He saw her as he had seen her the day that Marcus had introduced them: saw her pale, round face; her narrow, half-open eyes, blue like the eyes of a baby; her tiny, pale ears, suggestive of anaemia; the freckles across the bridge of her nose; her pale lips; the tiara of royal black hair; and, above all, the delicious poise of the head, tipped back as though by the weight of all that hair—the poise that thrust out her chin a little, with the movement that was so confiding, so innocent, so nearly infantile.

McTeague went softly about the room from one object to another, beholding Trina in everything he touched or looked at. He came at last to the closet door. It was ajar. He opened it wide, and paused upon the threshold.

Trina's clothes were hanging there—skirts and waists, jackets, and stiff white petticoats. What a vision! For an instant McTeague caught his breath, spellbound. If he had suddenly discovered Trina herself there, smiling at him, holding out her hands, he could hardly have been more overcome. Instantly he recognized the black dress she had worn on that famous first day. There it was, the little jacket she had carried over her arm the day he had terrified her with his blundering declaration, and still others, and others—a whole group of Trinas faced him there. He went farther into the closet, touching the clothes gingerly, stroking them softly with his huge leathern palms. As he stirred them a delicate perfume disengaged itself from the folds. Ah, that exquisite feminine odor! It was not only her hair now, it was Trina herself— her mouth, her hands, her neck; the indescribably sweet, fleshly aroma that was a part of her, pure and clean, and redolent of youth and freshness. All at once, seized with an unreasoned impulse, McTeague opened his huge arms and gathered the little garments close to him, plunging his face deep amongst them, savoring their delicious odor with long breaths of luxury and supreme content.

The picnic at Schuetzen Park decided matters. McTeague began to call on Trina regularly Sunday and Wednesday afternoons. He took Marcus Schouler's place. Sometimes Marcus accompanied him, but it was generally to meet Selina by appointment at the Sieppes's house.

But Marcus made the most of his renunciation of his cousin. He remembered his pose from time to time. He made McTeague unhappy and bewildered by wringing his hand, by venting sighs that seemed to tear his heart out, or by giving evidences of an infinite melancholy. "What is my life!" he would exclaim. "What is left for me? Nothing, by damn!" And when McTeague would attempt remonstrance, he would cry: "Never mind, old man. Never mind me. Go, be happy. I forgive you."

Forgive what? McTeague was all at sea, was harassed with the thought of some shadowy, irreparable injury he had done his friend.

"Oh, don't think of me!" Marcus would exclaim at other times, even when Trina was by. "Don't think of me; I don't count any more. I ain't in it." Marcus seemed to take great pleasure in contemplating the wreck of his life. There is no doubt he enjoyed himself hugely during these days.

The Sieppes were at first puzzled as well over this change of front.

"Trina has den a new younge man," cried Mr. Sieppe. "First Schouler, now der doktor, eh? What die tevil, I say!"

Weeks passed, February went, March came in very rainy, putting a stop to all their picnics and Sunday excursions.

One Wednesday afternoon in the second week in March McTeague came over to call on Trina, bringing his concertina with him, as was his custom nowadays. As he got off the train at the station he was surprised to find Trina waiting for him.

"This is the first day it hasn't rained in weeks," she explained, "an' I thought it would be nice to walk."

"Sure, sure," assented McTeague.

B Street station was nothing more than a little shed. There was no ticket office, nothing but a couple of whittled and carven benches. It was built close to the railroad tracks, just across which was the dirty, muddy shore of San Francisco Bay. About a quarter of a mile back from the station was the edge of the town of Oakland. Between the station and the first houses of the town lay immense salt flats, here and there broken by winding streams of black water. They were covered with a growth of wiry grass, strangely discolored in places by enormous stains of orange yellow.

Near the station a bit of fence painted with a cigar advertisement reeled over into the mud, while under its lee lay an abandoned gravel wagon with dished wheels. The station was connected with the town by the extension of B Street, which struck across the flats geometrically straight, a file of tall poles with intervening wires marching along with it. At the station these were headed by an iron electric-light pole that, with its supports and outriggers, looked for all the world like an immense grasshopper on its hind legs.

Across the flats, at the fringe of the town, were the dump heaps, the figures of a few Chinese rag-pickers moving over them. Far to the left the view was shut off by the immense red-brown drum of the gas-works; to the right it was bounded by the chimneys and workshops of an iron foundry.

Across the railroad tracks, to seaward, one saw the long stretch of black mud bank left bare by the tide, which was far out, nearly half a mile. Clouds of sea-gulls were forever rising and settling upon this mud bank; a wrecked and abandoned wharf crawled over it on tottering legs; close in an old sailboat lay canted on her bilge.

But farther on, across the yellow waters of the bay, beyond Goat Island, lay San Francisco, a blue line of hills, rugged with roofs and spires. Far to the westward opened the Golden Gate, a bleak cutting in the sand-hills, through which one caught a glimpse of the open Pacific.

The station at B Street was solitary; no trains passed at this hour; except the distant rag-pickers, not a soul was in sight. The wind blew strong, carrying with it the mingled smell of salt, of tar, of dead seaweed, and of bilge. The sky hung low and brown; at long intervals a few drops of rain fell.

Near the station Trina and McTeague sat on the roadbed of the tracks, at the edge of the mud bank, making the most out of the landscape, enjoying the open air, the salt marshes, and the sight of the distant water. From time to time McTeague played his six mournful airs upon his concertina.

After a while they began walking up and down the tracks, McTeague talking about his profession, Trina listening, very interested and absorbed, trying to understand.

"For pulling the roots of the upper molars we use the cowhorn forceps," continued the dentist, monotonously. "We get the inside beak over the palatal roots and the cow-horn beak over the buccal roots—that's the roots on the outside, you see. Then we close the forceps, and that breaks right through the alveolus—that's the part of the socket in the jaw, you understand."

At another moment he told her of his one unsatisfied desire. "Some day I'm going to have a big gilded tooth outside my window for a sign. Those big gold teeth are beautiful, beautiful—only they cost so much, I can't afford one just now."

"Oh, it's raining," suddenly exclaimed Trina, holding out her palm. They turned back and reached the station in a drizzle. The afternoon was closing in dark and rainy. The tide was coming back, talking and lapping for miles along the mud bank. Far off across the flats, at the edge of the town, an electric car went by, stringing out a long row of diamond sparks on the overhead wires.

"Say, Miss Trina," said McTeague, after a while, "what's the good of waiting any longer? Why can't us two get married?"

Trina still shook her head, saying "No" instinctively, in spite of herself.

"Why not?" persisted McTeague. "Don't you like me well enough?"

"Yes."

"Then why not?"

"Because."

"Ah, come on," he said, but Trina still shook her head.

"Ah, come on," urged McTeague. He could think of nothing else to say, repeating the same phrase over and over again to all her refusals.

"Ah, come on! Ah, come on!"

Suddenly he took her in his enormous arms, crushing down her struggle with his immense strength. Then Trina gave up, all in an instant, turning her head to his. They kissed each other, grossly, full in the mouth.

A roar and a jarring of the earth suddenly grew near and passed them in a reek of steam and hot air. It was the Overland, with its flaming headlight, on its way across the continent.

The passage of the train startled them both. Trina struggled to free herself from McTeague. "Oh, please! please!" she pleaded, on the point of tears. McTeague released her, but in that moment a slight, a barely perceptible, revulsion of feeling had taken place in him. The instant that Trina gave up, the instant she allowed him to kiss her, he thought less of her. She was not so desirable, after all. But this reaction was so faint, so subtle, so intangible, that in another moment he had doubted its occurrence. Yet afterward it returned. Was there not something gone from Trina now? Was he not disappointed in her for doing that very thing for which he had longed? Was Trina the submissive, the compliant, the attainable just the same, just as delicate and adorable as Trina the inaccessible? Perhaps he dimly saw that this must be so, that it belonged to the changeless order of things—the man desiring the woman only for what she withholds; the woman worshipping the man for that which she yields up to him. With each concession gained the man's desire cools; with every surrender made the woman's adoration increases. But why should it be so?

Trina wrenched herself free and drew back from McTeague, her little chin quivering; her face, even to the lobes of her pale ears, flushed scarlet; her narrow blue eyes brimming. Suddenly she put her head between her hands and began to sob.

"Say, say, Miss Trina, listen—listen here, Miss Trina," cried McTeague, coming forward a step.

"Oh, don't!" she gasped, shrinking. "I must go home," she cried, springing to her feet. "It's late. I must. I must. Don't come with me, please. Oh, I'm so—so,"—she could not find any words. "Let me go alone," she went on. "You may—you come Sunday. Good-by."

"Good-by," said McTeague, his head in a whirl at this sudden, unaccountable change. "Can't I kiss you again?" But Trina was firm now. When it came to his pleading—a mere matter of words—she was strong enough.

"No, no, you must not!" she exclaimed, with energy. She was gone in another instant. The dentist, stunned, bewildered, gazed stupidly after her as she ran up the extension of B Street through the rain.

But suddenly a great joy took possession of him. He had won her. Trina was to be for him, after all. An enormous smile distended his thick lips; his eyes grew wide, and flashed; and he drew his breath quickly, striking his mallet-like fist upon his knee, and exclaiming under his breath:

"I got her, by God! I got her, by God!" At the same time he thought better of himself; his self-respect increased enormously. The man that could win Trina Sieppe was a man of extraordinary ability.

Trina burst in upon her mother while the latter was setting a mousetrap in the kitchen.

"Oh, mamma!"

"Eh? Trina? Ach, what has happun?"

Trina told her in a breath.

"Soh soon?" was Mrs. Sieppe's first comment. "Eh, well, what you cry for, then?"

"I don't know," wailed Trina, plucking at the end of her handkerchief.

"You loaf der younge doktor?"

"I don't know."

"Well, what for you kiss him?"

"I don't know."

"You don' know, you don' know? Where haf your sensus gone, Trina? You kiss der doktor. You cry, and you don' know. Is ut Marcus den?"

"No, it's not Cousin Mark."

"Den ut must be der doktor."

Trina made no answer.

"Eh?"

"I—I guess so."

"You loaf him?"

"I don't know."

Mrs. Sieppe set down the mousetrap with such violence that it sprung with a sharp snap.

CHAPTER 6

No, Trina did not know. "Do I love him? Do I love him?" A thousand times she put the question to herself during the next two or three days. At night she hardly slept, but lay broad awake for hours in her little, gayly painted bed, with its white netting, torturing herself with doubts and questions. At times she remembered the scene in the station with a veritable agony of shame, and at other times she was ashamed to recall it with a thrill of joy. Nothing could have been more sudden, more unexpected, than that surrender of herself. For over a year she had thought that Marcus would some day be her husband. They would be married, she supposed, some time in the future, she did not know exactly when; the matter did not take definite shape in her mind. She liked Cousin Mark very well. And then suddenly this cross-current had set in; this blond giant had appeared, this huge, stolid fellow, with his immense, crude strength. She had not loved him at first, that was certain. The day he had spoken to her in his "Parlors" she had only been terrified. If he had confined himself to merely speaking, as did Marcus, to pleading with her, to wooing her at a distance, forestalling her wishes, showing her little attentions, sending her boxes of candy, she could have easily withstood him. But he had only to take her in his arms, to crush down her struggle with his enormous strength, to subdue her, conquer her by sheer brute force, and she gave up in an instant.

But why—why had she done so? Why did she feel the desire, the necessity of being conquered by a superior strength? Why did it please her? Why had it suddenly thrilled her from head to foot with a quick, terrifying gust of passion, the like of which she had never known? Never at his best had Marcus made her feel like that, and yet she had always thought she cared for Cousin Mark more than for any one else.

When McTeague had all at once caught her in his huge arms, something had leaped to life in her—something that had hitherto lain dormant, something strong and overpowering. It frightened her now as she thought of it, this second self that had wakened within her, and that shouted and clamored for recognition. And yet, was it to be feared? Was it something to be ashamed of? Was it not, after all, natural, clean, spontaneous? Trina knew that she was a pure girl; knew that this sudden commotion within her carried with it no suggestion of vice.

Dimly, as figures seen in a waking dream, these ideas floated through Trina's mind. It was quite beyond her to realize them clearly; she could not know what they meant. Until that rainy day by the shore of the bay Trina had lived her life with as little self-consciousness as a tree. She was frank, straightforward, a healthy, natural human being, without sex as yet. She was almost like a boy. At once there had been a mysterious disturbance. The woman within her suddenly awoke.

Did she love McTeague? Difficult question. Did she choose him for better or for worse, deliberately, of her own free will, or was Trina herself allowed even a choice in the taking of that step that was to make or mar her life? The Woman is awakened, and, starting from her sleep, catches blindly at what first her newly opened eyes light upon. It is a spell, a witchery, ruled by chance alone, inexplicable—a fairy queen enamored of a clown with ass's ears.

McTeague had awakened the Woman, and, whether she would or no, she was his now irrevocably; struggle against it as she would, she belonged to him, body and soul, for life or for death. She had not sought it, she had not desired it. The spell was laid upon her. Was it a blessing? Was it a curse? It was all one; she was his, indissolubly, for evil or for good.

And he? The very act of submission that bound the woman to him forever had made her seem less desirable in his eyes. Their undoing had already begun. Yet neither of them was to blame. From the first they had not sought each other. Chance had brought them face to face, and mysterious instincts as ungovernable as the winds of heaven were at work knitting their lives together. Neither of them had asked that this thing should be—that their destinies, their very souls, should be the sport of chance. If they could have known, they would have shunned the fearful risk. But they were allowed no voice in the matter. Why should it all be?

It had been on a Wednesday that the scene in the B Street station had taken place. Throughout the rest of the week, at every hour of the day, Trina asked herself the same question: "Do I love him? Do I really love him? Is this what love is like?" As she recalled McTeague—recalled his huge, square-cut head, his salient jaw, his shock of yellow hair, his heavy, lumbering body, his slow wits—she found little to admire in him beyond his physical strength, and at such moments she shook her head decisively. "No, surely she did not love him." Sunday afternoon, however, McTeague called. Trina had prepared a little speech for him. She was to tell him that she did not know what had been the matter with her that Wednesday afternoon; that she had acted like a bad girl; that she did not love him well enough to marry him; that she had told him as much once before.

McTeague saw her alone in the little front parlor. The instant she appeared he came straight towards her. She saw what he was bent upon doing. "Wait a minute," she cried, putting out her hands. "Wait. You don't understand. I have got something to say to you." She might as well have talked to the wind. McTeague put aside her hands with a single gesture, and gripped her to him in a bearlike embrace that all but smothered her. Trina was but a reed before that giant strength. McTeague turned her face to his and kissed her again upon the mouth. Where was all Trina's resolve then? Where was her carefully prepared little speech? Where was all her hesitation and torturing doubts of the last few days? She clasped McTeague's huge red neck with both her slender arms; she raised her adorable little chin and kissed him in return, exclaiming: "Oh, I do love you! I do love you!" Never afterward were the two so happy as at that moment.

A little later in that same week, when Marcus and McTeague were taking lunch at the car conductors' coffee-joint, the former suddenly exclaimed:

"Say, Mac, now that you've got Trina, you ought to do more for her. By damn! you ought to, for a fact. Why don't you take her out somewhere—to the theatre, or somewhere? You ain't on to your job."

Naturally, McTeague had told Marcus of his success with Trina. Marcus had taken on a grand air.

"You've got her, have you? Well, I'm glad of it, old man. I am, for a fact. I know you'll be happy with her. I know how I would have been. I forgive you; yes, I forgive you, freely."

McTeague had not thought of taking Trina to the theatre.

"You think I ought to, Mark?" he inquired, hesitating. Marcus answered, with his mouth full of suet pudding:

"Why, of course. That's the proper caper."

"Well—well, that's so. The theatre—that's the word."

"Take her to the variety show at the Orpheum. There's a good show there this week; you'll have to take Mrs. Sieppe, too, of course," he added. Marcus was not sure of himself as regarded certain proprieties, nor, for that matter, were any of the people of the little world of Polk Street. The shop girls, the plumbers' apprentices, the small tradespeople, and their like, whose social position was not clearly defined, could never be sure how far they could go and yet preserve their "respectability." When they wished to be "proper," they invariably overdid the thing. It was not as if they belonged to the "tough" element, who had no appearances to keep up. Polk Street rubbed elbows with the "avenue" one block above. There were certain limits which its dwellers could not overstep; but unfortunately for them, these limits were poorly defined. They could never be sure of themselves. At an unguarded moment they might be taken for "toughs," so they generally erred in the other direction, and were absurdly formal. No people have a keener eye for the amenities than those whose social position is not assured.

"Oh, sure, you'll have to take her mother," insisted Marcus. "It wouldn't be the proper racket if you didn't."

McTeague undertook the affair. It was an ordeal. Never in his life had he been so perturbed, so horribly anxious. He called upon Trina the following Wednesday and made arrangements. Mrs. Sieppe asked if little August might be included. It would console him for the loss of his steamboat.

"Sure, sure," said McTeague. "August too—everybody," he added, vaguely.

"We always have to leave so early," complained Trina, "in order to catch the last boat. Just when it's becoming interesting."

At this McTeague, acting upon a suggestion of Marcus Schouler's, insisted they should stay at the flat over night. Marcus and the dentist would give up their rooms to them and sleep at the dog hospital. There was a bed there in the sick ward that old Grannis sometimes occupied when a bad case needed watching. All at once McTeague had an idea, a veritable inspiration.

"And we'll—we'll—we'll have—what's the matter with having something to eat afterward in my 'Parlors'?"

"Vairy goot," commented Mrs. Sieppe. "Bier, eh? And some damales."

"Oh, I love tamales!" exclaimed Trina, clasping her hands.

McTeague returned to the city, rehearsing his instructions over and over. The theatre party began to assume tremendous proportions. First of all, he was to get the seats, the third or fourth row from the front, on the left-hand side, so as to be out of the hearing of the drums in the orchestra; he must make arrangements about the rooms with Marcus, must get in the beer, but not the tamales; must buy for himself a white lawn tie—so Marcus directed; must look to it that Maria Macapa put his room in perfect order; and, finally, must meet the Sieppes at the ferry slip at half-past seven the following Monday night.

The real labor of the affair began with the buying of the tickets. At the theatre McTeague got into wrong entrances; was sent from one wicket to another; was bewildered, confused; misunderstood directions; was at one moment suddenly convinced that he had not enough money with him, and started to return home. Finally he found himself at the box-office wicket.

"Is it here you buy your seats?"

"How many?"

"Is it here—"

"What night do you want 'em? Yes, sir, here's the place."

McTeague gravely delivered himself of the formula he had been reciting for the last dozen hours.

"I want four seats for Monday night in the fourth row from the front, and on the right-hand side."

"Right hand as you face the house or as you face the stage?" McTeague was dumfounded.

"I want to be on the right-hand side," he insisted, stolidly; adding, "in order to be away from the drums."

"Well, the drums are on the right of the orchestra as you face the stage," shouted the other impatiently; "you want to the left, then, as you face the house."

"I want to be on the right-hand side," persisted the dentist.

Without a word the seller threw out four tickets with a magnificent, supercilious gesture.

"There's four seats on the right-hand side, then, and you're right up against the drums."

"But I don't want to be near the drums," protested McTeague, beginning to perspire.

"Do you know what you want at all?" said the ticket seller with calmness, thrusting his head at McTeague. The dentist knew that he had hurt this young man's feelings.

"I want—I want," he stammered. The seller slammed down a plan of the house in front of him and began to explain excitedly. It was the one thing lacking to complete McTeague's confusion.

"There are your seats," finished the seller, shoving the tickets into McTeague's hands. "They are the fourth row from the front, and away from the drums. Now are you satisfied?"

"Are they on the right-hand side? I want on the right—no, I want on the left. I want—I don' know, I don' know."

The seller roared. McTeague moved slowly away, gazing stupidly at the blue slips of pasteboard. Two girls took his place at the wicket. In another moment McTeague came back, peering over the girls' shoulders and calling to the seller:

"Are these for Monday night?"

The other disdained reply. McTeague retreated again timidly, thrusting the tickets into his immense wallet. For a moment he stood thoughtful on the steps of the entrance. Then all at once he became enraged, he did not know exactly why; somehow he felt himself slighted. Once more he came back to the wicket.

"You can't make small of me," he shouted over the girls' shoulders; "you—you can't make small of me. I'll thump you in the head, you little—you little—you little—little—little pup." The ticket seller shrugged his shoulders wearily. "A dollar and a half," he said to the two girls.

McTeague glared at him and breathed loudly. Finally he decided to let the matter drop. He moved away, but on the steps was once more seized with a sense of injury and outraged dignity.

"You can't make small of me," he called back a last time, wagging his head and shaking his fist. "I will—I will—I will—yes, I will." He went off muttering.

At last Monday night came. McTeague met the Sieppes at the ferry, dressed in a black Prince Albert coat and his best slate-blue trousers, and wearing the made-up lawn necktie that Marcus had selected for him. Trina was very pretty in the black dress that McTeague knew so well. She wore a pair of new gloves. Mrs. Sieppe had on lisle-thread mits, and carried two bananas and an orange in a net reticule. "For Owgooste," she confided to him. Owgooste was in a Fauntleroy "costume" very much too small for him. Already he had been crying.

"Woult you pelief, Doktor, dot bube has torn his stockun alreatty? Walk in der front, you; stop cryun. Where is dot berliceman?"

At the door of the theatre McTeague was suddenly seized with a panic terror. He had lost the tickets. He tore through his pockets, ransacked his wallet. They were nowhere to be found. All at once he remembered, and with a gasp of relief removed his hat and took them out from beneath the sweatband.

The party entered and took their places. It was absurdly early. The lights were all darkened, the ushers stood under the galleries in groups, the empty auditorium echoing with their noisy talk. Occasionally a waiter with his tray and clean white apron sauntered up and doun the aisle. Directly in front of them was the great iron curtain of the stage, painted with all manner of advertisements. From behind this came a noise of hammering and of occasional loud voices.

While waiting they studied their programmes. First was an overture by the orchestra, after which came "The Gleasons, in their mirth-moving musical farce, entitled 'McMonnigal's Court-ship.'" This was to be followed by "The Lamont Sisters, Winnie and Violet, serio-comiques and skirt dancers." And after this came a great array of other "artists" and "specialty performers," musical wonders, acrobats, lightning artists, ventriloquists, and last of all, "The feature of the evening, the crowning scientific achievement of the nineteenth century, the kinetoscope." McTeague was excited, dazzled. In five years he had not been twice to the theatre. Now he beheld himself inviting his "girl" and her mother to accompany him. He began to feel that he was a man of the world. He ordered a cigar.

Meanwhile the house was filling up. A few side brackets were turned on. The ushers ran up and down the aisles, stubs of tickets between their thumb and finger, and from every part of the auditorium could be heard the sharp clap-clapping of the seats as the ushers flipped them down. A buzz of talk arose. In the gallery a street gamin whistled shrilly, and called to some friends on the other side of the house.

"Are they go-wun to begin pretty soon, ma?" whined Owgooste for the fifth or sixth time; adding, "Say, ma, can't I have some candy?" A cadaverous little boy had appeared in their aisle, chanting, "Candies, French mixed candies, popcorn, peanuts and candy." The orchestra entered, each man crawling out from an opening under the stage, hardly larger than the gate of a rabbit hutch. At every instant now the crowd increased; there were but few seats that were not taken. The waiters hurried up and down the aisles, their trays laden with beer glasses. A smell of cigar-smoke filled the air, and soon a faint blue haze rose from all corners of the house.

"Ma, when are they go-wun to begin?" cried Owgooste. As he spoke the iron advertisement curtain rose, disclosing the curtain proper underneath. This latter curtain was quite an affair. Upon it was painted a wonderful picture. A flight of marble steps led down to a stream of water; two white swans, their necks arched like the capital letter S, floated about. At the head of the marble steps were two vases filled with red and yellow flowers, while at the foot was moored a gondola. This gondola was full of red velvet rugs that hung over the side and trailed in the water. In the prow of the gondola a young man in vermilion tights held a mandolin in his left hand, and gave his right to a girl in white satin. A King Charles spaniel, dragging a leading-string in the shape of a huge pink sash, followed the girl. Seven scarlet roses were scattered upon the two lowest steps, and eight floated in the water.

"Ain't that pretty, Mac?" exclaimed Trina, turning to the dentist.

"Ma, ain't they go-wun to begin now-wow?" whined Owgooste. Suddenly the lights all over the house blazed up. "Ah!" said everybody all at once.

"Ain't ut crowdut?" murmured Mr. Sieppe. Every seat was taken; many were even standing up.

"I always like it better when there is a crowd," said Trina. She was in great spirits that evening. Her round, pale face was positively pink.

The orchestra banged away at the overture, suddenly finishing with a great flourish of violins. A short pause followed. Then the orchestra played a quick-step strain, and the curtain rose on an interior furnished with two red chairs and a green sofa. A girl in a short blue dress and black stockings entered in a hurry and began to dust the two chairs. She was in a great temper, talking very fast, disclaiming against the "new lodger." It appeared that this latter never paid his rent; that he was given to late hours. Then she came down to the footlights and began to sing in a tremendous voice, hoarse and flat, almost like a man's. The chorus, of a feeble originality, ran:

> "Oh, how happy I will be,
> When my darling's face I'll see;
> Oh, tell him for to meet me in the moonlight,
> Down where the golden lilies bloom."

The orchestra played the tune of this chorus a second time, with certain variations, while the girl danced to it. She sidled to one side of the stage and kicked, then sidled to the other and kicked again. As she finished with the song, a man, evidently the lodger in question, came in. Instantly McTeague exploded in a roar of laughter. The man was intoxicated, his hat was knocked in, one end of his collar was unfastened and stuck up into his face, his watch-chain dangled from his pocket, and a yellow satin slipper was tied to a button-hole of his vest; his nose was vermilion, one eye was black and blue. After a short dialogue with the girl, a third actor appeared. He was dressed like a little boy, the girl's younger brother. He wore an immense turned-down collar, and was continually doing hand-springs and wonderful back somersaults. The "act" devolved upon these three people; the lodger making love to the girl in the short blue dress, the boy playing all manner of tricks upon him, giving him tremendous digs in the ribs or slaps upon the back that made him cough, pulling chairs from under him, running on all fours between his legs and upsetting him, knocking him over at inopportune moments. Every one of his falls was accentuated by a bang upon the bass drum. The whole humor of the "act" seemed to consist in the tripping up of the intoxicated lodger.

This horse-play delighted McTeague beyond measure. He roared and shouted every time the lodger went down, slapping his knee, wagging his head. Owgooste crowed shrilly, clapping his hands and continually asking, "What did he say, ma? What did he say?" Mrs. Sieppe laughed immoderately, her huge fat body shaking like a mountain of jelly. She exclaimed from time to time, "Ach, Gott, dot fool!" Even Trina was moved, laughing demurely, her lips closed, putting one hand with its new glove to her mouth.

The performance went on. Now it was the "musical marvels," two men extravagantly made up as negro minstrels, with immense shoes and plaid vests. They seemed to be able to wrestle a tune out of almost anything—glass bottles, cigar-box fiddles, strings of sleigh-bells, even graduated brass tubes, which they rubbed with resined fingers. McTeague was stupefied with admiration.

"That's what you call musicians," he announced gravely. "'Home, Sweet Home,' played upon a trombone. Think of that! Art could go no farther."

The acrobats left him breathless. They were dazzling young men with beautifully parted hair, continually making graceful gestures to the audience. In one of them the dentist fancied he saw a strong resemblance to the boy who had tormented the intoxicated lodger and who had turned such marvellous somersaults. Trina could not bear to watch their antics. She turned away her head with a little shudder. "It always makes me sick," she explained.

The beautiful young lady, "The Society Contralto," in evening dress, who sang the sentimental songs, and carried the sheets of music at which she never looked, pleased McTeague less. Trina, however, was captivated. She grew pensive over

"*You do not love me—no;*
Bid me good-by and go;"

and split her new gloves in her enthusiasm when it was finished.

"Don't you love sad music, Mac?" she murmured.

Then came the two comedians. They talked with fearful rapidity; their wit and repartee seemed inexhaustible.

"As I was going down the street yesterday—"

"Ah! as YOU were going down the street—all right."

"I saw a girl at a window——"

"YOU saw a girl at a window."

"And this girl she was a corker——"

"Ah! as YOU were going down the street yesterday YOU saw a girl at a window, and this girl she was a corker. All right, go on."

The other comedian went on. The joke was suddenly evolved. A certain phrase led to a song, which was sung with lightning rapidity, each performer making precisely the same gestures at precisely the same instant. They were irresistible. McTeague, though he caught but a third of the jokes, could have listened all night.

After the comedians had gone out, the iron advertisement curtain was let down.

"What comes now?" said McTeague, bewildered.

"It's the intermission of fifteen minutes now."

The musicians disappeared through the rabbit hutch, and the audience stirred and stretched itself. Most of the young men left their seats.

During this intermission McTeague and his party had "refreshments." Mrs. Sieppe and Trina had Queen Charlottes, McTeague drank a glass of beer, Owgooste ate the orange and one of the bananas. He begged for a glass of lemonade, which was finally given him.

"Joost to geep um quiet," observed Mrs. Sieppe.

But almost immediately after drinking his lemonade Owgooste was seized with a sudden restlessness. He twisted and wriggled in his seat, swinging his legs violently, looking about him with eyes full of a vague distress. At length, just as the musicians were returning, he stood up and whispered energetically in his mother's ear. Mrs. Sieppe was exasperated at once.

"No, no," she cried, reseating him brusquely.

The performance was resumed. A lightning artist appeared, drawing caricatures and portraits with incredible swiftness. He even went so far as to ask for subjects from the audience, and the names of prominent men were shouted to him from the gallery. He drew portraits of the President, of Grant, of Washington, of Napoleon Bonaparte, of Bismarck, of Garibaldi, of P. T. Barnum.

And so the evening passed. The hall grew very hot, and the smoke of innumerable cigars made the eyes smart. A thick blue mist hung low over the heads of the audience. The air was full of varied smells—the smell of stale cigars, of flat beer, of orange peel, of gas, of sachet powders, and of cheap perfumery.

One "artist" after another came upon the stage. McTeague's attention never wandered for a minute. Trina and her mother enjoyed themselves hugely. At every moment they made comments to one another, their eyes never leaving the stage.

"Ain't dot fool joost too funny?"

"That's a pretty song. Don't you like that kind of a song?"

"Wonderful! It's wonderful! Yes, yes, wonderful! That's the word."

Owgooste, however, lost interest. He stood up in his place, his back to the stage, chewing a piece of orange peel and watching a little girl in her father's lap across the aisle, his eyes fixed in a glassy, ox-like stare. But he was uneasy. He danced from one foot to the other, and at intervals appealed in hoarse whispers to his mother, who disdained an answer.

"Ma, say, ma-ah," he whined, abstractedly chewing his orange peel, staring at the little girl.

"Ma-ah, say, ma." At times his monotonous plaint reached his mother's consciousness. She suddenly realized what this was that was annoying her.

"Owgooste, will you sit down?" She caught him up all at once, and jammed him down into his place. "Be quiet, den; loog; listun at der yunge girls."

Three young women and a young man who played a zither occupied the stage. They were dressed in Tyrolese costume; they were yodlers, and sang in German about "mountain tops" and "bold hunters" and the like. The yodling chorus was a marvel of flute-like modulations. The girls were really pretty, and were not made up in the least. Their "turn" had a great success. Mrs. Sieppe was entranced. Instantly she remembered her girlhood and her native Swiss village.

"Ach, dot is heavunly; joost like der old country. Mein gran'mutter used to be one of der mos' famous yodlers. When I was leedle, I haf seen dem joost like dat."

"Ma-ah," began Owgooste fretfully, as soon as the yodlers had departed. He could not keep still an instant; he twisted from side to side, swinging his legs with incredible swiftness.

"Ma-ah, I want to go ho-ome."

"Pehave!" exclaimed his mother, shaking him by the arm; "loog, der leedle girl is watchun you. Dis is der last dime I take you to der blay, you see."

"I don't ca-are; I'm sleepy." At length, to their great relief, he went to sleep, his head against his mother's arm.

The kinetoscope fairly took their breaths away.

"What will they do next?" observed Trina, in amazement. "Ain't that wonderful, Mac?"

McTeague was awe-struck.

"Look at that horse move his head," he cried excitedly, quite carried away. "Look at that cable car coming—and the man going across the street. See, here comes a truck. Well, I never in all my life! What would Marcus say to this?"

"It's all a drick!" exclaimed Mrs. Sieppe, with sudden conviction. "I ain't no fool; dot's nothun but a drick."

"Well, of course, mamma," exclaimed Trina, "it's——"

But Mrs. Sieppe put her head in the air.

"I'm too old to be fooled," she persisted. "It's a drick." Nothing more could be got out of her than this.

The party stayed to the very end of the show, though the kinetoscope was the last number but one on the programme, and fully half the audience left immediately afterward. However, while the unfortunate Irish comedian went through his "act" to the backs of the departing people, Mrs. Sieppe woke Owgooste, very cross and sleepy, and began getting her "things together." As soon as he was awake Owgooste began fidgeting again.

"Save der brogramme, Trina," whispered Mrs. Sieppe. "Take ut home to popper. Where is der hat of Owgooste? Haf you got mein handkerchief, Trina?"

But at this moment a dreadful accident happened to Owgooste; his distress reached its climax; his fortitude collapsed. What a misery! It was a veritable catastrophe, deplorable, lamentable, a thing beyond words! For a moment he gazed wildly about him, helpless and petrified with astonishment and terror. Then his grief found utterance, and the closing strains of the orchestra were mingled with a prolonged wail of infinite sadness.

"Owgooste, what is ut?" cried his mother eyeing him with dawning suspicion; then suddenly, "What haf you done? You haf ruin your new Vauntleroy gostume!" Her face blazed; without more ado she smacked him soundly. Then it was that Owgooste touched the limit of his misery, his unhappiness, his horrible discomfort; his utter wretchedness was complete. He filled the air with his doleful outcries. The more he was smacked and shaken, the louder he wept.

"What—what is the matter?" inquired McTeague.

Trina's face was scarlet. "Nothing, nothing," she exclaimed hastily, looking away. "Come, we must be going. It's about over." The end of the show and the breaking up of the audience tided over the embarrassment of the moment.

The party filed out at the tail end of the audience. Already the lights were being extinguished and the ushers spreading druggeting over the upholstered seats.

McTeague and the Sieppes took an uptown car that would bring them near Polk Street. The car was crowded; McTeague and Owgooste were obliged to stand. The little boy fretted to be taken in his mother's lap, but Mrs. Sieppe emphatically refused.

On their way home they discussed the performance.

"I—I like best der yodlers."

"Ah, the soloist was the best—the lady who sang those sad songs."

"Wasn't—wasn't that magic lantern wonderful, where the figures moved? Wonderful—ah, wonderful! And wasn't that first act funny, where the fellow fell down all the time? And that musical act, and the fellow with the burnt-cork face who played 'Nearer, My God, to Thee' on the beer bottles."

They got off at Polk Street and walked up a block to the flat. The street was dark and empty; opposite the flat, in the back of the deserted market, the ducks and geese were calling persistently.

As they were buying their tamales from the half-breed Mexican at the street corner, McTeague observed:

"Marcus ain't gone to bed yet. See, there's a light in his window. There!" he exclaimed at once, "I forgot the doorkey. Well, Marcus can let us in."

Hardly had he rung the bell at the street door of the flat when the bolt was shot back. In the hall at the top of the long, narrow staircase there was the sound of a great scurrying. Maria Macapa stood there, her hand upon the rope that drew the bolt; Marcus was at her side; Old Grannis was in the background, looking over their shoulders; while little Miss Baker leant over the banisters, a strange man in a drab overcoat at her side. As McTeague's party stepped into the doorway a half-dozen voices cried:

"Yes, it's them."

"Is that you, Mac?"

"Is that you, Miss Sieppe?"

"Is your name Trina Sieppe?"

Then, shriller than all the rest, Maria Macapa screamed:

"Oh, Miss Sieppe, come up here quick. Your lottery ticket has won five thousand dollars!"

CHAPTER 7

"What nonsense!" answered Trina.

"Ach Gott! What is ut?" cried Mrs. Sieppe, misunderstanding, supposing a calamity.

"What—what—what," stammered the dentist, confused by the lights, the crowded stairway, the medley of voices. The party reached the landing. The others surrounded them. Marcus alone seemed to rise to the occasion.

"Le' me be the first to congratulate you," he cried, catching Trina's hand. Every one was talking at once.

"Miss Sieppe, Miss Sieppe, your ticket has won five thousand dollars," cried Maria. "Don't you remember the lottery ticket I sold you in Doctor McTeague's office?"

"Trina!" almost screamed her mother. "Five tausend thalers! five tausend thalers! If popper were only here!"

"What is it—what is it?" exclaimed McTeague, rolling his eyes.

"What are you going to do with it, Trina?" inquired Marcus.

"You're a rich woman, my dear," said Miss Baker, her little false curls quivering with excitement, "and I'm glad for your sake. Let me kiss you. To think I was in the room when you bought the ticket!"

"Oh, oh!" interrupted Trina, shaking her head, "there is a mistake. There must be. Why—why should I win five thousand dollars? It's nonsense!"

"No mistake, no mistake," screamed Maria. "Your number was 400,012. Here it is in the paper this evening. I remember it well, because I keep an account."

"But I know you're wrong," answered Trina, beginning to tremble in spite of herself. "Why should I win?"

"Eh? Why shouldn't you?" cried her mother.

In fact, why shouldn't she? The idea suddenly occurred to Trina. After all, it was not a question of effort or merit on her part. Why should she suppose a mistake? What if it were true, this wonderful fillip of fortune striking in there like some chance-driven bolt?

"Oh, do you think so?" she gasped.

The stranger in the drab overcoat came forward.

"It's the agent," cried two or three voices, simultaneously.

"I guess you're one of the lucky ones, Miss Sieppe," he said. "I suppose you have kept your ticket."

"Yes, yes; four three oughts twelve—I remember."

"That's right," admitted the other. "Present your ticket at the local branch office as soon as possible—the address is printed on the back of the ticket—and you'll receive a check on our bank for five thousand dollars. Your number will have to be verified on our official list, but there's hardly a chance of a mistake. I congratulate you."

All at once a great shrill of gladness surged up in Trina. She was to possess five thousand dollars. She was carried away with the joy of her good fortune, a natural, spontaneous joy—the gaiety of a child with a new and wonderful toy.

"Oh, I've won, I've won, I've won!" she cried, clapping her hands. "Mamma, think of it. I've won five thousand dollars, just by buying a ticket. Mac, what do you say to that? I've got five thousand dollars. August, do you hear what's happened to sister?"

"Kiss your mommer, Trina," suddenly commanded Mrs. Sieppe. "What efer will you do mit all dose money, eh, Trina?"

"Huh!" exclaimed Marcus. "Get married on it for one thing." Thereat they all shouted with laughter. McTeague grinned, and looked about sheepishly. "Talk about luck," muttered Marcus, shaking his head at the dentist; then suddenly he added:

"Well, are we going to stay talking out here in the hall all night? Can't we all come into your 'Parlors', Mac?"

"Sure, sure," exclaimed McTeague, hastily unlocking his door.

"Efery botty gome," cried Mrs. Sieppe, genially. "Ain't ut so, Doktor?"

"Everybody," repeated the dentist. "There's—there's some beer."

"We'll celebrate, by damn!" exclaimed Marcus. "It ain't every day you win five thousand dollars. It's only Sundays and legal holidays." Again he set the company off into a gale of laughter. Anything was funny at a time like this. In some way every one of them felt elated. The wheel of fortune had come spinning close to them. They were near to this great sum of money. It was as though they too had won.

"Here's right where I sat when I bought that ticket," cried Trina, after they had come into the "Parlors," and Marcus had lit the gas. "Right here in this chair." She sat down in one of the rigid chairs under the steel engraving. "And, Marcus, you sat here— —"

"And I was just getting out of the operating chair," interposed Miss Baker.

"Yes, yes. That's so; and you," continued Trina, pointing to Maria, "came up and said, 'Buy a ticket in the lottery; just a dollar.' Oh, I remember it just as plain as though it was yesterday, and I wasn't going to at first— —"

"And don't you know I told Maria it was against the law?"

"Yes, I remember, and then I gave her a dollar and put the ticket in my pocketbook. It's in my pocketbook now at home in the top drawer of my bureau—oh, suppose it should be stolen now," she suddenly exclaimed.

"It's worth big money now," asserted Marcus.

"Five thousand dollars. Who would have thought it? It's wonderful." Everybody started and turned. It was McTeague. He stood in the middle of the floor, wagging his huge head. He seemed to have just realized what had happened.

"Yes, sir, five thousand dollars!" exclaimed Marcus, with a sudden unaccountable mirthlessness. "Five thousand dollars! Do you get on to that? Cousin Trina and you will be rich people."

"At six per cent, that's twenty-five dollars a month," hazarded the agent.

"Think of it. Think of it," muttered McTeague. He went aimlessly about the room, his eyes wide, his enormous hands dangling.

"A cousin of mine won forty dollars once," observed Miss Baker. "But he spent every cent of it buying more tickets, and never won anything."

Then the reminiscences began. Maria told about the butcher on the next block who had won twenty dollars the last drawing. Mrs. Sieppe knew a gasfitter in Oakland who had won several times; once a hundred dollars. Little Miss Baker announced that she had always believed that lotteries were wrong; but, just the same, five thousand was five thousand.

"It's all right when you win, ain't it, Miss Baker?" observed Marcus, with a certain sarcasm. What was the matter with Marcus? At moments he seemed singularly out of temper.

But the agent was full of stories. He told his experiences, the legends and myths that had grown up around the history of the lottery; he told of the poor newsboy with a dying mother to support who had drawn a prize of fifteen thousand; of the man who was driven to suicide through want, but who held (had he but known it) the number that two days after his death drew the capital prize of thirty thousand dollars; of the little milliner who for ten years had played the lottery without success, and who had one day declared that she would buy but one more ticket and then give up trying, and of how this last ticket had brought her a fortune upon which she could retire; of tickets that had been lost or destroyed, and whose numbers had won fabulous sums at the drawing; of criminals, driven to vice by poverty, and who had reformed after winning competencies; of gamblers who played the lottery as they would play a faro bank, turning in their winnings again as soon as made, buying thousands of tickets all over the country; of superstitions as to terminal and initial numbers, and as to lucky days of purchase; of marvellous coincidences—three capital prizes drawn consecutively by the same town; a ticket bought by a millionaire and given to his boot-black, who won a thousand dollars upon it; the same number winning the same amount an indefinite number of times; and so on to infinity. Invariably it was the needy who won, the destitute and starving woke to wealth and plenty, the virtuous toiler suddenly found his reward in a ticket bought at a hazard; the lottery was a great charity, the friend of the people, a vast beneficent machine that recognized neither rank nor wealth nor station.

 The company began to be very gay. Chairs and tables were brought in from the adjoining rooms, and Maria was sent out for more beer and tamales, and also commissioned to buy a bottle of wine and some cake for Miss Baker, who abhorred beer.

 The "Dental Parlors" were in great confusion. Empty beer bottles stood on the movable rack where the instruments were kept; plates and napkins were upon the seat of the operating chair and upon the stand of shelves in the corner, side by side with the concertina and the volumes of "Allen's Practical Dentist." The canary woke and chittered crossly, his feathers puffed out; the husks of tamales littered the floor; the stone pug dog sitting before the little stove stared at the unusual scene, his glass eyes starting from their sockets.

 They drank and feasted in impromptu fashion. Marcus Schouler assumed the office of master of ceremonies; he was in a lather of excitement, rushing about here and there, opening beer bottles, serving the tamales, slapping McTeague upon the back, laughing and joking continually. He made McTeague sit at the head of the table, with Trina at his right and the agent at his left; he—when he sat down at all—occupied the foot, Maria

Macapa at his left, while next to her was Mrs. Sieppe, opposite Miss Baker. Owgooste had been put to bed upon the bed-lounge.

"Where's Old Grannis?" suddenly exclaimed Marcus. Sure enough, where had the old Englishman gone? He had been there at first.

"I called him down with everybody else," cried Maria Macapa, "as soon as I saw in the paper that Miss Sieppe had won. We all came down to Mr. Schouler's room and waited for you to come home. I think he must have gone back to his room. I'll bet you'll find him sewing up his books."

"No, no," observed Miss Baker, "not at this hour."

Evidently the timid old gentleman had taken advantage of the confusion to slip unobtrusively away.

"I'll go bring him down," shouted Marcus; "he's got to join us."

Miss Baker was in great agitation.

"I—I hardly think you'd better," she murmured; "he—he—I don't think he drinks beer."

"He takes his amusement in sewin' up books," cried Maria.

Marcus brought him down, nevertheless, having found him just preparing for bed.

"I—I must apologize," stammered Old Grannis, as he stood in the doorway. "I had not quite expected—I—find—find myself a little unprepared." He was without collar and cravat, owing to Marcus Schouler's precipitate haste. He was annoyed beyond words that Miss Baker saw him thus. Could anything be more embarrassing?

Old Grannis was introduced to Mrs. Sieppe and to Trina as Marcus's employer. They shook hands solemnly.

"I don't believe that he an' Miss Baker have ever been introduced," cried Maria Macapa, shrilly, "an' they've been livin' side by side for years."

The two old people were speechless, avoiding each other's gaze. It had come at last; they were to know each other, to talk together, to touch each other's hands.

Marcus brought Old Grannis around the table to little Miss Baker, dragging him by the coat sleeve, exclaiming: "Well, I thought you two people knew each other long ago. Miss Baker, this is Mr. Grannis; Mr. Grannis, this is Miss Baker." Neither spoke. Like two little children they faced each other, awkward, constrained, tongue-tied with embarrassment. Then Miss Baker put out her hand shyly. Old Grannis touched it for an instant and let it fall.

"Now you know each other," cried Marcus, "and it's about time." For the first time their eyes met; Old Grannis trembled a little, putting his hand uncertainly to his chin. Miss Baker flushed ever so slightly, but Maria Macapa passed suddenly between them, carrying a half empty beer bottle. The two old people fell back from one another, Miss Baker resuming her seat.

"Here's a place for you over here, Mr. Grannis," cried Marcus, making room for him at his side. Old Grannis slipped into the chair, withdrawing at once from the company's notice. He stared fixedly at his plate and did not speak again. Old Miss Baker began to talk volubly across the table to Mrs. Sieppe about hot-house flowers and medicated flannels.

It was in the midst of this little impromptu supper that the engagement of Trina and the dentist was announced. In a pause in the chatter of conversation Mrs. Sieppe leaned forward and, speaking to the agent, said:

"Vell, you know also my daughter Trina get married bretty soon. She and der dentist, Doktor McTeague, eh, yes?"

There was a general exclamation.

"I thought so all along," cried Miss Baker, excitedly. "The first time I saw them together I said, 'What a pair!'"

"Delightful!" exclaimed the agent, "to be married and win a snug little fortune at the same time."

"So—So," murmured Old Grannis, nodding at his plate.

"Good luck to you," cried Maria.

"He's lucky enough already," growled Marcus under his breath, relapsing for a moment into one of those strange moods of sullenness which had marked him throughout the evening.

Trina flushed crimson, drawing shyly nearer her mother. McTeague grinned from ear to ear, looking around from one to another, exclaiming "Huh! Huh!"

But the agent rose to his feet, a newly filled beer glass in his hand. He was a man of the world, this agent. He knew life. He was suave and easy. A diamond was on his little finger.

"Ladies and gentlemen," he began. There was an instant silence. "This is indeed a happy occasion. I—I am glad to be here to-night; to be a witness to such good fortune; to partake in these—in this celebration. Why, I feel almost as glad as if I had held four three oughts twelve myself; as if the five thousand were mine instead of belonging to our charming hostess. The good wishes of my humble self go out to Miss Sieppe in this moment of her good fortune, and I think—in fact, I am sure I can speak for the great institution, the great company I represent. The company congratulates Miss Sieppe. We—they—ah—They wish her every happiness her new fortune can procure her. It has been my duty, my—ah—cheerful duty to call upon the winners of large prizes and to offer the felicitation of the company. I have, in my experience, called upon many such; but never have I seen fortune so happily bestowed as in this case. The company have dowered the prospective bride. I am sure I but echo the sentiments of this assembly when I wish all joy and happiness to this happy pair, happy in the possession of a snug little fortune, and happy—happy in—" he finished with a sudden inspiration—"in the possession of each other; I drink to the health, wealth, and happiness of the future bride and groom. Let us drink standing up." They drank with enthusiasm. Marcus was carried away with the excitement of the moment.

"Outa sight, outa sight," he vociferated, clapping his hands. "Very well said. To the health of the bride. McTeague, McTeague, speech, speech!"

In an instant the whole table was clamoring for the dentist to speak. McTeague was terrified; he gripped the table with both hands, looking wildly about him.

"Speech, speech!" shouted Marcus, running around the table and endeavoring to drag McTeague up.

"No—no—no," muttered the other. "No speech." The company rattled upon the table with their beer glasses, insisting upon a speech. McTeague settled obstinately into his chair, very red in the face, shaking his head energetically.

"Ah, go on!" he exclaimed; "no speech."

"Ah, get up and say somethun, anyhow," persisted Marcus; "you ought to do it. It's the proper caper."

McTeague heaved himself up; there was a burst of applause; he looked slowly about him, then suddenly sat down again, shaking his head hopelessly.

"Oh, go on, Mac," cried Trina.

"Get up, say somethun, anyhow," cried Marcus, tugging at his arm; "you GOT to."

Once more McTeague rose to his feet.

"Huh!" he exclaimed, looking steadily at the table. Then he began:

"I don' know what to say—I—I—I ain't never made a speech before; I—I ain't never made a speech before. But I'm glad Trina's won the prize—"

"Yes, I'll bet you are," muttered Marcus.

"I—I—I'm glad Trina's won, and I—I want to—I want to—I want to—want to say that—you're—all—welcome, an' drink hearty, an' I'm much obliged to the agent. Trina and I are goin' to be married, an' I'm glad everybody's here to-night, an' you're—all—welcome, an' drink hearty, an' I hope you'll come again, an' you're always welcome—an'—I—an'—an'—That's—about—all—I—gotta say." He sat down, wiping his forehead, amidst tremendous applause.

Soon after that the company pushed back from the table and relaxed into couples and groups. The men, with the exception of Old Grannis, began to smoke, the smell of their tobacco mingling with the odors of ether, creosote, and stale bedding, which pervaded the "Parlors." Soon the windows had to be lowered from the top. Mrs. Sieppe and old Miss Baker sat together in the bay window exchanging confidences. Miss Baker had turned back the overskirt of her dress; a plate of cake was in her lap; from time to time she sipped her wine with the delicacy of a white cat. The two women were much interested in each other. Miss Baker told Mrs. Sieppe all about Old Grannis, not forgetting the fiction of the title and the unjust stepfather.

"He's quite a personage really," said Miss Baker.

Mrs. Sieppe led the conversation around to her children. "Ach, Trina is sudge a goote girl," she said; "always gay, yes, und sing from morgen to night. Und Owgooste, he is soh smart also, yes, eh? He has der genius for machines, always making somethun mit wheels und sbrings."

"Ah, if—if—I had children," murmured the little old maid a trifle wistfully, "one would have been a sailor; he would have begun as a midshipman on my brother's ship; in time he would have been an officer. The other would have been a landscape gardener."

"Oh, Mac!" exclaimed Trina, looking up into the dentist's face, "think of all this money coming to us just at this very moment. Isn't it wonderful? Don't it kind of scare you?"

"Wonderful, wonderful!" muttered McTeague, shaking his head. "Let's buy a lot of tickets," he added, struck with an idea.

"Now, that's how you can always tell a good cigar," observed the agent to Marcus as the two sat smoking at the end of the table. "The light end should be rolled to a point."

"Ah, the Chinese cigar-makers," cried Marcus, in a passion, brandishing his fist. "It's them as is ruining the cause of white labor. They are, they are for a FACT. Ah, the rat-eaters! Ah, the white-livered curs!"

Over in the corner, by the stand of shelves, Old Grannis was listening to Maria Macapa. The Mexican woman had been violently stirred over Trina's sudden wealth; Maria's mind had gone back to her younger days. She leaned forward, her elbows on her knees, her chin in her hands, her eyes wide and fixed. Old Grannis listened to her attentively.

"There wa'n't a piece that was so much as scratched," Maria was saying. "Every piece was just like a mirror, smooth and bright; oh, bright as a little sun. Such a service as that was—platters and soup tureens and an immense big punchbowl. Five thousand dollars, what does that amount to? Why, that punch-bowl alone was worth a fortune."

"What a wonderful story!" exclaimed Old Grannis, never for an instant doubting its truth. "And it's all lost now, you say?"

"Lost, lost," repeated Maria.

"Tut, tut! What a pity! What a pity!"

Suddenly the agent rose and broke out with:

"Well, I must be going, if I'm to get any car."

He shook hands with everybody, offered a parting cigar to Marcus, congratulated McTeague and Trina a last time, and bowed himself out.

"What an elegant gentleman," commented Miss Baker.

"Ah," said Marcus, nodding his head, "there's a man of the world for you. Right on to himself, by damn!"

The company broke up.

"Come along, Mac," cried Marcus; "we're to sleep with the dogs tonight, you know."

The two friends said "Good-night" all around and departed for the little dog hospital.

Old Grannis hurried to his room furtively, terrified lest he should again be brought face to face with Miss Baker. He bolted himself in and listened until he heard her foot in the hall and the soft closing of her door. She was there close beside him; as one might say, in the same room; for he, too, had made the discovery as to the similarity of the wallpaper. At long intervals he could hear a faint rustling as she moved about. What an evening that had been for him! He had met her, had spoken to her, had touched her hand; he was in a tremor of excitement. In a like manner the little old dressmaker listened and quivered. HE was there in that same room which they shared in common, separated only by the thinnest board partition. He was thinking of her, she was almost sure of it. They were strangers no longer; they were acquaintances, friends. What an event that evening had been in their lives!

Late as it was, Miss Baker brewed a cup of tea and sat down in her rocking chair close to the partition; she rocked gently, sipping her tea, calming herself after the emotions of that wonderful evening.

Old Grannis heard the clinking of the tea things and smelt the faint odor of the tea. It seemed to him a signal, an invitation. He drew his chair close to his side of the partition, before his work-table. A pile of half-bound "Nations" was in the little binding apparatus; he threaded his huge upholsterer's needle with stout twine and set to work.

It was their tete-a-tete. Instinctively they felt each other's presence, felt each other's thought coming to them through the thin partition. It was charming; they were perfectly happy. There in the stillness that settled over the flat in the half hour after midnight the two old people "kept company," enjoying after their fashion their little romance that had come so late into the lives of each.

On the way to her room in the garret Maria Macapa paused under the single gas-jet that burned at the top of the well of the staircase; she assured herself that she was alone, and then drew from her pocket one of McTeague's "tapes" of non-cohesive gold. It was the most valuable steal she had ever yet made in the dentist's "Parlors." She told herself that it was worth at least a couple of dollars. Suddenly an idea occurred to her, and she went hastily to a window at the end of the hall, and, shading her face with both hands, looked down into the little alley just back of the flat. On some nights Zerkow, the red-headed Polish Jew, sat up late, taking account of the week's ragpicking. There was a dim light in his window now.

Maria went to her room, threw a shawl around her head, and descended into the little back yard of the flat by the back stairs. As she let herself out of the back gate into the alley, Alexander, Marcus's Irish setter, woke suddenly with a gruff bark. The collie who lived on the other side of the fence, in the back yard of the branch post-office, answered with a snarl. Then in an instant the endless feud between the two dogs was resumed. They dragged their respective kennels to the fence, and through the cracks raged at each other in a frenzy of hate; their teeth snapped and gleamed; the hackles on their backs rose and stiffened. Their hideous clamor could have been heard for blocks around. What a massacre should the two ever meet!

Meanwhile, Maria was knocking at Zerkow's miserable hovel.

"Who is it? Who is it?" cried the rag-picker from within, in his hoarse voice, that was half whisper, starting nervously, and sweeping a handful of silver into his drawer.

"It's me, Maria Macapa;" then in a lower voice, and as if speaking to herself, "had a flying squirrel an' let him go."

"Ah, Maria," cried Zerkow, obsequiously opening the door. "Come in, come in, my girl; you're always welcome, even as late as this. No junk, hey? But you're welcome for all that. You'll have a drink, won't you?" He led her into his back room and got down the whiskey bottle and the broken red tumbler.

After the two had drunk together Maria produced the gold "tape." Zerkow's eyes glittered on the instant. The sight of gold invariably sent a qualm all through him; try as he would, he could not repress it. His fingers trembled and clawed at his mouth; his breath grew short.

"Ah, ah, ah!" he exclaimed, "give it here, give it here; give it to me, Maria. That's a good girl, come give it to me."

They haggled as usual over the price, but to-night Maria was too excited over other matters to spend much time in bickering over a few cents.

"Look here, Zerkow," she said as soon as the transfer was made, "I got something to tell you. A little while ago I sold a lottery ticket to a girl at the flat; the drawing was in this evening's papers. How much do you suppose that girl has won?"

"I don't know. How much? How much?"

"Five thousand dollars."

It was as though a knife had been run through the Jew; a spasm of an almost physical pain twisted his face—his entire body. He raised his clenched fists into the air, his eyes shut, his teeth gnawing his lip.

"Five thousand dollars," he whispered; "five thousand dollars. For what? For nothing, for simply buying a ticket; and I have worked so hard for it, so hard, so hard. Five thousand dollars, five thousand dollars. Oh, why couldn't it have come to me?" he cried, his voice choking, the tears starting to his eyes; "why couldn't it have come to me? To come so close, so close, and yet to miss me—me who have worked for it, fought for it, starved for it, am dying for it every day. Think of it, Maria, five thousand dollars, all bright, heavy pieces——"

"Bright as a sunset," interrupted Maria, her chin propped on her hands. "Such a glory, and heavy. Yes, every piece was heavy, and it was all you could do to lift the punch-bowl. Why, that punch-bowl was worth a fortune alone— —"

"And it rang when you hit it with your knuckles, didn't it?" prompted Zerkow, eagerly, his lips trembling, his fingers hooking themselves into claws.

"Sweeter'n any church bell," continued Maria.

"Go on, go on, go on," cried Zerkow, drawing his chair closer, and shutting his eyes in ecstasy.

"There were more than a hundred pieces, and every one of them gold— —"

"Ah, every one of them gold."

"You should have seen the sight when the leather trunk was opened. There wa'n't a piece that was so much as scratched; every one was like a mirror, smooth and bright, polished so that it looked black—you know how I mean."

"Oh, I know, I know," cried Zerkow, moistening his lips.

Then he plied her with questions—questions that covered every detail of that service of plate. It was soft, wasn't it? You could bite into a plate and leave a dent? The handles of the knives, now, were they gold, too? All the knife was made from one piece of gold, was it? And the forks the same? The interior of the trunk was quilted, of course? Did Maria ever polish the plates herself? When the company ate off this service, it must have made a fine noise—these gold knives and forks clinking together upon these gold plates.

"Now, let's have it all over again, Maria," pleaded Zerkow. "Begin now with 'There were more than a hundred pieces, and every one of them gold.' Go on, begin, begin, begin!"

The red-headed Pole was in a fever of excitement. Maria's recital had become a veritable mania with him. As he listened, with closed eyes and trembling lips, he fancied he could see that wonderful plate before him, there on the table, under his eyes, under his hand, ponderous, massive, gleaming. He tormented Maria into a second repetition of the story—into a third. The more his mind dwelt upon it, the sharper grew his desire. Then, with Maria's refusal to continue the tale, came the reaction. Zerkow awoke as from some ravishing dream. The plate was gone, was irretrievably lost. There was nothing in that miserable room but grimy rags and rust-corroded iron. What torment! what agony! to be so near—so near, to see it in one's distorted fancy as plain as in a mirror. To know every individual piece as an old friend; to feel its weight; to be dazzled by its glitter; to call it one's own, own; to have it to oneself, hugged to the breast; and then to start, to wake, to come down to the horrible reality.

"And you, YOU had it once," gasped Zerkow, clawing at her arm; "you had it once, all your own. Think of it, and now it's gone."

"Gone for good and all."

"Perhaps it's buried near your old place somewhere."

"It's gone—gone—gone," chanted Maria in a monotone.

Zerkow dug his nails into his scalp, tearing at his red hair.

"Yes, yes, it's gone, it's gone—lost forever! Lost forever!"

Marcus and the dentist walked up the silent street and reached the little dog hospital. They had hardly spoken on the way. McTeague's brain was in a whirl; speech failed him. He was busy thinking of the great thing that had happened that night, and was trying to realize what its effect would be upon his life—his life and Trina's. As soon as they had found themselves in the street, Marcus had relapsed at once to a sullen silence, which McTeague was too abstracted to notice.

They entered the tiny office of the hospital with its red carpet, its gas stove, and its colored prints of famous dogs hanging against the walls. In one corner stood the iron bed which they were to occupy.

"You go on an' get to bed, Mac," observed Marcus. "I'll take a look at the dogs before I turn in."

He went outside and passed along into the yard, that was bounded on three sides by pens where the dogs were kept. A bull terrier dying of gastritis recognized him and began to whimper feebly.

Marcus paid no attention to the dogs. For the first time that evening he was alone and could give vent to his thoughts. He took a couple of turns up and down the yard, then suddenly in a low voice exclaimed:

"You fool, you fool, Marcus Schouler! If you'd kept Trina you'd have had that money. You might have had it yourself. You've thrown away your chance in life—to give up the girl, yes—but this," he stamped his foot with rage—"to throw five thousand dollars out of the window—to stuff it into the pockets of someone else, when it might have been yours, when you might have had Trina AND the money—and all for what? Because we were pals. Oh, 'pals' is all right—but five thousand dollars—to have played it right into his hands—God DAMN the luck!"

CHAPTER 8

The next two months were delightful. Trina and McTeague saw each other regularly, three times a week. The dentist went over to B Street Sunday and Wednesday afternoons as usual; but on Fridays it was Trina who came to the city. She spent the morning between nine and twelve o'clock down town, for the most part in the cheap department stores, doing the weekly shopping for herself and the family. At noon she took an uptown car and met McTeague at the corner of Polk Street. The two lunched together at a small uptown hotel just around the corner on Sutter Street. They were given a little room to themselves. Nothing could have been more delicious. They had but to close the sliding door to shut themselves off from the whole world.

Trina would arrive breathless from her raids upon the bargain counters, her pale cheeks flushed, her hair blown about her face and into the corners of her lips, her mother's net reticule stuffed to bursting. Once in their tiny private room, she would drop into her chair with a little groan.

"Oh, MAC, I am so tired; I've just been all OVER town. Oh, it's good to sit down. Just think, I had to stand up in the car all the way, after being on my feet the whole blessed morning. Look here what I've bought. Just things and things. Look, there's some dotted veiling I got for myself; see now, do you think it looks pretty?"—she spread it over her face—"and I got a box of writing paper, and a roll of crepe paper to make a lamp shade for the front parlor; and—what do you suppose—I saw a pair of Nottingham lace curtains for FORTY-NINE CENTS; isn't that cheap? and some chenille portieres for two and a half. Now what have YOU been doing since I last saw you? Did Mr. Heise finally get up enough courage to have his tooth pulled yet?" Trina took off her hat and veil and rearranged her hair before the looking-glass.

"No, no—not yet. I went down to the sign painter's yesterday afternoon to see about that big gold tooth for a sign. It costs too much; I can't get it yet a while. There's two kinds, one German gilt and the other French gilt; but the German gilt is no good."

McTeague sighed, and wagged his head. Even Trina and the five thousand dollars could not make him forget this one unsatisfied longing.

At other times they would talk at length over their plans, while Trina sipped her chocolate and McTeague devoured huge chunks of butterless bread. They were to be married at the end of May, and the dentist already had his eye on a couple of rooms, part of the suite of a bankrupt photographer. They were situated in the flat, just back of his "Parlors," and he believed the photographer would sublet them furnished.

McTeague and Trina had no apprehensions as to their finances. They could be sure, in fact, of a tidy little income. The dentist's practice was fairly good, and they could count upon the interest of Trina's five thousand dollars. To McTeague's mind this interest seemed woefully small. He had had uncertain ideas about that five thousand dollars; had imagined that they would spend it in some lavish fashion; would buy a house, perhaps, or would furnish their new rooms with overwhelming luxury—luxury that implied red velvet carpets and continued feasting. The oldtime miner's idea of wealth easily gained and quickly spent persisted in his mind. But when Trina had begun to talk of investments and interests and per cents, he was troubled and not a little disappointed. The lump sum of five thousand dollars was one thing, a miserable little twenty or twenty-five a month was quite another; and then someone else had the money.

"But don't you see, Mac," explained Trina, "it's ours just the same. We could get it back whenever we wanted it; and then it's the reasonable way to do. We mustn't let it turn our heads, Mac, dear, like that man that spent all he won in buying more tickets. How foolish we'd feel after we'd spent it all! We ought to go on just the same as before; as if we hadn't won. We must be sensible about it, mustn't we?"

"Well, well, I guess perhaps that's right," the dentist would answer, looking slowly about on the floor.

Just what should ultimately be done with the money was the subject of endless discussion in the Sieppe family. The savings bank would allow only three per cent., but Trina's parents believed that something better could be got.

"There's Uncle Oelbermann," Trina had suggested, remembering the rich relative who had the wholesale toy store in the Mission.

Mr. Sieppe struck his hand to his forehead. "Ah, an idea," he cried. In the end an agreement was made. The money was invested in Mr. Oelbermann's business. He gave Trina six per cent.

Invested in this fashion, Trina's winning would bring in twenty-five dollars a month. But, besides this, Trina had her own little trade. She made Noah's ark animals for Uncle Oelbermann's store. Trina's ancestors on both sides were German-Swiss, and some long-forgotten forefather of the sixteenth century, some worsted-leggined wood-carver of the Tyrol, had handed down the talent of the national industry, to reappear in this strangely distorted guise.

She made Noah's ark animals, whittling them out of a block of soft wood with a sharp jack-knife, the only instrument she used. Trina was very proud to explain her work to McTeague as he had already explained his own to her.

"You see, I take a block of straight-grained pine and cut out the shape, roughly at first, with the big blade; then I go over it a second time with the little blade, more carefully; then I put in the ears and tail with a drop of glue, and paint it with a 'non-poisonous' paint—Vandyke brown for the horses, foxes, and cows; slate gray for the elephants and camels; burnt umber for the chickens, zebras, and so on; then, last, a dot of Chinese white for the eyes, and there you are, all finished. They sell for nine cents a dozen. Only I can't make the manikins."

"The manikins?"

"The little figures, you know—Noah and his wife, and Shem, and all the others."

It was true. Trina could not whittle them fast enough and cheap enough to compete with the turning lathe, that could throw off whole tribes and peoples of manikins while she was fashioning one family. Everything else, however, she made—the ark itself, all windows and no door; the box in which the whole was packed; even down to pasting on the label, which read, "Made in France." She earned from three to four dollars a week.

The income from these three sources, McTeague's profession, the interest of the five thousand dollars, and Trina's whittling, made a respectable little sum taken altogether. Trina declared they could even lay by something, adding to the five thousand dollars little by little.

It soon became apparent that Trina would be an extraordinarily good housekeeper. Economy was her strong point. A good deal of peasant blood still ran undiluted in her veins, and she had all the instinct of a hardy and penurious mountain race—the instinct which saves without any thought, without idea of consequence—saving for the sake of saving, hoarding without knowing why. Even McTeague did not know how closely Trina held to her new-found wealth.

But they did not always pass their luncheon hour in this discussion of incomes and economies. As the dentist came to know his little woman better she grew to be more and more of a puzzle and a joy to him. She would suddenly interrupt a grave discourse upon the rents of rooms and the cost of light and fuel with a brusque outburst of affection that set him all a-tremble with delight. All at once she would set down her chocolate, and, leaning across the narrow table, would exclaim:

"Never mind all that! Oh, Mac, do you truly, really love me—love me BIG?"

McTeague would stammer something, gasping, and wagging his head, beside himself for the lack of words.

"Old bear," Trina would answer, grasping him by both huge ears and swaying his head from side to side. "Kiss me, then. Tell me, Mac, did you think any less of me that first time I let you kiss me there in the station? Oh, Mac, dear, what a funny nose you've got, all full of hairs inside; and, Mac, do you know you've got a bald spot—" she dragged his head down towards her—"right on the top of your head." Then she would seriously kiss the bald spot in question, declaring:

"That'll make the hair grow."

Trina took an infinite enjoyment in playing with McTeague's great square-cut head, rumpling his hair till it stood on end, putting her fingers in his eyes, or stretching his ears out straight, and watching the effect with her head on one side. It was like a little child playing with some gigantic, good-natured Saint Bernard.

One particular amusement they never wearied of. The two would lean across the table towards each other, McTeague folding his arms under his breast. Then Trina, resting on her elbows, would part his mustache-the great blond mustache of a viking—with her two hands, pushing it up from his lips, causing his face to assume the appearance of a Greek mask. She would curl it around either forefinger, drawing it to a fine end. Then all at once McTeague would make a fearful snorting noise through his nose. Invariably—though she was expecting this, though it was part of the game—Trina would jump with a stifled shriek. McTeague would bellow with laughter till his eyes watered. Then they would recommence upon the instant, Trina protesting with a nervous tremulousness:

"Now—now—now, Mac, DON'T; you SCARE me so."

But these delicious tete-a-tetes with Trina were offset by a certain coolness that Marcus Schouler began to affect towards the dentist. At first McTeague was unaware of it; but by this time even his slow wits began to perceive that his best friend—his "pal"—was not the same to him as formerly. They continued to meet at lunch nearly every day but Friday at the car conductors' coffee-joint. But Marcus was sulky; there could be no doubt about that. He avoided talking to McTeague, read the paper continually, answering the dentist's timid efforts at conversation in gruff monosyllables. Sometimes, even, he turned sideways to the table and talked at great length to Heise the harness-maker, whose table was next to theirs. They took no more long walks together when Marcus went out to exercise the dogs. Nor did Marcus ever again recur to his generosity in renouncing Trina.

One Tuesday, as McTeague took his place at the table in the coffee-joint, he found Marcus already there.

"Hello, Mark," said the dentist, "you here already?"

"Hello," returned the other, indifferently, helping himself to tomato catsup. There was a silence. After a long while Marcus suddenly looked up.

"Say, Mac," he exclaimed, "when you going to pay me that money you owe me?"

McTeague was astonished.

"Huh? What? I don't—do I owe you any money, Mark?"

"Well, you owe me four bits," returned Marcus, doggedly. "I paid for you and Trina that day at the picnic, and you never gave it back."

"Oh—oh!" answered McTeague, in distress. "That's so, that's so. I—you ought to have told me before. Here's your money, and I'm obliged to you."

"It ain't much," observed Marcus, sullenly. "But I need all I can get now-a-days."

"Are you—are you broke?" inquired McTeague.

"And I ain't saying anything about your sleeping at the hospital that night, either," muttered Marcus, as he pocketed the coin.

"Well—well—do you mean—should I have paid for that?"

"Well, you'd 'a' had to sleep SOMEWHERES, wouldn't you?" flashed out Marcus. "You 'a' had to pay half a dollar for a bed at the flat."

"All right, all right," cried the dentist, hastily, feeling in his pockets. "I don't want you should be out anything on my account, old man. Here, will four bits do?"

"I don't WANT your damn money," shouted Marcus in a sudden rage, throwing back the coin. "I ain't no beggar."

McTeague was miserable. How had he offended his pal?

"Well, I want you should take it, Mark," he said, pushing it towards him.

"I tell you I won't touch your money," exclaimed the other through his clenched teeth, white with passion. "I've been played for a sucker long enough."

"What's the matter with you lately, Mark?" remonstrated McTeague. "You've got a grouch about something. Is there anything I've done?"

"Well, that's all right, that's all right," returned Marcus as he rose from the table. "That's all right. I've been played for a sucker long enough, that's all. I've been played for a sucker long enough." He went away with a parting malevolent glance.

At the corner of Polk Street, between the flat and the car conductors' coffee-joint, was Frenna's. It was a corner grocery; advertisements for cheap butter and eggs, painted in green marking-ink upon wrapping paper, stood about on the sidewalk outside. The doorway was decorated with a huge Milwaukee beer sign. Back of the store proper was a bar where white sand covered the floor. A few tables and chairs were scattered here and there. The walls were hung with gorgeously-colored tobacco advertisements and colored lithographs of trotting horses. On the wall behind the bar was a model of a full-rigged ship enclosed in a bottle.

It was at this place that the dentist used to leave his pitcher to be filled on Sunday afternoons. Since his engagement to Trina he had discontinued this habit. However, he still dropped into Frenna's one or two nights in the week. He spent a pleasant hour there, smoking his huge porcelain pipe and drinking his beer. He never joined any of the groups of piquet players around the tables. In fact, he hardly spoke to anyone but the bartender and Marcus.

For Frenna's was one of Marcus Schouler's haunts; a great deal of his time was spent there. He involved himself in fearful political and social discussions with Heise the harness-maker, and with one or two old German, habitues of the place. These discussions Marcus carried on, as was his custom, at the top of his voice, gesticulating fiercely, banging the table with his fists, brandishing the plates and glasses, exciting himself with his own clamor.

On a certain Saturday evening, a few days after the scene at the coffee-joint, the dentist bethought him to spend a quiet evening at Frenna's. He had not been there for some time, and, besides that, it occurred to him that the day was his birthday. He would permit himself an extra pipe and a few glasses of beer. When McTeague entered Frenna's back room by the street door, he found Marcus and Heise already installed at one of the tables. Two or three of the old Germans sat opposite them, gulping their beer from time to time. Heise was smoking a cigar, but Marcus had before him his fourth whiskey cocktail. At the moment of McTeague's entrance Marcus had the floor.

"It can't be proven," he was yelling. "I defy any sane politician whose eyes are not blinded by party prejudices, whose opinions are not warped by a personal bias, to substantiate such a statement. Look at your facts, look at your figures. I am a free American citizen, ain't I? I pay my taxes to support a good government, don't I? It's a contract between me and the government, ain't it? Well, then, by damn! if the authorities do not or will not afford me protection for life, liberty, and the pursuit of happiness, then my obligations are at an end; I withhold my taxes. I do—I do—I say I do. What?" He glared about him, seeking opposition.

"That's nonsense," observed Heise, quietly. "Try it once; you'll get jugged." But this observation of the harness-maker's roused Marcus to the last pitch of frenzy.

"Yes, ah, yes!" he shouted, rising to his feet, shaking his finger in the other's face. "Yes, I'd go to jail; but because I—I am crushed by a tyranny, does that make the tyranny right? Does might make right?"

"You must make less noise in here, Mister Schouler," said Frenna, from behind the bar.

"Well, it makes me mad," answered Marcus, subsiding into a growl and resuming his chair. "Hullo, Mac."

"Hullo, Mark."

But McTeague's presence made Marcus uneasy, rousing in him at once a sense of wrong. He twisted to and fro in his chair, shrugging first one shoulder and then another. Quarrelsome at all times, the heat of the previous discussion had awakened within him all his natural combativeness. Besides this, he was drinking his fourth cocktail.

McTeague began filling his big porcelain pipe. He lit it, blew a great cloud of smoke into the room, and settled himself comfortably in his chair. The smoke of his cheap tobacco drifted into the faces of the group at the adjoining table, and Marcus strangled and coughed. Instantly his eyes flamed.

"Say, for God's sake," he vociferated, "choke off on that pipe! If you've got to smoke rope like that, smoke it in a crowd of muckers; don't come here amongst gentlemen."

"Shut up, Schouler!" observed Heise in a low voice.

McTeague was stunned by the suddenness of the attack. He took his pipe from his mouth, and stared blankly at Marcus; his lips moved, but he said no word. Marcus turned his back on him, and the dentist resumed his pipe.

But Marcus was far from being appeased. McTeague could not hear the talk that followed between him and the harnessmaker, but it seemed to him that Marcus was telling Heise of some injury, some grievance, and that the latter was trying to pacify him. All at once their talk grew louder. Heise laid a retaining hand upon his companion's coat sleeve, but Marcus swung himself around in his chair, and, fixing his eyes on McTeague, cried as if in answer to some protestation on the part of Heise:

"All I know is that I've been soldiered out of five thousand dollars."

McTeague gaped at him, bewildered. He removed his pipe from his mouth a second time, and stared at Marcus with eyes full of trouble and perplexity.

"If I had my rights," cried Marcus, bitterly, "I'd have part of that money. It's my due—it's only justice." The dentist still kept silence.

"If it hadn't been for me," Marcus continued, addressing himself directly to McTeague, "you wouldn't have had a cent of it—no, not a cent. Where's my share, I'd like to know? Where do I come in? No, I ain't in it any more. I've been played for a sucker, an' now that you've got all you can out of me, now that you've done me out of my girl and out of my money, you give me the go-by. Why, where would you have been TO-DAY if it hadn't been for me?" Marcus shouted in a sudden exasperation, "You'd a been plugging teeth at two bits an hour. Ain't you got any gratitude? Ain't you got any sense of decency?"

"Ah, hold up, Schouler," grumbled Heise. "You don't want to get into a row."

"No, I don't, Heise," returned Marcus, with a plaintive, aggrieved air. "But it's too much sometimes when you think of it. He stole away my girl's affections, and now that he's rich and prosperous, and has got five thousand dollars that I might have had, he gives me the go-by; he's played me for a sucker. Look here," he cried, turning again to McTeague, "do I get any of that money?"

"It ain't mine to give," answered McTeague. "You're drunk, that's what you are."

"Do I get any of that money?" cried Marcus, persistently.

The dentist shook his head. "No, you don't get any of it."

"Now—NOW," clamored the other, turning to the harnessmaker, as though this explained everything. "Look at that, look at that. Well, I've done with you from now on." Marcus had risen to his feet by this time and made as if to leave, but at every instant he came back, shouting his phrases into McTeague's face, moving off again as he spoke the last words, in order to give them better effect.

"This settles it right here. I've done with you. Don't you ever dare speak to me again"—his voice was shaking with fury—"and don't you sit at my table in the restaurant again. I'm sorry I ever lowered myself to keep company with such dirt. Ah, one-horse dentist! Ah, ten-cent zinc-plugger—hoodlum—MUCKER! Get your damn smoke outa my face."

Then matters reached a sudden climax. In his agitation the dentist had been pulling hard on his pipe, and as Marcus for the last time thrust his face close to his own, McTeague, in opening his lips to reply, blew a stifling, acrid cloud directly in Marcus Schouler's eyes. Marcus knocked the pipe from his fingers with a sudden flash of his hand; it spun across the room and broke into a dozen fragments in a far corner.

McTeague rose to his feet, his eyes wide. But as yet he was not angry, only surprised, taken all aback by the suddenness of Marcus Schouler's outbreak as well as by its unreasonableness. Why had Marcus broken his pipe? What did it all mean, anyway? As he rose the dentist made a vague motion with his right hand. Did Marcus misinterpret it as a gesture of menace? He sprang back as though avoiding a blow. All at once there was a cry. Marcus had made a quick, peculiar motion, swinging his arm upward with a wide and sweeping gesture; his jack-knife lay open in his palm; it shot forward as he flung it, glinted sharply by McTeague's head, and struck quivering into the wall behind.

A sudden chill ran through the room; the others stood transfixed, as at the swift passage of some cold and deadly wind. Death had stooped there for an instant, had stooped and past, leaving a trail of terror and confusion. Then the door leading to the street slammed; Marcus had disappeared.

Thereon a great babel of exclamation arose. The tension of that all but fatal instant snapped, and speech became once more possible.

"He would have knifed you."

"Narrow escape."

"What kind of a man do you call THAT?"

"'Tain't his fault he ain't a murderer."

"I'd have him up for it."

"And they two have been the greatest kind of friends."

"He didn't touch you, did he?"

"No—no—no."

"What a—what a devil! What treachery! A regular greaser trick!"

"Look out he don't stab you in the back. If that's the kind of man he is, you never can tell."

Frenna drew the knife from the wall.

"Guess I'll keep this toad-stabber," he observed. "That fellow won't come round for it in a hurry; goodsized blade, too." The group examined it with intense interest.

"Big enough to let the life out of any man," observed Heise.

"What—what—what did he do it for?" stammered McTeague. "I got no quarrel with him."

He was puzzled and harassed by the strangeness of it all. Marcus would have killed him; had thrown his knife at him in the true, uncanny "greaser" style. It was inexplicable. McTeague sat down again, looking stupidly about on the floor. In a corner of the room his eye encountered his broken pipe, a dozen little fragments of painted porcelain and the stem of cherry wood and amber.

At that sight his tardy wrath, ever lagging behind the original affront, suddenly blazed up. Instantly his huge jaws clicked together.

"He can't make small of ME," he exclaimed, suddenly. "I'll show Marcus Schouler—I'll show him—I'll——"

He got up and clapped on his hat.

"Now, Doctor," remonstrated Heise, standing between him and the door, "don't go make a fool of yourself."

"Let 'um alone," joined in Frenna, catching the dentist by the arm; "he's full, anyhow."

"He broke my pipe," answered McTeague.

It was this that had roused him. The thrown knife, the attempt on his life, was beyond his solution; but the breaking of his pipe he understood clearly enough.

"I'll show him," he exclaimed.

As though they had been little children, McTeague set Frenna and the harness-maker aside, and strode out at the door like a raging elephant. Heise stood rubbing his shoulder.

"Might as well try to stop a locomotive," he muttered. "The man's made of iron."

Meanwhile, McTeague went storming up the street toward the flat, wagging his head and grumbling to himself. Ah, Marcus would break his pipe, would he? Ah, he was a zinc-plugger, was he? He'd show Marcus Schouler. No one should make small of him. He tramped up the stairs to Marcus's room. The door was locked. The dentist put one enormous hand on the knob and pushed the door in, snapping the wood-work, tearing off the lock. Nobody—the room was dark and empty. Never mind, Marcus would have to come home some time that night. McTeague would go down and wait for him in his "Parlors." He was bound to hear him as he came up the stairs.

As McTeague reached his room he stumbled over, in the darkness, a big packing-box that stood in the hallway just outside his door. Puzzled, he stepped over it, and lighting the gas in his room, dragged it inside and examined it.

It was addressed to him. What could it mean? He was expecting nothing. Never since he had first furnished his room had packing-cases been left for him in this fashion. No mistake was possible. There were his name and address unmistakably. "Dr. McTeague, dentist—Polk Street, San Francisco, Cal.," and the red Wells Fargo tag.

Seized with the joyful curiosity of an overgrown boy, he pried off the boards with the corner of his fireshovel. The case was stuffed full of excelsior. On the top lay an envelope addressed to him in Trina's handwriting. He opened it and read, "For my dear Mac's birthday, from Trina;" and below, in a kind of post-script, "The man will be round to-morrow to put it in place." McTeague tore away the excelsior. Suddenly he uttered an exclamation.

It was the Tooth—the famous golden molar with its huge prongs—his sign, his ambition, the one unrealized dream of his life; and it was French gilt, too, not the cheap German gilt that was no good. Ah, what a dear little woman was this Trina, to keep so quiet, to remember his birthday!

"Ain't she—ain't she just a—just a JEWEL," exclaimed McTeague under his breath, "a JEWEL—yes, just a JEWEL; that's the word."

Very carefully he removed the rest of the excelsior, and lifting the ponderous Tooth from its box, set it upon the marble-top centre table. How immense it looked in that little room! The thing was tremendous, overpowering—the tooth of a gigantic fossil, golden and dazzling. Beside it everything seemed dwarfed. Even McTeague himself, big boned and enormous as he was, shrank and dwindled in the presence of the monster. As for an instant he bore it in his hands, it was like a puny Gulliver struggling with the molar of some vast Brobdingnag.

The dentist circled about that golden wonder, gasping with delight and stupefaction, touching it gingerly with his hands as if it were something sacred. At every moment his thought returned to Trina. No, never was there such a little woman as his—the very thing he wanted—how had she remembered? And the money, where had that come from? No one knew better than he how expensive were these signs; not another dentist on Polk Street could afford one. Where, then, had Trina found the money? It came out of her five thousand dollars, no doubt.

But what a wonderful, beautiful tooth it was, to be sure, bright as a mirror, shining there in its coat of French gilt, as if with a light of its own! No danger of that tooth turning black with the weather, as did the cheap German gilt impostures. What would that other dentist, that poser, that rider of bicycles, that courser of greyhounds, say when he should see this marvellous molar run out from McTeague's bay window like a flag of defiance? No doubt he would suffer veritable convulsions of envy; would be positively sick with jealousy. If McTeague could only see his face at the moment!

For a whole hour the dentist sat there in his little "Parlor," gazing ecstatically at his treasure, dazzled, supremely content. The whole room took on a different aspect because of it. The stone pug dog before the little stove reflected it in his protruding eyes; the canary woke and chittered feebly at this new gilt, so much brighter than the bars of its little prison. Lorenzo de' Medici, in the steel engraving, sitting in the heart of his court, seemed to ogle the thing out of the corner of one eye, while the brilliant colors of the unused rifle manufacturer's calendar seemed to fade and pale in the brilliance of this greater glory.

At length, long after midnight, the dentist started to go to bed, undressing himself with his eyes still fixed on the great tooth. All at once he heard Marcus Schouler's foot on the stairs; he started up with his fists clenched, but immediately dropped back upon the bed-lounge with a gesture of indifference.

He was in no truculent state of mind now. He could not reinstate himself in that mood of wrath wherein he had left the corner grocery. The tooth had changed all that. What was Marcus Schouler's hatred to him, who had Trina's affection? What did he care about a broken pipe now that he had the tooth? Let him go. As Frenna said, he was not worth it. He heard Marcus come out into the hall, shouting aggrievedly to anyone within sound of his voice:

"An' now he breaks into my room—into my room, by damn! How do I know how many things he's stolen? It's come to stealing from me, now, has it?" He went into his room, banging his splintered door.

McTeague looked upward at the ceiling, in the direction of the voice, muttering:

"Ah, go to bed, you."

He went to bed himself, turning out the gas, but leaving the window-curtains up so that he could see the tooth the last thing before he went to sleep and the first thing as he arose in the morning.

But he was restless during the night. Every now and then he was awakened by noises to which he had long since become accustomed. Now it was the cackling of the geese in the deserted market across the street; now it was the stoppage of the cable, the sudden silence coming almost like a shock; and now it was the infuriated barking of the dogs in the back yard—Alec, the Irish setter, and the collie that belonged to the branch post-office raging at each other through the fence, snarling their endless hatred into each other's faces. As often as he woke, McTeague turned and looked for the tooth, with a sudden suspicion that he had only that moment dreamed the whole business. But he always found it—Trina's gift, his birthday from his little woman—a huge, vague bulk, looming there through the half darkness in the centre of the room, shining dimly out as if with some mysterious light of its own.

CHAPTER 9

Trina and McTeague were married on the first day of June, in the photographer's rooms that the dentist had rented. All through May the Sieppe household had been turned upside down. The little box of a house vibrated with excitement and confusion, for not only were the preparations for Trina's marriage to be made, but also the preliminaries were to be arranged for the hegira of the entire Sieppe family.

They were to move to the southern part of the State the day after Trina's marriage, Mr. Sieppe having bought a third interest in an upholstering business in the suburbs of Los Angeles. It was possible that Marcus Schouler would go with them.

Not Stanley penetrating for the first time into the Dark Continent, not Napoleon leading his army across the Alps, was more weighted with responsibility, more burdened with care, more overcome with the sense of the importance of his undertaking, than was Mr. Sieppe during this period of preparation. From dawn to dark, from dark to early dawn, he toiled and planned and fretted, organizing and reorganizing, projecting and devising. The trunks were lettered, A, B, and C, the packages and smaller bundles numbered. Each member of the family had his especial duty to perform, his particular bundles to oversee. Not a detail was forgotten—fares, prices, and tips were calculated to two places of decimals. Even the amount of food that it would be necessary to carry for the black greyhound was determined. Mrs. Sieppe was to look after the lunch, "der gomisariat." Mr. Sieppe would assume charge of the checks, the money, the tickets, and, of course, general supervision. The twins would be under the command of Owgooste, who, in turn, would report for orders to his father.

Day in and day out these minutiae were rehearsed. The children were drilled in their parts with a military exactitude; obedience and punctuality became cardinal virtues. The vast importance of the undertaking was insisted upon with scrupulous iteration. It was a manoeuvre, an army changing its base of operations, a veritable tribal migration.

On the other hand, Trina's little room was the centre around which revolved another and different order of things. The dressmaker came and went, congratulatory visitors invaded the little front parlor, the chatter of unfamiliar voices resounded from the front steps; bonnet-boxes and yards of dress-goods littered the beds and chairs; wrapping paper, tissue paper, and bits of string strewed the floor; a pair of white satin slippers stood on a corner of the toilet table; lengths of white veiling, like a snow-flurry, buried the little work-table; and a mislaid box of artificial orange blossoms was finally discovered behind the bureau.

The two systems of operation often clashed and tangled. Mrs. Sieppe was found by her harassed husband helping Trina with the waist of her gown when she should have been slicing cold chicken in the kitchen. Mr. Sieppe packed his frock coat, which he would have to wear at the wedding, at the very bottom of "Trunk C." The minister, who called to offer his congratulations and to make arrangements, was mistaken for the expressman.

McTeague came and went furtively, dizzied and made uneasy by all this bustle. He got in the way; he trod upon and tore breadths of silk; he tried to help carry the packing-boxes, and broke the hall gas fixture; he came in upon Trina and the dress-maker at an ill-timed moment, and retiring precipitately, overturned the piles of pictures stacked in the hall.

There was an incessant going and coming at every moment of the day, a great calling up and down stairs, a shouting from room to room, an opening and shutting of doors, and an intermittent sound of hammering from the laundry, where Mr. Sieppe in his shirt sleeves labored among the packing-boxes. The twins clattered about on the carpetless floors of the denuded rooms. Owgooste was smacked from hour to hour, and wept upon the front stairs; the dressmaker called over the banisters for a hot flatiron; expressmen tramped up and down the stairway. Mrs. Sieppe stopped in the preparation of the lunches to call "Hoop, Hoop" to the greyhound, throwing lumps of coal. The dog-wheel creaked, the front door bell rang, delivery wagons rumbled away, windows rattled—the little house was in a positive uproar.

Almost every day of the week now Trina was obliged to run over to town and meet McTeague. No more philandering over their lunch now-a-days. It was business now. They haunted the house-furnishing floors of the great department houses, inspecting and pricing ranges, hardware, china, and the like. They rented the photographer's rooms furnished, and fortunately only the kitchen and dining-room utensils had to be bought.

The money for this as well as for her trousseau came out of Trina's five thousand dollars. For it had been finally decided that two hundred dollars of this amount should be devoted to the establishment of the new household.

Now that Trina had made her great winning, Mr. Sieppe no longer saw the necessity of dowering her further, especially when he considered the enormous expense to which he would be put by the voyage of his own family.

It had been a dreadful wrench for Trina to break in upon her precious five thousand. She clung to this sum with a tenacity that was surprising; it had become for her a thing miraculous, a god-from-the-machine, suddenly descending upon the stage of her humble little life; she regarded it as something almost sacred and inviolable. Never, never should a penny of it be spent. Before she could be induced to part with two hundred dollars of it, more than one scene had been enacted between her and her parents.

Did Trina pay for the golden tooth out of this two hundred? Later on, the dentist often asked her about it, but Trina invariably laughed in his face, declaring that it was her secret. McTeague never found out.

One day during this period McTeague told Trina about his affair with Marcus. Instantly she was aroused.

"He threw his knife at you! The coward! He wouldn't of dared stand up to you like a man. Oh, Mac, suppose he HAD hit you?"

"Came within an inch of my head," put in McTeague, proudly.

"Think of it!" she gasped; "and he wanted part of my money. Well, I do like his cheek; part of my five thousand! Why, it's mine, every single penny of it. Marcus hasn't the least bit of right to it. It's mine, mine.—I mean, it's ours, Mac, dear."

The elder Sieppes, however, made excuses for Marcus. He had probably been drinking a good deal and didn't know what he was about. He had a dreadful temper, anyhow. Maybe he only wanted to scare McTeague.

The week before the marriage the two men were reconciled. Mrs. Sieppe brought them together in the front parlor of the B Street house.

"Now, you two fellers, don't be dot foolish. Schake hands und maig ut oop, soh."

Marcus muttered an apology. McTeague, miserably embarrassed, rolled his eyes about the room, murmuring, "That's all right—that's all right—that's all right."

However, when it was proposed that Marcus should be McTeague's best man, he flashed out again with renewed violence. Ah, no! ah, NO! He'd make up with the dentist now that he was going away, but he'd be damned—yes, he would—before he'd be his best man. That was rubbing it in. Let him get Old Grannis.

"I'm friends with um all right," vociferated Marcus, "but I'll not stand up with um. I'll not be ANYBODY'S best man, I won't."

The wedding was to be very quiet; Trina preferred it that way. McTeague would invite only Miss Baker and Heise the harness-maker. The Sieppes sent cards to Selina, who was counted on to furnish the music; to Marcus, of course; and to Uncle Oelbermann.

At last the great day, the first of June, arrived. The Sieppes had packed their last box and had strapped the last trunk. Trina's two trunks had already been sent to her new home—the remodelled photographer's rooms. The B Street house was deserted; the whole family came over to the city on the last day of May and stopped over night at one of the cheap downtown hotels. Trina would be married the following evening, and immediately after the wedding supper the Sieppes would leave for the South.

McTeague spent the day in a fever of agitation, frightened out of his wits each time that Old Grannis left his elbow.

Old Grannis was delighted beyond measure at the prospect of acting the part of best man in the ceremony. This wedding in which he was to figure filled his mind with vague ideas and half-formed thoughts. He found himself continually wondering what Miss Baker would think of it. During all that day he was in a reflective mood.

"Marriage is a—a noble institution, is it not, Doctor?" he observed to McTeague. "The—the foundation of society. It is not good that man should be alone. No, no," he added, pensively, "it is not good."

"Huh? Yes, yes," McTeague answered, his eyes in the air, hardly hearing him. "Do you think the rooms are all right? Let's go in and look at them again."

They went down the hall to where the new rooms were situated, and the dentist inspected them for the twentieth time.

The rooms were three in number—first, the sitting-room, which was also the dining-room; then the bedroom, and back of this the tiny kitchen.

The sitting-room was particularly charming. Clean matting covered the floor, and two or three bright colored rugs were scattered here and there. The backs of the chairs were hung with knitted worsted tidies, very gay. The bay window should have been occupied by Trina's sewing machine, but this had been moved to the other side of the room to give place to a little black walnut table with spiral legs, before which the pair were to be married. In one corner stood the parlor melodeon, a family possession of the Sieppes, but given now to Trina as one of her parents' wedding presents.

Three pictures hung upon the walls. Two were companion pieces. One of these represented a little boy wearing huge spectacles and trying to smoke an enormous pipe. This was called "I'm Grandpa," the title being printed in large black letters; the companion picture was entitled "I'm Grandma," a little girl in cap and "specs," wearing mitts, and knitting. These pictures were hung on either side of the mantelpiece. The other picture was quite an affair, very large and striking. It was a colored lithograph of two little golden-haired girls in their nightgowns. They were kneeling down and saying their prayers; their eyes—very large and very blue—rolled upward. This picture had for name, "Faith," and was bordered with a red plush mat and a frame of imitation beaten brass.

A door hung with chenille portieres—a bargain at two dollars and a half—admitted one to the bedroom. The bedroom could boast a carpet, three-ply ingrain, the design being bunches of red and green flowers in yellow baskets on a white ground. The wall-paper was admirable— hundreds and hundreds of tiny Japanese mandarins, all identically alike, helping hundreds of almond-eyed ladies into hundreds of impossible junks, while hundreds of bamboo palms overshadowed the pair, and hundreds of long-legged storks trailed contemptuously away from the scene. This room was prolific in pictures. Most of them were framed colored prints from Christmas editions of the London "Graphic" and "Illustrated News," the subject of each picture inevitably involving very alert fox terriers and very pretty moon-faced little girls.

Back of the bedroom was the kitchen, a creation of Trina's, a dream of a kitchen, with its range, its porcelain-lined sink, its copper boiler, and its overpowering array of flashing tinware. Everything was new; everything was complete.

Maria Macapa and a waiter from one of the restaurants in the street were to prepare the wedding supper here. Maria had already put in an appearance. The fire was crackling in the new stove, that smoked badly; a smell of cooking was in the air. She drove McTeague and Old Grannis from the room with great gestures of her bare arms.

This kitchen was the only one of the three rooms they had been obliged to furnish throughout. Most of the sitting-room and bedroom furniture went with the suite; a few pieces they had bought; the remainder Trina had brought over from the B Street house.

The presents had been set out on the extension table in the sitting-room. Besides the parlor melodeon, Trina's parents had given her an ice-water set, and a carving knife and fork with elk-horn handles. Selina had painted a view of the Golden Gate upon a polished slice of redwood that answered the purposes of a paper weight. Marcus Schouler—after impressing upon Trina that his gift was to HER, and not to McTeague—had sent a chatelaine watch of German silver; Uncle Oelbermann's present, however, had been awaited with a good deal of curiosity. What would he send? He was very rich; in a sense Trina was his protege. A couple of days before that upon which the wedding was to take place, two boxes arrived with his card. Trina and McTeague, assisted by Old Grannis, had opened them. The first was a box of all sorts of toys.

"But what—what—I don't make it out," McTeague had exclaimed. "Why should he send us toys? We have no need of toys." Scarlet to her hair, Trina dropped into a chair and laughed till she cried behind her handkerchief.

"We've no use of toys," muttered McTeague, looking at her in perplexity. Old Grannis smiled discreetly, raising a tremulous hand to his chin.

The other box was heavy, bound with withes at the edges, the letters and stamps burnt in.

"I think—I really think it's champagne," said Old Grannis in a whisper. So it was. A full case of Monopole. What a wonder! None of them had seen the like before. Ah, this Uncle Oelbermann! That's what it was to be rich. Not one of the other presents produced so deep an impression as this.

After Old Grannis and the dentist had gone through the rooms, giving a last look around to see that everything was ready, they returned to McTeague's "Parlors." At the door Old Grannis excused himself.

At four o'clock McTeague began to dress, shaving himself first before the hand-glass that was hung against the woodwork of the bay window. While he shaved he sang with strange inappropriateness:

"No one to love, none to Caress,
Left all alone in this world's wilderness."

But as he stood before the mirror, intent upon his shaving, there came a roll of wheels over the cobbles in front of the house. He rushed to the window. Trina had arrived with her father and mother. He saw her get out, and as she glanced upward at his window, their eyes met.

Ah, there she was. There she was, his little woman, looking up at him, her adorable little chin thrust upward with that familiar movement of innocence and confidence. The dentist saw again, as if for the first time, her small, pale face looking out from beneath her royal tiara of black hair; he saw again her long, narrow blue eyes; her lips, nose, and tiny ears, pale and bloodless, and suggestive of anaemia, as if all the vitality that should have lent them color had been sucked up into the strands and coils of that wonderful hair.

As their eyes met they waved their hands gayly to each other; then McTeague heard Trina and her mother come up the stairs and go into the bedroom of the photographer's suite, where Trina was to dress.

No, no; surely there could be no longer any hesitation. He knew that he loved her. What was the matter with him, that he should have doubted it for an instant? The great difficulty was that she was too good, too adorable, too sweet, too delicate for him, who was so huge, so clumsy, so brutal.

There was a knock at the door. It was Old Grannis. He was dressed in his one black suit of broadcloth, much wrinkled; his hair was carefully brushed over his bald forehead.

"Miss Trina has come," he announced, "and the minister. You have an hour yet."

The dentist finished dressing. He wore a suit bought for the occasion—a ready made "Prince Albert" coat too short in the sleeves, striped "blue" trousers, and new patent leather shoes—veritable instruments of torture. Around his collar was a wonderful necktie that Trina had given him; it was of salmon-pink satin; in its centre Selina had painted a knot of blue forget-me-nots.

At length, after an interminable period of waiting, Mr. Sieppe appeared at the door.

"Are you reatty?" he asked in a sepulchral whisper. "Gome, den." It was like King Charles summoned to execution. Mr. Sieppe preceded them into the hall, moving at a funereal pace. He paused. Suddenly, in the direction of the sitting-room, came the strains of the parlor melodeon. Mr. Sieppe flung his arm in the air.

"Vowaarts!" he cried.

He left them at the door of the sitting-room, he himself going into the bedroom where Trina was waiting, entering by the hall door. He was in a tremendous state of nervous tension, fearful lest something should go wrong. He had employed the period of waiting in going through his part for the fiftieth time, repeating what he had to say in a low voice. He had even made chalk marks on the matting in the places where he was to take positions.

The dentist and Old Grannis entered the sitting-room; the minister stood behind the little table in the bay window, holding a book, one finger marking the place; he was rigid, erect, impassive. On either side of him, in a semi-circle, stood the invited guests. A little pock-marked gentleman in glasses, no doubt the famous Uncle Oelbermann; Miss Baker, in her black grenadine, false curls, and coral brooch; Marcus Schouler, his arms folded, his brows bent, grand and gloomy; Heise the harness-maker, in yellow gloves, intently studying the pattern of the matting; and Owgooste, in his Fauntleroy "costume," stupefied and a little frightened, rolling his eyes from face to face. Selina sat at the parlor melodeon, fingering the keys, her glance wandering to the chenille portieres. She stopped playing as McTeague and Old Grannis entered and took their places. A profound silence ensued. Uncle Oelbermann's shirt front could be heard creaking as he breathed. The most solemn expression pervaded every face.

All at once the portieres were shaken violently. It was a signal. Selina pulled open the stops and swung into the wedding march.

Trina entered. She was dressed in white silk, a crown of orange blossoms was around her swarthy hair—dressed high for the first time— her veil reached to the floor. Her face was pink, but otherwise she was calm. She looked quietly around the room as she crossed it, until her glance rested on McTeague, smiling at him then very prettily and with perfect self-possession.

She was on her father's arm. The twins, dressed exactly alike, walked in front, each carrying an enormous bouquet of cut flowers in a "lace-paper" holder. Mrs. Sieppe followed in the rear. She was crying; her handkerchief was rolled into a wad. From time to time she looked at the train of Trina's dress through her tears. Mr. Sieppe marched his daughter to the exact middle of the floor, wheeled at right angles, and brought her up to the minister. He stepped back three paces, and stood planted upon one of his chalk marks, his face glistening with perspiration.

Then Trina and the dentist were married. The guests stood in constrained attitudes, looking furtively out of the corners of their eyes. Mr. Sieppe never moved a muscle; Mrs. Sieppe cried into her handkerchief all the time. At the melodeon Selina played "Call Me Thine Own," very softly, the tremulo stop pulled out. She looked over her shoulder from time to time. Between the pauses of the music one could hear the low tones of the minister, the responses of the participants, and the suppressed sounds of Mrs. Sieppe's weeping. Outside the noises of the street rose to the windows in muffled undertones, a cable car rumbled past, a newsboy went by chanting the evening papers; from somewhere in the building itself came a persistent noise of sawing.

Trina and McTeague knelt. The dentist's knees thudded on the floor and he presented to view the soles of his shoes, painfully new and unworn, the leather still yellow, the brass nail heads still glittering. Trina sank at his side very gracefully, setting her dress and train with a little gesture of her free hand. The company bowed their heads, Mr. Sieppe shutting his eyes tight. But Mrs. Sieppe took advantage of the moment to stop crying and make furtive gestures towards Owgooste, signing him to pull down his coat. But Owgooste gave no heed; his eyes were starting from their sockets, his chin had dropped upon his lace collar, and his head turned vaguely from side to side with a continued and maniacal motion.

All at once the ceremony was over before any one expected it. The guests kept their positions for a moment, eyeing one another, each fearing to make the first move, not quite certain as to whether or not everything were finished. But the couple faced the room, Trina throwing back her veil. She—perhaps McTeague as well—felt that there was a certain inadequateness about the ceremony. Was that all there was to it? Did just those few muttered phrases make them man and wife? It had been over in a few moments, but it had bound them for life. Had not something been left out? Was not the whole affair cursory, superficial? It was disappointing.

But Trina had no time to dwell upon this. Marcus Schouler, in the manner of a man of the world, who knew how to act in every situation, stepped forward and, even before Mr. or Mrs. Sieppe, took Trina's hand.

"Let me be the first to congratulate Mrs. McTeague," he said, feeling very noble and heroic. The strain of the previous moments was relaxed immediately, the guests crowded around the pair, shaking hands—a babel of talk arose.

"Owgooste, WILL you pull down your goat, den?"

"Well, my dear, now you're married and happy. When I first saw you two together, I said, 'What a pair!' We're to be neighbors now; you must come up and see me very often and we'll have tea together."

"Did you hear that sawing going on all the time? I declare it regularly got on my nerves."

Trina kissed her father and mother, crying a little herself as she saw the tears in Mrs. Sieppe's eyes.

Marcus came forward a second time, and, with an air of great gravity, kissed his cousin upon the forehead. Heise was introduced to Trina and Uncle Oelbermann to the dentist.

For upwards of half an hour the guests stood about in groups, filling the little sitting-room with a great chatter of talk. Then it was time to make ready for supper.

This was a tremendous task, in which nearly all the guests were obliged to assist. The sitting-room was transformed into a dining-room. The presents were removed from the extension table and the table drawn out to its full length. The cloth was laid, the chairs—rented from the dancing academy hard by—drawn up, the dishes set out, and the two bouquets of cut flowers taken from the twins under their shrill protests, and "arranged" in vases at either end of the table.

There was a great coming and going between the kitchen and the sitting-room. Trina, who was allowed to do nothing, sat in the bay window and fretted, calling to her mother from time to time:

"The napkins are in the right-hand drawer of the pantry."

"Yes, yes, I got um. Where do you geep der zoup blates?"

"The soup plates are here already."

"Say, Cousin Trina, is there a corkscrew? What is home without a corkscrew?"

"In the kitchen-table drawer, in the left-hand corner."

"Are these the forks you want to use, Mrs. McTeague?"

"No, no, there's some silver forks. Mamma knows where."

They were all very gay, laughing over their mistakes, getting in one another's way, rushing into the sitting-room, their hands full of plates or knives or glasses, and darting out again after more. Marcus and Mr. Sieppe took their coats off. Old Grannis and Miss Baker passed each other in the hall in a constrained silence, her grenadine brushing against the elbow of his wrinkled frock coat. Uncle Oelbermann superintended Heise opening the case of champagne with the gravity of a magistrate. Owgooste was assigned the task of filling the new salt and pepper canisters of red and blue glass.

In a wonderfully short time everything was ready. Marcus Schouler resumed his coat, wiping his forehead, and remarking:

"I tell you, I've been doing CHORES for MY board."

"To der table!" commanded Mr. Sieppe.

The company sat down with a great clatter, Trina at the foot, the dentist at the head, the others arranged themselves in haphazard fashion. But it happened that Marcus Schouler crowded into the seat beside Selina, towards which Old Grannis was directing himself. There was but one other chair vacant, and that at the side of Miss Baker. Old Grannis hesitated, putting his hand to his chin. However, there was no escape. In great trepidation he sat down beside the retired dressmaker. Neither of them spoke. Old Grannis dared not move, but sat rigid, his eyes riveted on his empty soup plate.

All at once there was a report like a pistol. The men started in their places. Mrs. Sieppe uttered a muffled shriek. The waiter from the cheap restaurant, hired as Maria's assistant, rose from a bending posture, a champagne bottle frothing in his hand; he was grinning from ear to ear.

"Don't get scairt," he said, reassuringly, "it ain't loaded."

When all their glasses had been filled, Marcus proposed the health of the bride, "standing up." The guests rose and drank. Hardly one of them had ever tasted champagne before. The moment's silence after the toast was broken by McTeague exclaiming with a long breath of satisfaction: "That's the best beer I ever drank."

There was a roar of laughter. Especially was Marcus tickled over the dentist's blunder; he went off in a very spasm of mirth, banging the table with his fist, laughing until his eyes watered. All through the meal he kept breaking out into cackling imitations of McTeague's words: "That's the best BEER I ever drank. Oh, Lord, ain't that a break!"

What a wonderful supper that was! There was oyster soup; there were sea bass and barracuda; there was a gigantic roast goose stuffed with chestnuts; there were egg-plant and sweet potatoes—Miss Baker called them "yams." There was calf's head in oil, over which Mr. Sieppe went into ecstasies; there was lobster salad; there were rice pudding, and strawberry ice cream, and wine jelly, and stewed prunes, and cocoanuts, and mixed nuts, and raisins, and fruit, and tea, and coffee, and mineral waters, and lemonade.

For two hours the guests ate; their faces red, their elbows wide, the perspiration beading their foreheads. All around the table one saw the same incessant movement of jaws and heard the same uninterrupted sound of chewing. Three times Heise passed his plate for more roast goose. Mr. Sieppe devoured the calf's head with long breaths of contentment; McTeague ate for the sake of eating, without choice; everything within reach of his hands found its way into his enormous mouth.

There was but little conversation, and that only of the food; one exchanged opinions with one's neighbor as to the soup, the egg-plant, or the stewed prunes. Soon the room became very warm, a faint moisture appeared upon the windows, the air was heavy with the smell of cooked food. At every moment Trina or Mrs. Sieppe urged some one of the company to have his or her plate refilled. They were constantly employed in dishing potatoes or carving the goose or ladling gravy. The hired waiter circled around the room, his limp napkin over his arm, his hands full of plates and dishes. He was a great joker; he had names of his own for different articles of food, that sent gales of laughter around the table. When he spoke of a bunch of parsley as "scenery," Heise all but strangled himself over a mouthful of potato. Out in the kitchen Maria Macapa did the work of three, her face scarlet, her sleeves rolled up; every now and then she uttered shrill but unintelligible outcries, supposedly addressed to the waiter.

"Uncle Oelbermann," said Trina, "let me give you another helping of prunes."

The Sieppes paid great deference to Uncle Oelbermann, as indeed did the whole company. Even Marcus Schouler lowered his voice when he addressed him. At the beginning of the meal he had nudged the harness-maker and had whispered behind his hand, nodding his head toward the wholesale toy dealer, "Got thirty thousand dollars in the bank; has, for a fact."

"Don't have much to say," observed Heise.

"No, no. That's his way; never opens his face."

As the evening wore on, the gas and two lamps were lit. The company were still eating. The men, gorged with food, had unbuttoned their vests. McTeague's cheeks were distended, his eyes wide, his huge, salient jaw moved with a machine-like regularity; at intervals he drew a series of short breaths through his nose. Mrs. Sieppe wiped her forehead with her napkin.

"Hey, dere, poy, gif me some more oaf dat—what you call—'bubble-water.'"

That was how the waiter had spoken of the champagne—"bubble-water." The guests had shouted applause, "Outa sight." He was a heavy josher was that waiter.

Bottle after bottle was opened, the women stopping their ears as the corks were drawn. All of a sudden the dentist uttered an exclamation, clapping his hand to his nose, his face twisting sharply.

"Mac, what is it?" cried Trina in alarm.

"That champagne came to my nose," he cried, his eyes watering. "It stings like everything."

"Great BEER, ain't ut?" shouted Marcus.

"Now, Mark," remonstrated Trina in a low voice. "Now, Mark, you just shut up; that isn't funny any more. I don't want you should make fun of Mac. He called it beer on purpose. I guess HE knows."

Throughout the meal old Miss Baker had occupied herself largely with Owgooste and the twins, who had been given a table by themselves—the black walnut table before which the ceremony had taken place. The little dressmaker was continually turning about in her place, inquiring of the children if they wanted for anything; inquiries they rarely answered other than by stare, fixed, ox-like, expressionless.

Suddenly the little dressmaker turned to Old Grannis and exclaimed:

"I'm so very fond of little children."

"Yes, yes, they're very interesting. I'm very fond of them, too."

The next instant both of the old people were overwhelmed with confusion. What! They had spoken to each other after all these years of silence; they had for the first time addressed remarks to each other.

The old dressmaker was in a torment of embarrassment. How was it she had come to speak? She had neither planned nor wished it. Suddenly the words had escaped her, he had answered, and it was all over—over before they knew it.

Old Grannis's fingers trembled on the table ledge, his heart beat heavily, his breath fell short. He had actually talked to the little dressmaker. That possibility to which he had looked forward, it seemed to him for years—that companionship, that intimacy with his fellow-lodger, that delightful acquaintance which was only to ripen at some far distant time, he could not exactly say when—behold, it had suddenly come to a head, here in this overcrowded, over-heated room, in the midst of all this feeding, surrounded by odors of hot dishes, accompanied by the sounds of incessant mastication. How different he had imagined it would be! They were to be alone—he and Miss Baker—in the evening somewhere, withdrawn from the world, very quiet, very calm and peaceful. Their talk was to be of their lives, their lost illusions, not of other people's children.

The two old people did not speak again. They sat there side by side, nearer than they had ever been before, motionless, abstracted; their thoughts far away from that scene of feasting. They were thinking of each other and they were conscious of it. Timid, with the timidity of their second childhood, constrained and embarrassed by each other's presence, they were, nevertheless, in a little Elysium of their own creating. They walked hand in hand in a delicious garden where it was always autumn; together and alone they entered upon the long retarded romance of their commonplace and uneventful lives.

At last that great supper was over, everything had been eaten; the enormous roast goose had dwindled to a very skeleton. Mr. Sieppe had reduced the calf's head to a mere skull; a row of empty champagne bottles—"dead soldiers," as the facetious waiter had called them—lined the mantelpiece. Nothing of the stewed prunes remained but the juice, which was given to Owgooste and the twins. The platters were as clean as if they had been washed; crumbs of bread, potato parings, nutshells, and bits of cake littered the table; coffee and ice-cream stains and spots of congealed gravy marked the position of each plate. It was a devastation, a pillage; the table presented the appearance of an abandoned battlefield.

"Ouf," cried Mrs. Sieppe, pushing back, "I haf eatun und eatun, ach, Gott, how I haf eatun!"

"Ah, dot kaf's het," murmured her husband, passing his tongue over his lips.

The facetious waiter had disappeared. He and Maria Macapa foregathered in the kitchen. They drew up to the washboard of the sink, feasting off the remnants of the supper, slices of goose, the remains of the lobster salad, and half a bottle of champagne. They were obliged to drink the latter from teacups.

"Here's how," said the waiter gallantly, as he raised his tea-cup, bowing to Maria across the sink. "Hark," he added, "they're singing inside."

The company had left the table and had assembled about the melodeon, where Selina was seated. At first they attempted some of the popular songs of the day, but were obliged to give over as none of them knew any of the words beyond the first line of the chorus. Finally they pitched upon "Nearer, My God, to Thee," as the only song which they all knew. Selina sang the "alto," very much off the key; Marcus intoned the bass, scowling fiercely, his chin drawn into his collar. They sang in very slow time. The song became a dirge, a lamentable, prolonged wail of distress:

"Nee-rah, my Gahd, to Thee,
Nee-rah to Thee-ah."

At the end of the song, Uncle Oelbermann put on his hat without a word of warning. Instantly there was a hush. The guests rose.

"Not going so soon, Uncle Oelbermann?" protested Trina, politely. He only nodded. Marcus sprang forward to help him with his overcoat. Mr. Sieppe came up and the two men shook hands.

Then Uncle Oelbermann delivered himself of an oracular phrase. No doubt he had been meditating it during the supper. Addressing Mr. Sieppe, he said:

"You have not lost a daughter, but have gained a son."

These were the only words he had spoken the entire evening. He departed; the company was profoundly impressed.

About twenty minutes later, when Marcus Schouler was entertaining the guests by eating almonds, shells and all, Mr. Sieppe started to his feet, watch in hand.

"Haf-bast elevun," he shouted. "Attention! Der dime haf arrive, shtop eferyting. We depart."

This was a signal for tremendous confusion. Mr. Sieppe immediately threw off his previous air of relaxation, the calf's head was forgotten, he was once again the leader of vast enterprises.

"To me, to me," he cried. "Mommer, der tervins, Owgooste." He marshalled his tribe together, with tremendous commanding gestures. The sleeping twins were suddenly shaken into a dazed consciousness; Owgooste, whom the almond-eating of Marcus Schouler had petrified with admiration, was smacked to a realization of his surroundings.

Old Grannis, with a certain delicacy that was one of his characteristics, felt instinctively that the guests—the mere outsiders—should depart before the family began its leave-taking of Trina. He withdrew unobtrusively, after a hasty good-night to the bride and groom. The rest followed almost immediately.

"Well, Mr. Sieppe," exclaimed Marcus, "we won't see each other for some time." Marcus had given up his first intention of joining in the Sieppe migration. He spoke in a large way of certain affairs that would keep him in San Francisco till the fall. Of late he had entertained ambitions of a ranch life, he would breed cattle, he had a little money and was only looking for some one "to go in with." He dreamed of a cowboy's life and saw himself in an entrancing vision involving silver spurs and untamed bronchos. He told himself that Trina had cast him off, that his best friend had "played him for a sucker," that the "proper caper" was to withdraw from the world entirely.

"If you hear of anybody down there," he went on, speaking to Mr. Sieppe, "that wants to go in for ranching, why just let me know."

"Soh, soh," answered Mr. Sieppe abstractedly, peering about for Owgooste's cap.

Marcus bade the Sieppes farewell. He and Heise went out together. One heard them, as they descended the stairs, discussing the possibility of Frenna's place being still open.

Then Miss Baker departed after kissing Trina on both cheeks. Selina went with her. There was only the family left.

Trina watched them go, one by one, with an increasing feeling of uneasiness and vague apprehension. Soon they would all be gone.

"Well, Trina," exclaimed Mr. Sieppe, "goot-py; perhaps you gome visit us somedime."

Mrs. Sieppe began crying again.

"Ach, Trina, ven shall I efer see you again?"

Tears came to Trina's eyes in spite of herself. She put her arms around her mother.

"Oh, sometime, sometime," she cried. The twins and Owgooste clung to Trina's skirts, fretting and whimpering.

McTeague was miserable. He stood apart from the group, in a corner. None of them seemed to think of him; he was not of them.

"Write to me very often, mamma, and tell me about everything—about August and the twins."

"It is dime," cried Mr. Sieppe, nervously. "Goot-py, Trina. Mommer, Owgooste, say goot-py, den we must go. Goot-py, Trina." He kissed her. Owgooste and the twins were lifted up. "Gome, gome," insisted Mr. Sieppe, moving toward the door.

"Goot-py, Trina," exclaimed Mrs. Sieppe, crying harder than ever. "Doktor—where is der doktor—Doktor, pe goot to her, eh? pe vairy goot, eh, won't you? Zum day, Dokter, you vill haf a daughter, den you know berhaps how I feel, yes."

They were standing at the door by this time. Mr. Sieppe, half way down the stairs, kept calling "Gome, gome, we miss der drain."

Mrs. Sieppe released Trina and started down the hall, the twins and Owgooste following. Trina stood in the doorway, looking after them through her tears. They were going, going. When would she ever see them again? She was to be left alone with this man to whom she had just been married. A sudden vague terror seized her; she left McTeague and ran down the hall and caught her mother around the neck.

"I don't WANT you to go," she whispered in her mother's ear, sobbing. "Oh, mamma, I—I'm 'fraid."

"Ach, Trina, you preak my heart. Don't gry, poor leetle girl." She rocked Trina in her arms as though she were a child again. "Poor leetle scairt girl, don' gry—soh—soh—soh, dere's nuttun to pe 'fraid oaf. Dere, go to your hoasban'. Listen, popper's galling again; go den; goot-by."

She loosened Trina's arms and started down the stairs. Trina leaned over the banisters, straining her eyes after her mother.

"What is ut, Trina?"

"Oh, good-by, good-by."

"Gome, gome, we miss der drain."

"Mamma, oh, mamma!"

"What is ut, Trina?"

"Good-by."

"Goot-py, leetle daughter."

"Good-by, good-by, good-by."

The street door closed. The silence was profound.

For another moment Trina stood leaning over the banisters, looking down into the empty stairway. It was dark. There was nobody. They—her father, her mother, the children—had left her, left her alone. She faced about toward the rooms—faced her husband, faced her new home, the new life that was to begin now.

The hall was empty and deserted. The great flat around her seemed new and huge and strange; she felt horribly alone. Even Maria and the hired waiter were gone. On one of the floors above she heard a baby crying. She stood there an instant in the dark hall, in her wedding finery, looking about her, listening. From the open door of the sitting-room streamed a gold bar of light.

She went down the hall, by the open door of the sitting-room, going on toward the hall door of the bedroom.

As she softly passed the sitting-room she glanced hastily in. The lamps and the gas were burning brightly, the chairs were pushed back from the table just as the guests had left them, and the table itself, abandoned, deserted, presented to view the vague confusion of its dishes, its knives and forks, its empty platters and crumpled napkins. The dentist sat there leaning on his elbows, his back toward her; against the white blur of the table he looked colossal. Above his giant shoulders rose his thick, red neck and mane of yellow hair. The light shone pink through the gristle of his enormous ears.

Trina entered the bedroom, closing the door after her. At the sound, she heard McTeague start and rise.

"Is that you, Trina?"

She did not answer; but paused in the middle of the room, holding her breath, trembling.

The dentist crossed the outside room, parted the chenille portieres, and came in. He came toward her quickly, making as if to take her in his arms. His eyes were alight.

"No, no," cried Trina, shrinking from him. Suddenly seized with the fear of him—the intuitive feminine fear of the male—her whole being quailed before him. She was terrified at his huge, square-cut head; his powerful, salient jaw; his huge, red hands; his enormous, resistless strength.

"No, no—I'm afraid," she cried, drawing back from him to the other side of the room.

"Afraid?" answered the dentist in perplexity. "What are you afraid of, Trina? I'm not going to hurt you. What are you afraid of?"

What, indeed, was Trina afraid of? She could not tell. But what did she know of McTeague, after all? Who was this man that had come into her life, who had taken her from her home and from her parents, and with whom she was now left alone here in this strange, vast flat?

"Oh, I'm afraid. I'm afraid," she cried.

McTeague came nearer, sat down beside her and put one arm around her.

"What are you afraid of, Trina?" he said, reassuringly. "I don't want to frighten you."

She looked at him wildly, her adorable little chin quivering, the tears brimming in her narrow blue eyes. Then her glance took on a certain intentness, and she peered curiously into his face, saying almost in a whisper:

"I'm afraid of YOU."

But the dentist did not heed her. An immense joy seized upon him—the joy of possession. Trina was his very own now. She lay there in the hollow of his arm, helpless and very pretty.

Those instincts that in him were so close to the surface suddenly leaped to life, shouting and clamoring, not to be resisted. He loved her. Ah, did he not love her? The smell of her hair, of her neck, rose to him.

Suddenly he caught her in both his huge arms, crushing down her struggle with his immense strength, kissing her full upon the mouth. Then her great love for McTeague suddenly flashed up in Trina's breast; she gave up to him as she had done before, yielding all at once to that strange desire of being conquered and subdued. She clung to him, her hands clasped behind his neck, whispering in his ear:

"Oh, you must be good to me—very, very good to me, dear—for you're all that I have in the world now."

CHAPTER 10

That summer passed, then the winter. The wet season began in the last days of September and continued all through October, November, and December. At long intervals would come a week of perfect days, the sky without a cloud, the air motionless, but touched with a certain nimbleness, a faint effervescence that was exhilarating. Then, without warning, during a night when a south wind blew, a gray scroll of cloud would unroll and hang high over the city, and the rain would come pattering down again, at first in scattered showers, then in an uninterrupted drizzle.

All day long Trina sat in the bay window of the sitting-room that commanded a view of a small section of Polk Street. As often as she raised her head she could see the big market, a confectionery store, a bell-hanger's shop, and, farther on, above the roofs, the glass skylights and water tanks of the big public baths. In the nearer foreground ran the street itself; the cable cars trundled up and down, thumping heavily over the joints of the rails; market carts by the score came and went, driven at a great rate by preoccupied young men in their shirt sleeves, with pencils behind their ears, or by reckless boys in blood-stained butcher's aprons. Upon the sidewalks the little world of Polk Street swarmed and jostled through its daily round of life. On fine days the great ladies from the avenue, one block above, invaded the street, appearing before the butcher stalls, intent upon their day's marketing. On rainy days their servants—the Chinese cooks or the second girls—took their places. These servants gave themselves great airs, carrying their big cotton umbrellas as they had seen their mistresses carry their parasols, and haggling in supercilious fashion with the market men, their chins in the air.

The rain persisted. Everything in the range of Trina's vision, from the tarpaulins on the market-cart horses to the panes of glass in the roof of the public baths, looked glazed and varnished. The asphalt of the sidewalks shone like the surface of a patent leather boot; every hollow in the street held its little puddle, that winked like an eye each time a drop of rain struck into it.

Trina still continued to work for Uncle Oelbermann. In the mornings she busied herself about the kitchen, the bedroom, and the sitting-room; but in the afternoon, for two or three hours after lunch, she was occupied with the Noah's ark animals. She took her work to the bay window, spreading out a great square of canvas underneath her chair, to catch the chips and shavings, which she used afterwards for lighting fires. One after another she caught up the little blocks of straight-grained pine, the knife flashed between her fingers, the little figure grew rapidly under her touch, was finished and ready for painting in a wonderfully short time, and was tossed into the basket that stood at her elbow.

But very often during that rainy winter after her marriage Trina would pause in her work, her hands falling idly into her lap, her eyes—her narrow, pale blue eyes—growing wide and thoughtful as she gazed, unseeing, out into the rain-washed street.

She loved McTeague now with a blind, unreasoning love that admitted of no doubt or hesitancy. Indeed, it seemed to her that it was only AFTER her marriage with the dentist that she had really begun to love him. With the absolute final surrender of herself, the irrevocable, ultimate submission, had come an affection the like of which she had never dreamed in the old B Street days. But Trina loved her husband, not because she fancied she saw in him any of those noble and generous qualities that inspire affection. The dentist might or might not possess them, it was all one with Trina. She loved him because she had given herself to him freely, unreservedly; had merged her individuality into his; she was his, she belonged to him forever and forever. Nothing that he could do (so she told herself), nothing that she herself could do, could change her in this respect. McTeague might cease to love her, might leave her, might even die; it would be all the same, SHE WAS HIS.

But it had not been so at first. During those long, rainy days of the fall, days when Trina was left alone for hours, at that time when the excitement and novelty of the honeymoon were dying down, when the new household was settling into its grooves, she passed through many an hour of misgiving, of doubt, and even of actual regret.

Never would she forget one Sunday afternoon in particular. She had been married but three weeks. After dinner she and little Miss Baker had gone for a bit of a walk to take advantage of an hour's sunshine and to look at some wonderful geraniums in a florist's window on Sutter Street. They had been caught in a shower, and on returning to the flat the little dressmaker had insisted on fetching Trina up to her tiny room and brewing her a cup of strong tea, "to take the chill off." The two women had chatted over their teacups the better part of the afternoon, then Trina had returned to her rooms. For nearly three hours McTeague had been out of her thoughts, and as she came through their little suite, singing softly to herself, she suddenly came upon him quite unexpectedly. Her husband was in the "Dental Parlors," lying back in his operating chair, fast asleep. The little stove was crammed with coke, the room was overheated, the air thick and foul with the odors of ether, of coke gas, of stale beer and cheap tobacco. The dentist sprawled his gigantic limbs over the worn velvet of the operating chair; his coat and vest and shoes were off, and his huge feet, in their thick gray socks, dangled over the edge of the foot-rest; his pipe, fallen from his half-open mouth, had spilled the ashes into his lap; while on the floor, at his side stood the half-empty pitcher of steam beer. His head had rolled limply upon one shoulder, his face was red with sleep, and from his open mouth came a terrific sound of snoring.

For a moment Trina stood looking at him as he lay thus, prone, inert, half-dressed, and stupefied with the heat of the room, the steam beer, and the fumes of the cheap tobacco. Then her little chin quivered and a sob rose to her throat; she fled from the "Parlors," and locking herself in her bedroom, flung herself on the bed and burst into an agony of weeping. Ah, no, ah, no, she could not love him. It had all been a dreadful mistake, and now it was irrevocable; she was bound to this man for life. If it was as bad as this now, only three weeks after her marriage, how would it be in the years to come? Year after year, month after month, hour after hour, she was to see this same face, with its salient jaw, was to feel the touch of those enormous red hands, was to hear the heavy, elephantine tread of those huge feet—in thick gray socks. Year after year, day after day, there would be no change, and it would last all her life. Either it would be one long continued revulsion, or else—worse than all—she would come to be content with him, would come to be like him, would sink to the level of steam beer and cheap tobacco, and all her pretty ways, her clean, trim little habits, would be forgotten, since they would be thrown away upon her stupid, brutish husband. "Her husband!" THAT, was her husband in there—she could yet hear his snores—for life, for life. A great despair seized upon her. She buried her face in the pillow and thought of her mother with an infinite longing.

Aroused at length by the chittering of the canary, McTeague had awakened slowly. After a while he had taken down his concertina and played upon it the six very mournful airs that he knew.

Face downward upon the bed, Trina still wept. Throughout that little suite could be heard but two sounds, the lugubrious strains of the concertina and the noise of stifled weeping.

That her husband should be ignorant of her distress seemed to Trina an additional grievance. With perverse inconsistency she began to wish him to come to her, to comfort her. He ought to know that she was in trouble, that she was lonely and unhappy.

"Oh, Mac," she called in a trembling voice. But the concertina still continued to wail and lament. Then Trina wished she were dead, and on the instant jumped up and ran into the "Dental Parlors," and threw herself into her husband's arms, crying: "Oh, Mac, dear, love me, love me big! I'm so unhappy."

"What—what—what—" the dentist exclaimed, starting up bewildered, a little frightened.

"Nothing, nothing, only LOVE me, love me always and always."

But this first crisis, this momentary revolt, as much a matter of high-strung feminine nerves as of anything else, passed, and in the end Trina's affection for her "old bear" grew in spite of herself. She began to love him more and more, not for what he was, but for what she had given up to him. Only once again did Trina undergo a reaction against her husband, and then it was but the matter of an instant, brought on, curiously enough, by the sight of a bit of egg on McTeague's heavy mustache one morning just after breakfast.

Then, too, the pair had learned to make concessions, little by little, and all unconsciously they adapted their modes of life to suit each other. Instead of sinking to McTeague's level as she had feared, Trina found that she could make McTeague rise to hers, and in this saw a solution of many a difficult and gloomy complication.

For one thing, the dentist began to dress a little better, Trina even succeeding in inducing him to wear a high silk hat and a frock coat of a Sunday. Next he relinquished his Sunday afternoon's nap and beer in favor of three or four hours spent in the park with her—the weather permitting. So that gradually Trina's misgivings ceased, or when they did assail her, she could at last meet them with a shrug of the shoulders, saying to herself meanwhile, "Well, it's done now and it can't be helped; one must make the best of it."

During the first months of their married life these nervous relapses of hers had alternated with brusque outbursts of affection when her only fear was that her husband's love did not equal her own. Without an instant's warning, she would clasp him about the neck, rubbing her cheek against his, murmuring:

"Dear old Mac, I love you so, I love you so. Oh, aren't we happy together, Mac, just us two and no one else? You love me as much as I love you, don't you, Mac? Oh, if you shouldn't—if you SHOULDN'T."

But by the middle of the winter Trina's emotions, oscillating at first from one extreme to another, commenced to settle themselves to an equilibrium of calmness and placid quietude. Her household duties began more and more to absorb her attention, for she was an admirable housekeeper, keeping the little suite in marvellous good order and regulating the schedule of expenditure with an economy that often bordered on positive niggardliness. It was a passion with her to save money. In the bottom of her trunk, in the bedroom, she hid a brass match-safe that answered the purposes of a savings bank. Each time she added a quarter or a half dollar to the little store she laughed and sang with a veritable childish delight; whereas, if the butcher or milkman compelled her to pay an overcharge she was unhappy for the rest of the day. She did not save this money for any ulterior purpose, she hoarded instinctively, without knowing why, responding to the dentist's remonstrances with:

"Yes, yes, I know I'm a little miser, I know it."

Trina had always been an economical little body, but it was only since her great winning in the lottery that she had become especially penurious. No doubt, in her fear lest their great good luck should demoralize them and lead to habits of extravagance, she had recoiled too far in the other direction. Never, never, never should a penny of that miraculous fortune be spent; rather should it be added to. It was a nest egg, a monstrous, roc-like nest egg, not so large, however, but that it could be made larger. Already by the end of that winter Trina had begun to make up the deficit of two hundred dollars that she had been forced to expend on the preparations for her marriage.

McTeague, on his part, never asked himself now-a-days whether he loved Trina the wife as much as he had loved Trina the young girl. There had been a time when to kiss Trina, to take her in his arms, had thrilled him from head to heel with a happiness that was beyond words; even the smell of her wonderful odorous hair had sent a sensation of faintness all through him. That time was long past now. Those sudden outbursts of affection on the part of his little woman, outbursts that only increased in vehemence the longer they lived together, puzzled rather than pleased him. He had come to submit to them good-naturedly, answering her passionate inquiries with a "Sure, sure, Trina, sure I love you. What—what's the matter with you?"

There was no passion in the dentist's regard for his wife. He dearly liked to have her near him, he took an enormous pleasure in watching her as she moved about their rooms, very much at home, gay and singing from morning till night; and it was his great delight to call her into the "Dental Parlors" when a patient was in the chair and, while he held the plugger, to have her rap in the gold fillings with the little box-wood mallet as he had taught her. But that tempest of passion, that overpowering desire that had suddenly taken possession of him that day when he had given her ether, again when he had caught her in his arms in the B Street station, and again and again during the early days of their married life, rarely stirred him now. On the other hand, he was never assailed with doubts as to the wisdom of his marriage.

McTeague had relapsed to his wonted stolidity. He never questioned himself, never looked for motives, never went to the bottom of things. The year following upon the summer of his marriage was a time of great contentment for him; after the novelty of the honeymoon had passed he slipped easily into the new order of things without a question. Thus his life would be for years to come. Trina was there; he was married and settled. He accepted the situation. The little animal comforts which for him constituted the enjoyment of life were ministered to at every turn, or when they were interfered with—as in the case of his Sunday afternoon's nap and beer—some agreeable substitute was found. In her attempts to improve McTeague—to raise him from the stupid animal life to which he had been accustomed in his bachelor days—Trina was tactful enough to move so cautiously and with such slowness that the dentist was unconscious of any process of change. In the matter of the high silk hat, it seemed to him that the initiative had come from himself.

Gradually the dentist improved under the influence of his little wife. He no longer went abroad with frayed cuffs about his huge red wrists— or worse, without any cuffs at all. Trina kept his linen clean and mended, doing most of his washing herself, and insisting that he should change his flannels—thick red flannels they were, with enormous bone buttons—once a week, his linen shirts twice a week, and his collars and cuffs every second day. She broke him of the habit of eating with his knife, she caused him to substitute bottled beer in the place of steam beer, and she induced him to take off his hat to Miss Baker, to Heise's wife, and to the other women of his acquaintance. McTeague no longer spent an evening at Frenna's. Instead of this he brought a couple of bottles of beer up to the rooms and shared it with Trina. In his "Parlors" he was no longer gruff and indifferent to his female patients; he arrived at that stage where he could work and talk to them at the same time; he even accompanied them to the door, and held it open for them when the operation was finished, bowing them out with great nods of his huge square-cut head.

Besides all this, he began to observe the broader, larger interests of life, interests that affected him not as an individual, but as a member of a class, a profession, or a political party. He read the papers, he subscribed to a dental magazine; on Easter, Christmas, and New Year's he went to church with Trina. He commenced to have opinions, convictions—it was not fair to deprive tax-paying women of the privilege to vote; a university education should not be a prerequisite for admission to a dental college; the Catholic priests were to be restrained in their efforts to gain control of the public schools.

But most wonderful of all, McTeague began to have ambitions—very vague, very confused ideas of something better—ideas for the most part borrowed from Trina. Some day, perhaps, he and his wife would have a house of their own. What a dream! A little home all to themselves, with six rooms and a bath, with a grass plat in front and calla-lilies. Then there would be children. He would have a son, whose name would be Daniel, who would go to High School, and perhaps turn out to be a prosperous plumber or house painter. Then this son Daniel would marry a wife, and they would all live together in that six-room-and-bath house; Daniel would have little children. McTeague would grow old among them all. The dentist saw himself as a venerable patriarch surrounded by children and grandchildren.

So the winter passed. It was a season of great happiness for the McTeagues; the new life jostled itself into its grooves. A routine began.

On weekdays they rose at half-past six, being awakened by the boy who brought the bottled milk, and who had instructions to pound upon the bedroom door in passing. Trina made breakfast—coffee, bacon and eggs, and a roll of Vienna bread from the bakery. The breakfast was eaten in the kitchen, on the round deal table covered with the shiny oilcloth table-spread tacked on. After breakfast the dentist immediately betook himself to his "Parlors" to meet his early morning appointments—those made with the clerks and shop girls who stopped in for half an hour on their way to their work.

Trina, meanwhile, busied herself about the suite, clearing away the breakfast, sponging off the oilcloth table-spread, making the bed, pottering about with a broom or duster or cleaning rag. Towards ten o'clock she opened the windows to air the rooms, then put on her drab jacket, her little round turban with its red wing, took the butcher's and grocer's books from the knife basket in the drawer of the kitchen table, and descended to the street, where she spent a delicious hour—now in the huge market across the way, now in the grocer's store with its fragrant aroma of coffee and spices, and now before the counters of the haberdasher's, intent on a bit of shopping, turning over ends of veiling, strips of elastic, or slivers of whalebone. On the street she rubbed elbows with the great ladies of the avenue in their beautiful dresses, or at intervals she met an acquaintance or two—Miss Baker, or Heise's lame wife, or Mrs. Ryer. At times she passed the flat and looked up at the windows of her home, marked by the huge golden molar that projected, flashing, from the bay window of the "Parlors." She saw the open windows of the sitting-room, the Nottingham lace curtains stirring and billowing in the draft, and she caught sight of Maria Macapa's towelled head as the Mexican maid-of-all-work went to and fro in the suite, sweeping or carrying away the ashes. Occasionally in the windows of the "Parlors" she beheld McTeague's rounded back as he bent to his work. Sometimes, even, they saw each other and waved their hands gayly in recognition.

By eleven o'clock Trina returned to the flat, her brown net reticule—once her mother's—full of parcels. At once she set about getting lunch—sausages, perhaps, with mashed potatoes; or last evening's joint warmed over or made into a stew; chocolate, which Trina adored, and a side dish or two—a salted herring or a couple of artichokes or a salad. At half-past twelve the dentist came in from the "Parlors," bringing with him the smell of creosote and of ether. They sat down to lunch in the sitting-room. They told each other of their doings throughout the forenoon; Trina showed her purchases, McTeague recounted the progress of an operation. At one o'clock they separated, the dentist returning to the "Parlors," Trina settling to her work on the Noah's ark animals. At about three o'clock she put this work away, and for the rest of the afternoon was variously occupied—sometimes it was the mending, sometimes the wash, sometimes new curtains to be put up, or a bit of carpet to be tacked down, or a letter to be written, or a visit—generally to Miss Baker—to be returned. Towards five o'clock the old woman whom they had hired for that purpose came to cook supper, for even Trina was not equal to the task of preparing three meals a day.

This woman was French, and was known to the flat as Augustine, no one taking enough interest in her to inquire for her last name; all that was known of her was that she was a decayed French laundress, miserably poor, her trade long since ruined by Chinese competition. Augustine cooked well, but she was otherwise undesirable, and Trina lost patience with her at every moment. The old French woman's most marked characteristic was her timidity. Trina could scarcely address her a simple direction without Augustine quailing and shrinking; a reproof, however gentle, threw her into an agony of confusion; while Trina's anger promptly reduced her to a state of nervous collapse, wherein she lost all power of speech, while her head began to bob and nod with an incontrollable twitching of the muscles, much like the oscillations of the head of a toy donkey. Her timidity was exasperating, her very presence in the room unstrung the nerves, while her morbid eagerness to avoid offence only served to develop in her a clumsiness that was at times beyond belief. More than once Trina had decided that she could no longer put up with Augustine but each time she had retained her as she reflected upon her admirably cooked cabbage soups and tapioca puddings, and—which in Trina's eyes was her chiefest recommendation— the pittance for which she was contented to work.

Augustine had a husband. He was a spirit-medium—a "professor." At times he held seances in the larger rooms of the flat, playing vigorously upon a mouth-organ and invoking a familiar whom he called "Edna," and whom he asserted was an Indian maiden.

The evening was a period of relaxation for Trina and McTeague. They had supper at six, after which McTeague smoked his pipe and read the papers for half an hour, while Trina and Augustine cleared away the table and washed the dishes. Then, as often as not, they went out together. One of their amusements was to go "down town" after dark and promenade Market and Kearney Streets. It was very gay; a great many others were promenading there also. All of the stores were brilliantly lighted and many of them still open. They walked about aimlessly, looking into the shop windows. Trina would take McTeague's arm, and he, very much embarrassed at that, would thrust both hands into his pockets and pretend not to notice. They stopped before the jewellers' and milliners' windows, finding a great delight in picking out things for each other, saying how they would choose this and that if they were rich. Trina did most of the talking. McTeague merely approving by a growl or a movement of the head or shoulders; she was interested in the displays of some of the cheaper stores, but he found an irresistible charm in an enormous golden molar with four prongs that hung at a corner of Kearney Street. Sometimes they would look at Mars or at the moon through the street telescopes or sit for a time in the rotunda of a vast department store where a band played every evening.

Occasionally they met Heise the harness-maker and his wife, with whom they had become acquainted. Then the evening was concluded by a four-cornered party in the Luxembourg, a quiet German restaurant under a theatre. Trina had a tamale and a glass of beer, Mrs. Heise (who was a decayed writing teacher) ate salads, with glasses of grenadine and currant syrups. Heise drank cocktails and whiskey straight, and urged the dentist to join him. But McTeague was obstinate, shaking his head. "I can't drink that stuff," he said. "It don't agree with me, somehow; I go kinda crazy after two glasses." So he gorged himself with beer and frankfurter sausages plastered with German mustard.

When the annual Mechanic's Fair opened, McTeague and Trina often spent their evenings there, studying the exhibits carefully (since in Trina's estimation education meant knowing things and being able to talk about them). Wearying of this they would go up into the gallery, and, leaning over, look down into the huge amphitheatre full of light and color and movement.

There rose to them the vast shuffling noise of thousands of feet and a subdued roar of conversation like the sound of a great mill. Mingled with this was the purring of distant machinery, the splashing of a temporary fountain, and the rhythmic jangling of a brass band, while in the piano exhibit a hired performer was playing upon a concert grand with a great flourish. Nearer at hand they could catch ends of conversation and notes of laughter, the noise of moving dresses, and the rustle of stiffly starched skirts. Here and there school children elbowed their way through the crowd, crying shrilly, their hands full of advertisement pamphlets, fans, picture cards, and toy whips, while the air itself was full of the smell of fresh popcorn.

They even spent some time in the art gallery. Trina's cousin Selina, who gave lessons in hand painting at two bits an hour, generally had an exhibit on the walls, which they were interested to find. It usually was a bunch of yellow poppies painted on black velvet and framed in gilt. They stood before it some little time, hazarding their opinions, and then moved on slowly from one picture to another. Trina had McTeague buy a catalogue and made a duty of finding the title of every picture. This, too, she told McTeague, as a kind of education one ought to cultivate. Trina professed to be fond of art, having perhaps acquired a taste for painting and sculpture from her experience with the Noah's ark animals.

"Of course," she told the dentist, "I'm no critic, I only know what I like." She knew that she liked the "Ideal Heads," lovely girls with flowing straw-colored hair and immense, upturned eyes. These always had for title, "Reverie," or "An Idyll," or "Dreams of Love."

"I think those are lovely, don't you, Mac?" she said.

"Yes, yes," answered McTeague, nodding his head, bewildered, trying to understand. "Yes, yes, lovely, that's the word. Are you dead sure now, Trina, that all that's hand-painted just like the poppies?"

Thus the winter passed, a year went by, then two. The little life of Polk Street, the life of small traders, drug clerks, grocers, stationers, plumbers, dentists, doctors, spirit-mediums, and the like, ran on monotonously in its accustomed grooves. The first three years of their married life wrought little change in the fortunes of the McTeagues. In the third summer the branch post-office was moved from the ground floor of the flat to a corner farther up the street in order to be near the cable line that ran mail cars. Its place was taken by a German saloon, called a "Wein Stube," in the face of the protests of every female lodger. A few months later quite a little flurry of excitement ran through the street on the occasion of "The Polk Street Open Air Festival," organized to celebrate the introduction there of electric lights. The festival lasted three days and was quite an affair. The street was garlanded with yellow and white bunting; there were processions and "floats" and brass bands. Marcus Schouler was in his element during the whole time of the celebration. He was one of the marshals of the parade, and was to be seen at every hour of the day, wearing a borrowed high hat and cotton gloves, and galloping a broken-down cab-horse over the cobbles. He carried a baton covered with yellow and white calico, with which he made furious passes and gestures. His voice was soon reduced to a whisper by continued shouting, and he raged and fretted over trifles till he wore himself thin. McTeague was disgusted with him. As often as Marcus passed the window of the flat the dentist would mutter:

"Ah, you think you're smart, don't you?"

The result of the festival was the organizing of a body known as the "Polk Street Improvement Club," of which Marcus was elected secretary. McTeague and Trina often heard of him in this capacity through Heise the harness-maker. Marcus had evidently come to have political aspirations. It appeared that he was gaining a reputation as a maker of speeches, delivered with fiery emphasis, and occasionally reprinted in the "Progress," the organ of the club—"outraged constituencies," "opinions warped by personal bias," "eyes blinded by party prejudice," etc.

Of her family, Trina heard every fortnight in letters from her mother. The upholstery business which Mr. Sieppe had bought was doing poorly, and Mrs. Sieppe bewailed the day she had ever left B Street. Mr. Sieppe was losing money every month. Owgooste, who was to have gone to school, had been forced to go to work in "the store," picking waste. Mrs. Sieppe was obliged to take a lodger or two. Affairs were in a very bad way. Occasionally she spoke of Marcus. Mr. Sieppe had not forgotten him despite his own troubles, but still had an eye out for some one whom Marcus could "go in with" on a ranch.

It was toward the end of this period of three years that Trina and McTeague had their first serious quarrel. Trina had talked so much about having a little house of their own at some future day, that McTeague had at length come to regard the affair as the end and object of all their labors. For a long time they had had their eyes upon one house in particular. It was situated on a cross street close by, between Polk Street and the great avenue one block above, and hardly a Sunday afternoon passed that Trina and McTeague did not go and look at it. They stood for fully half an hour upon the other side of the street, examining every detail of its exterior, hazarding guesses as to the arrangement of the rooms, commenting upon its immediate neighborhood—which was rather sordid. The house was a wooden two-story arrangement, built by a misguided contractor in a sort of hideous Queen Anne style, all scrolls and meaningless mill work, with a cheap imitation of stained glass in the light over the door. There was a microscopic front yard full of dusty calla-lilies. The front door boasted an electric bell. But for the McTeagues it was an ideal home. Their idea was to live in this little house, the dentist retaining merely his office in the flat. The two places were but around the corner from each other, so that McTeague could lunch with his wife, as usual, and could even keep his early morning appointments and return to breakfast if he so desired.

However, the house was occupied. A Hungarian family lived in it. The father kept a stationery and notion "bazaar" next to Heise's harness-shop on Polk Street, while the oldest son played a third violin in the orchestra of a theatre. The family rented the house unfurnished for thirty-five dollars, paying extra for the water.

But one Sunday as Trina and McTeague on their way home from their usual walk turned into the cross street on which the little house was situated, they became promptly aware of an unwonted bustle going on upon the sidewalk in front of it. A dray was back against the curb, an express wagon drove away loaded with furniture; bedsteads, looking-glasses, and washbowls littered the sidewalks. The Hungarian family were moving out.

"Oh, Mac, look!" gasped Trina.

"Sure, sure," muttered the dentist.

After that they spoke but little. For upwards of an hour the two stood upon the sidewalk opposite, watching intently all that went forward, absorbed, excited.

On the evening of the next day they returned and visited the house, finding a great delight in going from room to room and imagining themselves installed therein. Here would be the bedroom, here the dining-room, here a charming little parlor. As they came out upon the front steps once more they met the owner, an enormous, red-faced fellow, so fat that his walking seemed merely a certain movement of his feet by which he pushed his stomach along in front of him. Trina talked with him a few moments, but arrived at no understanding, and the two went away after giving him their address. At supper that night McTeague said:

"Huh—what do you think, Trina?"

Trina put her chin in the air, tilting back her heavy tiara of swarthy hair.

"I am not so sure yet. Thirty-five dollars and the water extra. I don't think we can afford it, Mac."

"Ah, pshaw!" growled the dentist, "sure we can."

"It isn't only that," said Trina, "but it'll cost so much to make the change."

"Ah, you talk's though we were paupers. Ain't we got five thousand dollars?"

Trina flushed on the instant, even to the lobes of her tiny pale ears, and put her lips together.

"Now, Mac, you know I don't want you should talk like that. That money's never, never to be touched."

"And you've been savun up a good deal, besides," went on McTeague, exasperated at Trina's persistent economies. "How much money have you got in that little brass match-safe in the bottom of your trunk? Pretty near a hundred dollars, I guess—ah, sure." He shut his eyes and nodded his great head in a knowing way.

Trina had more than that in the brass match-safe in question, but her instinct of hoarding had led her to keep it a secret from her husband. Now she lied to him with prompt fluency.

"A hundred dollars! What are you talking of, Mac? I've not got fifty. I've not got THIRTY."

"Oh, let's take that little house," broke in McTeague. "We got the chance now, and it may never come again. Come on, Trina, shall we? Say, come on, shall we, huh?"

"We'd have to be awful saving if we did, Mac."

"Well, sure, I say let's take it."

"I don't know," said Trina, hesitating. "Wouldn't it be lovely to have a house all to ourselves? But let's not decide until to-morrow."

The next day the owner of the house called. Trina was out at her morning's marketing and the dentist, who had no one in the chair at the time, received him in the "Parlors." Before he was well aware of it, McTeague had concluded the bargain. The owner bewildered him with a world of phrases, made him believe that it would be a great saving to move into the little house, and finally offered it to him "water free."

"All right, all right," said McTeague, "I'll take it."

The other immediately produced a paper.

"Well, then, suppose you sign for the first month's rent, and we'll call it a bargain. That's business, you know," and McTeague, hesitating, signed.

"I'd like to have talked more with my wife about it first," he said, dubiously.

"Oh, that's all right," answered the owner, easily. "I guess if the head of the family wants a thing, that's enough."

McTeague could not wait until lunch time to tell the news to Trina. As soon as he heard her come in, he laid down the plaster-of-paris mould he was making and went out into the kitchen and found her chopping up onions.

"Well, Trina," he said, "we got that house. I've taken it."

"What do you mean?" she answered, quickly. The dentist told her.

"And you signed a paper for the first month's rent?"

"Sure, sure. That's business, you know."

"Well, why did you DO it?" cried Trina. "You might have asked ME something about it. Now, what have you done? I was talking with Mrs. Ryer about that house while I was out this morning, and she said the Hungarians moved out because it was absolutely unhealthy; there's water been standing in the basement for months. And she told me, too," Trina went on indignantly, "that she knew the owner, and she was sure we could get the house for thirty if we'd bargain for it. Now what have you gone and done? I hadn't made up my mind about taking the house at all. And now I WON'T take it, with the water in the basement and all."

"Well—well," stammered McTeague, helplessly, "we needn't go in if it's unhealthy."

"But you've signed a PAPER," cried Trina, exasperated. "You've got to pay that first month's rent, anyhow—to forfeit it. Oh, you are so stupid! There's thirty-five dollars just thrown away. I SHAN'T go into that house; we won't move a FOOT out of here. I've changed my mind about it, and there's water in the basement besides."

"Well, I guess we can stand thirty-five dollars," mumbled the dentist, "if we've got to."

"Thirty-five dollars just thrown out of the window," cried Trina, her teeth clicking, every instinct of her parsimony aroused. "Oh, you the thick-wittedest man that I ever knew. Do you think we're millionaires? Oh, to think of losing thirty-five dollars like that." Tears were in her eyes, tears of grief as well as of anger. Never had McTeague seen his little woman so aroused. Suddenly she rose to her feet and slammed the chopping-bowl down upon the table. "Well, I won't pay a nickel of it," she exclaimed.

"Huh? What, what?" stammered the dentist, taken all aback by her outburst.

"I say that you will find that money, that thirty-five dollars, yourself."

"Why—why——"

"It's your stupidity got us into this fix, and you'll be the one that'll suffer by it."

"I can't do it, I WON'T do it. We'll—we'll share and share alike. Why, you said—you told me you'd take the house if the water was free."

"I NEVER did. I NEVER did. How can you stand there and say such a thing?"

"You did tell me that," vociferated McTeague, beginning to get angry in his turn.

"Mac, I didn't, and you know it. And what's more, I won't pay a nickel. Mr. Heise pays his bill next week, it's forty-three dollars, and you can just pay the thirty-five out of that."

"Why, you got a whole hundred dollars saved up in your match-safe," shouted the dentist, throwing out an arm with an awkward gesture. "You pay half and I'll pay half, that's only fair."

"No, no, NO," exclaimed Trina. "It's not a hundred dollars. You won't touch it; you won't touch my money, I tell you."

"Ah, how does it happen to be yours, I'd like to know?"

"It's mine! It's mine! It's mine!" cried Trina, her face scarlet, her teeth clicking like the snap of a closing purse.

"It ain't any more yours than it is mine."

"Every penny of it is mine."

"Ah, what a fine fix you'd get me into," growled the dentist. "I've signed the paper with the owner; that's business, you know, that's business, you know; and now you go back on me. Suppose we'd taken the house, we'd 'a' shared the rent, wouldn't we, just as we do here?"

Trina shrugged her shoulders with a great affectation of indifference and began chopping the onions again.

"You settle it with the owner," she said. "It's your affair; you've got the money." She pretended to assume a certain calmness as though the matter was something that no longer affected her. Her manner exasperated McTeague all the more.

"No, I won't; no, I won't; I won't either," he shouted. "I'll pay my half and he can come to you for the other half." Trina put a hand over her ear to shut out his clamor.

"Ah, don't try and be smart," cried McTeague. "Come, now, yes or no, will you pay your half?"

"You heard what I said."

"Will you pay it?"

"No."

"Miser!" shouted McTeague. "Miser! you're worse than old Zerkow. All right, all right, keep your money. I'll pay the whole thirty-five. I'd rather lose it than be such a miser as you."

"Haven't you got anything to do," returned Trina, "instead of staying here and abusing me?"

"Well, then, for the last time, will you help me out?" Trina cut the heads of a fresh bunch of onions and gave no answer.

"Huh? will you?"

"I'd like to have my kitchen to myself, please," she said in a mincing way, irritating to a last degree. The dentist stamped out of the room, banging the door behind him.

For nearly a week the breach between them remained unhealed. Trina only spoke to the dentist in monosyllables, while he, exasperated at her calmness and frigid reserve, sulked in his "Dental Parlors," muttering terrible things beneath his mustache, or finding solace in his concertina, playing his six lugubrious airs over and over again, or swearing frightful oaths at his canary. When Heise paid his bill, McTeague, in a fury, sent the amount to the owner of the little house.

There was no formal reconciliation between the dentist and his little woman. Their relations readjusted themselves inevitably. By the end of the week they were as amicable as ever, but it was long before they spoke of the little house again. Nor did they ever revisit it of a Sunday afternoon. A month or so later the Ryers told them that the owner himself had moved in. The McTeagues never occupied that little house.

But Trina suffered a reaction after the quarrel. She began to be sorry she had refused to help her husband, sorry she had brought matters to such an issue. One afternoon as she was at work on the Noah's ark animals, she surprised herself crying over the affair. She loved her "old bear" too much to do him an injustice, and perhaps, after all, she had been in the wrong. Then it occurred to her how pretty it would be to come up behind him unexpectedly, and slip the money, thirty-five dollars, into his hand, and pull his huge head down to her and kiss his bald spot as she used to do in the days before they were married.

Then she hesitated, pausing in her work, her knife dropping into her lap, a half-whittled figure between her fingers. If not thirty-five dollars, then at least fifteen or sixteen, her share of it. But a feeling of reluctance, a sudden revolt against this intended generosity, arose in her.

"No, no," she said to herself. "I'll give him ten dollars. I'll tell him it's all I can afford. It IS all I can afford."

She hastened to finish the figure of the animal she was then at work upon, putting in the ears and tail with a drop of glue, and tossing it into the basket at her side. Then she rose and went into the bedroom and opened her trunk, taking the key from under a corner of the carpet where she kept it hid.

At the very bottom of her trunk, under her bridal dress, she kept her savings. It was all in change—half dollars and dollars for the most part, with here and there a gold piece. Long since the little brass match-box had overflowed. Trina kept the surplus in a chamois-skin sack she had made from an old chest protector. Just now, yielding to an impulse which often seized her, she drew out the match-box and the chamois sack, and emptying the contents on the bed, counted them carefully. It came to one hundred and sixty-five dollars, all told. She counted it and recounted it and made little piles of it, and rubbed the gold pieces between the folds of her apron until they shone.

"Ah, yes, ten dollars is all I can afford to give Mac," said Trina, "and even then, think of it, ten dollars—it will be four or five months before I can save that again. But, dear old Mac, I know it would make him feel glad, and perhaps," she added, suddenly taken with an idea, "perhaps Mac will refuse to take it."

She took a ten-dollar piece from the heap and put the rest away. Then she paused:

"No, not the gold piece," she said to herself. "It's too pretty. He can have the silver." She made the change and counted out ten silver dollars into her palm. But what a difference it made in the appearance and weight of the little chamois bag! The bag was shrunken and withered, long wrinkles appeared running downward from the draw-string. It was a lamentable sight. Trina looked longingly at the ten broad pieces in her hand. Then suddenly all her intuitive desire of saving, her instinct of hoarding, her love of money for the money's sake, rose strong within her.

"No, no, no," she said. "I can't do it. It may be mean, but I can't help it. It's stronger than I." She returned the money to the bag and locked it and the brass match-box in her trunk, turning the key with a long breath of satisfaction.

She was a little troubled, however, as she went back into the sitting-room and took up her work.

"I didn't use to be so stingy," she told herself. "Since I won in the lottery I've become a regular little miser. It's growing on me, but never mind, it's a good fault, and, anyhow, I can't help it."

CHAPTER 11

On that particular morning the McTeagues had risen a half hour earlier than usual and taken a hurried breakfast in the kitchen on the deal table with its oilcloth cover. Trina was house-cleaning that week and had a presentiment of a hard day's work ahead of her, while McTeague remembered a seven o'clock appointment with a little German shoemaker.

At about eight o'clock, when the dentist had been in his office for over an hour, Trina descended upon the bedroom, a towel about her head and the roller-sweeper in her hand. She covered the bureau and sewing machine with sheets, and unhooked the chenille portieres between the bedroom and the sitting-room. As she was tying the Nottingham lace curtains at the window into great knots, she saw old Miss Baker on the opposite sidewalk in the street below, and raising the sash called down to her.

"Oh, it's you, Mrs. McTeague," cried the retired dressmaker, facing about, her head in the air. Then a long conversation was begun, Trina, her arms folded under her breast, her elbows resting on the window ledge, willing to be idle for a moment; old Miss Baker, her market-basket on her arm, her hands wrapped in the ends of her worsted shawl against the cold of the early morning. They exchanged phrases, calling to each other from window to curb, their breath coming from their lips in faint puffs of vapor, their voices shrill, and raised to dominate the clamor of the waking street. The newsboys had made their appearance on the street, together with the day laborers. The cable cars had begun to fill up; all along the street could be seen the shopkeepers taking down their shutters; some were still breakfasting. Now and then a waiter from one of the cheap restaurants crossed from one sidewalk to another, balancing on one palm a tray covered with a napkin.

"Aren't you out pretty early this morning, Miss Baker?" called Trina.

"No, no," answered the other. "I'm always up at half-past six, but I don't always get out so soon. I wanted to get a nice head of cabbage and some lentils for a soup, and if you don't go to market early, the restaurants get all the best."

"And you've been to market already, Miss Baker?"

"Oh, my, yes; and I got a fish—a sole—see." She drew the sole in question from her basket.

"Oh, the lovely sole!" exclaimed Trina.

"I got this one at Spadella's; he always has good fish on Friday. How is the doctor, Mrs. McTeague?"

"Ah, Mac is always well, thank you, Miss Baker."

"You know, Mrs. Ryer told me," cried the little dressmaker, moving forward a step out of the way of a "glass-put-in" man, "that Doctor McTeague pulled a tooth of that Catholic priest, Father—oh, I forget his name—anyhow, he pulled his tooth with his fingers. Was that true, Mrs. McTeague?"

"Oh, of course. Mac does that almost all the time now, 'specially with front teeth. He's got a regular reputation for it. He says it's brought him more patients than even the sign I gave him," she added, pointing to the big golden molar projecting from the office window.

"With his fingers! Now, think of that," exclaimed Miss Baker, wagging her head. "Isn't he that strong! It's just wonderful. Cleaning house to-day?" she inquired, glancing at Trina's towelled head.

"Um hum," answered Trina. "Maria Macapa's coming in to help pretty soon."

At the mention of Maria's name the little old dressmaker suddenly uttered an exclamation.

"Well, if I'm not here talking to you and forgetting something I was just dying to tell you. Mrs. McTeague, what ever in the world do you suppose? Maria and old Zerkow, that red-headed Polish Jew, the rag-bottles-sacks man, you know, they're going to be married."

"No!" cried Trina, in blank amazement. "You don't mean it."

"Of course I do. Isn't it the funniest thing you ever heard of?"

"Oh, tell me all about it," said Trina, leaning eagerly from the window. Miss Baker crossed the street and stood just beneath her.

"Well, Maria came to me last night and wanted me to make her a new gown, said she wanted something gay, like what the girls at the candy store wear when they go out with their young men. I couldn't tell what had got into the girl, until finally she told me she wanted something to get married in, and that Zerkow had asked her to marry him, and that she was going to do it. Poor Maria! I guess it's the first and only offer she ever received, and it's just turned her head."

"But what DO those two see in each other?" cried Trina. "Zerkow is a horror, he's an old man, and his hair is red and his voice is gone, and then he's a Jew, isn't he?"

"I know, I know; but it's Maria's only chance for a husband, and she don't mean to let it pass. You know she isn't quite right in her head, anyhow. I'm awfully sorry for poor Maria. But I can't see what Zerkow wants to marry her for. It's not possible that he's in love with Maria, it's out of the question. Maria hasn't a sou, either, and I'm just positive that Zerkow has lots of money."

"I'll bet I know why," exclaimed Trina, with sudden conviction; "yes, I know just why. See here, Miss Baker, you know how crazy old Zerkow is after money and gold and those sort of things."

"Yes, I know; but you know Maria hasn't——"

"Now, just listen. You've heard Maria tell about that wonderful service of gold dishes she says her folks used to own in Central America; she's crazy on that subject, don't you know. She's all right on everything else, but just start her on that service of gold plate and she'll talk you deaf. She can describe it just as though she saw it, and she can make you see it, too, almost. Now, you see, Maria and Zerkow have known each other pretty well. Maria goes to him every two weeks or so to sell him junk; they got acquainted that way, and I know Maria's been dropping in to see him pretty often this last year, and sometimes he comes here to see her. He's made Maria tell him the story of that plate over and over and over again, and Maria does it and is glad to, because he's the only one that believes it. Now he's going to marry her just so's he can hear that story every day, every hour. He's pretty near as crazy on the subject as Maria is. They're a pair for you, aren't they? Both crazy over a lot of gold dishes that never existed. Perhaps Maria'll marry him because it's her only chance to get a husband, but I'm sure it's more for the reason that she's got some one to talk to now who believes her story. Don't you think I'm right?"

"Yes, yes, I guess you're right," admitted Miss Baker.

"But it's a queer match anyway you put it," said Trina, musingly.

"Ah, you may well say that," returned the other, nodding her head. There was a silence. For a long moment the dentist's wife and the retired dressmaker, the one at the window, the other on the sidewalk, remained lost in thought, wondering over the strangeness of the affair.

But suddenly there was a diversion. Alexander, Marcus Schouler's Irish setter, whom his master had long since allowed the liberty of running untrammelled about the neighborhood, turned the corner briskly and came trotting along the sidewalk where Miss Baker stood. At the same moment the Scotch collie who had at one time belonged to the branch post-office issued from the side door of a house not fifty feet away. In an instant the two enemies had recognized each other. They halted abruptly, their fore feet planted rigidly. Trina uttered a little cry.

"Oh, look out, Miss Baker. Those two dogs hate each other just like humans. You best look out. They'll fight sure." Miss Baker sought safety in a nearby vestibule, whence she peered forth at the scene, very interested and curious. Maria Macapa's head thrust itself from one of the top-story windows of the flat, with a shrill cry. Even McTeague's huge form appeared above the half curtains of the "Parlor" windows, while over his shoulder could be seen the face of the "patient," a napkin tucked in his collar, the rubber dam depending from his mouth. All the flat knew of the feud between the dogs, but never before had the pair been brought face to face.

Meanwhile, the collie and the setter had drawn near to each other; five feet apart they paused as if by mutual consent. The collie turned sidewise to the setter; the setter instantly wheeled himself flank on to the collie. Their tails rose and stiffened, they raised their lips over their long white fangs, the napes of their necks bristled, and they showed each other the vicious whites of their eyes, while they drew in their breaths with prolonged and rasping snarls. Each dog seemed to be the personification of fury and unsatisfied hate. They began to circle about each other with infinite slowness, walking stiffed-legged and upon the very points of their feet. Then they wheeled about and began to circle in the opposite direction. Twice they repeated this motion, their snarls growing louder. But still they did not come together, and the distance of five feet between them was maintained with an almost mathematical precision. It was magnificent, but it was not war. Then the setter, pausing in his walk, turned his head slowly from his enemy. The collie sniffed the air and pretended an interest in an old shoe lying in the gutter. Gradually and with all the dignity of monarchs they moved away from each other. Alexander stalked back to the corner of the street. The collie paced toward the side gate whence he had issued, affecting to remember something of great importance. They disappeared. Once out of sight of one another they began to bark furiously.

"Well, I NEVER!" exclaimed Trina in great disgust. "The way those two dogs have been carrying on you'd 'a' thought they would 'a' just torn each other to pieces when they had the chance, and here I'm wasting the whole morning——" she closed her window with a bang.

"Sick 'im, sick 'im," called Maria Macapa, in a vain attempt to promote a fight.

Old Miss Baker came out of the vestibule, pursing her lips, quite put out at the fiasco. "And after all that fuss," she said to herself aggrievedly.

The little dressmaker bought an envelope of nasturtium seeds at the florist's, and returned to her tiny room in the flat. But as she slowly mounted the first flight of steps she suddenly came face to face with Old Grannis, who was coming down. It was between eight and nine, and he was on his way to his little dog hospital, no doubt. Instantly Miss Baker was seized with trepidation, her curious little false curls shook, a faint—a very faint—flush came into her withered cheeks, and her heart beat so violently under the worsted shawl that she felt obliged to shift the market-basket to her other arm and put out her free hand to steady herself against the rail.

On his part, Old Grannis was instantly overwhelmed with confusion. His awkwardness seemed to paralyze his limbs, his lips twitched and turned dry, his hand went tremblingly to his chin. But what added to Miss Baker's miserable embarrassment on this occasion was the fact that the old Englishman should meet her thus, carrying a sordid market-basket full of sordid fish and cabbage. It seemed as if a malicious fate persisted in bringing the two old people face to face at the most inopportune moments.

Just now, however, a veritable catastrophe occurred. The little old dressmaker changed her basket to her other arm at precisely the wrong moment, and Old Grannis, hastening to pass, removing his hat in a hurried salutation, struck it with his fore arm, knocking it from her grasp, and sending it rolling and bumping down the stairs. The sole fell flat upon the first landing; the lentils scattered themselves over the entire flight; while the cabbage, leaping from step to step, thundered down the incline and brought up against the street door with a shock that reverberated through the entire building.

The little retired dressmaker, horribly vexed, nervous and embarrassed, was hard put to it to keep back the tears. Old Grannis stood for a moment with averted eyes, murmuring: "Oh, I'm so sorry, I'm so sorry. I—I really—I beg your pardon, really—really."

Marcus Schouler, coming down stairs from his room, saved the situation.

"Hello, people," he cried. "By damn! you've upset your basket—you have, for a fact. Here, let's pick um up." He and Old Grannis went up and down the flight, gathering up the fish, the lentils, and the sadly battered cabbage. Marcus was raging over the pusillanimity of Alexander, of which Maria had just told him.

"I'll cut him in two—with the whip," he shouted. "I will, I will, I say I will, for a fact. He wouldn't fight, hey? I'll give um all the fight he wants, nasty, mangy cur. If he won't fight he won't eat. I'm going to get the butcher's bull pup and I'll put um both in a bag and shake um up. I will, for a fact, and I guess Alec will fight. Come along, Mister Grannis," and he took the old Englishman away.

Little Miss Baker hastened to her room and locked herself in. She was excited and upset during all the rest of the day, and listened eagerly for Old Grannis's return that evening. He went instantly to work binding up "The Breeder and Sportsman," and back numbers of the "Nation." She heard him softly draw his chair and the table on which he had placed his little binding apparatus close to the wall. At once she did the same, brewing herself a cup of tea. All through that evening the two old people "kept company" with each other, after their own peculiar fashion. "Setting out with each other" Miss Baker had begun to call it. That they had been presented, that they had even been forced to talk together, had made no change in their relative positions. Almost immediately they had fallen back into their old ways again, quite unable to master their timidity, to overcome the stifling embarrassment that seized upon them when in each other's presence. It was a sort of hypnotism, a thing stronger than themselves. But they were not altogether dissatisfied with the way things had come to be. It was their little romance, their last, and they were living through it with supreme enjoyment and calm contentment.

Marcus Schouler still occupied his old room on the floor above the McTeagues. They saw but little of him, however. At long intervals the dentist or his wife met him on the stairs of the flat. Sometimes he would stop and talk with Trina, inquiring after the Sieppes, asking her if Mr. Sieppe had yet heard of any one with whom he, Marcus, could "go in with on a ranch." McTeague, Marcus merely nodded to. Never had the quarrel between the two men been completely patched up. It did not seem possible to the dentist now that Marcus had ever been his "pal," that they had ever taken long walks together. He was sorry that he had treated Marcus gratis for an ulcerated tooth, while Marcus daily recalled the fact that he had given up his "girl" to his friend—the girl who had won a fortune—as the great mistake of his life. Only once since the wedding had he called upon Trina, at a time when he knew McTeague would be out. Trina had shown him through the rooms and had told him, innocently enough, how gay was their life there. Marcus had come away fairly sick with envy; his rancor against the dentist—and against himself, for that matter—knew no bounds. "And you might 'a' had it all yourself, Marcus Schouler," he muttered to himself on the stairs. "You mushhead, you damn fool!"

Meanwhile, Marcus was becoming involved in the politics of his ward. As secretary of the Polk Street Improvement Club—which soon developed into quite an affair and began to assume the proportions of a Republican political machine—he found he could make a little, a very little more than enough to live on. At once he had given up his position as Old Grannis's assistant in the dog hospital. Marcus felt that he needed a wider sphere. He had his eye upon a place connected with the city pound. When the great railroad strike occurred, he promptly got himself engaged as deputy-sheriff, and spent a memorable week in Sacramento, where he involved himself in more than one terrible melee with the strikers. Marcus had that quickness of temper and passionate readiness to take offence which passes among his class for bravery. But whatever were his motives, his promptness to face danger could not for a moment be doubted. After the strike he returned to Polk Street, and throwing himself into the Improvement Club, heart, soul, and body, soon became one of its ruling spirits. In a certain local election, where a huge paving contract was at stake, the club made itself felt in the ward, and Marcus so managed his cards and pulled his wires that, at the end of the matter, he found himself some four hundred dollars to the good.

When McTeague came out of his "Parlors" at noon of the day upon which Trina had heard the news of Maria Macapa's intended marriage, he found Trina burning coffee on a shovel in the sitting-room. Try as she would, Trina could never quite eradicate from their rooms a certain faint and indefinable odor, particularly offensive to her. The smell of the photographer's chemicals persisted in spite of all Trina could do to combat it. She burnt pastilles and Chinese punk, and even, as now, coffee on a shovel, all to no purpose. Indeed, the only drawback to their delightful home was the general unpleasant smell that pervaded it—a smell that arose partly from the photographer's chemicals, partly from the cooking in the little kitchen, and partly from the ether and creosote of the dentist's "Parlors."

As McTeague came in to lunch on this occasion, he found the table already laid, a red cloth figured with white flowers was spread, and as he took his seat his wife put down the shovel on a chair and brought in the stewed codfish and the pot of chocolate. As he tucked his napkin into his enormous collar, McTeague looked vaguely about the room, rolling his eyes.

During the three years of their married life the McTeagues had made but few additions to their furniture, Trina declaring that they could not afford it. The sitting-room could boast of but three new ornaments. Over the melodeon hung their marriage certificate in a black frame. It was balanced upon one side by Trina's wedding bouquet under a glass case, preserved by some fearful unknown process, and upon the other by the photograph of Trina and the dentist in their wedding finery. This latter picture was quite an affair, and had been taken immediately after the wedding, while McTeague's broadcloth was still new, and before Trina's silks and veil had lost their stiffness. It represented Trina, her veil thrown back, sitting very straight in a rep armchair, her elbows well in at her sides, holding her bouquet of cut flowers directly before her. The dentist stood at her side, one hand on her shoulder, the other thrust into the breast of his "Prince Albert," his chin in the air, his eyes to one side, his left foot forward in the attitude of a statue of a Secretary of State.

"Say, Trina," said McTeague, his mouth full of codfish, "Heise looked in on me this morning. He says 'What's the matter with a basket picnic over at Schuetzen Park next Tuesday?' You know the paper-hangers are going to be in the 'Parlors' all that day, so I'll have a holiday. That's what made Heise think of it. Heise says he'll get the Ryers to go too. It's the anniversary of their wedding day. We'll ask Selina to go; she can meet us on the other side. Come on, let's go, huh, will you?"

Trina still had her mania for family picnics, which had been one of the Sieppes most cherished customs; but now there were other considerations.

"I don't know as we can afford it this month, Mac," she said, pouring the chocolate. "I got to pay the gas bill next week, and there's the papering of your office to be paid for some time."

"I know, I know," answered her husband. "But I got a new patient this week, had two molars and an upper incisor filled at the very first sitting, and he's going to bring his children round. He's a barber on the next block."

"Well you pay half, then," said Trina. "It'll cost three or four dollars at the very least; and mind, the Heises pay their own fare both ways, Mac, and everybody gets their OWN lunch. Yes," she added, after a pause, "I'll write and have Selina join us. I haven't seen Selina in months. I guess I'll have to put up a lunch for her, though," admitted Trina, "the way we did last time, because she lives in a boarding-house now, and they make a fuss about putting up a lunch."

They could count on pleasant weather at this time of the year—it was May—and that particular Tuesday was all that could be desired. The party assembled at the ferry slip at nine o'clock, laden with baskets. The McTeagues came last of all; Ryer and his wife had already boarded the boat. They met the Heises in the waiting-room.

"Hello, Doctor," cried the harness-maker as the McTeagues came up. "This is what you'd call an old folks' picnic, all married people this time."

The party foregathered on the upper deck as the boat started, and sat down to listen to the band of Italian musicians who were playing outside this morning because of the fineness of the weather.

"Oh, we're going to have lots of fun," cried Trina. "If it's anything I do love it's a picnic. Do you remember our first picnic, Mac?"

"Sure, sure," replied the dentist; "we had a Gotha truffle."

"And August lost his steamboat," put in Trina, "and papa smacked him. I remember it just as well."

"Why, look there," said Mrs. Heise, nodding at a figure coming up the companion-way. "Ain't that Mr. Schouler?"

It was Marcus, sure enough. As he caught sight of the party he gaped at them a moment in blank astonishment, and then ran up, his eyes wide.

"Well, by damn!" he exclaimed, excitedly. "What's up? Where you all going, anyhow? Say, ain't ut queer we should all run up against each other like this?" He made great sweeping bows to the three women, and shook hands with "Cousin Trina," adding, as he turned to the men of the party, "Glad to see you, Mister Heise. How do, Mister Ryer?" The dentist, who had formulated some sort of reserved greeting, he ignored completely. McTeague settled himself in his seat, growling inarticulately behind his mustache.

"Say, say, what's all up, anyhow?" cried Marcus again.

"It's a picnic," exclaimed the three women, all speaking at once; and Trina added, "We're going over to the same old Schuetzen Park again. But you're all fixed up yourself, Cousin Mark; you look as though you were going somewhere yourself."

In fact, Marcus was dressed with great care. He wore a new pair of slate-blue trousers, a black "cutaway," and a white lawn "tie" (for him the symbol of the height of elegance). He carried also his cane, a thin wand of ebony with a gold head, presented to him by the Improvement Club in "recognition of services."

"That's right, that's right," said Marcus, with a grin. "I'm takun a holiday myself to-day. I had a bit of business to do over at Oakland, an' I thought I'd go up to B Street afterward and see Selina. I haven't called on——"

But the party uttered an exclamation.

"Why, Selina is going with us."

"She's going to meet us at the Schuetzen Park station" explained Trina.

Marcus's business in Oakland was a fiction. He was crossing the bay that morning solely to see Selina. Marcus had "taken up with" Selina a little after Trina had married, and had been "rushing" her ever since, dazzled and attracted by her accomplishments, for which he pretended a great respect. At the prospect of missing Selina on this occasion, he was genuinely disappointed. His vexation at once assumed the form of exasperation against McTeague. It was all the dentist's fault. Ah, McTeague was coming between him and Selina now as he had come between him and Trina. Best look out, by damn! how he monkeyed with him now. Instantly his face flamed and he glanced over furiously at the dentist, who, catching his eye, began again to mutter behind his mustache.

"Well, say," began Mrs. Ryer, with some hesitation, looking to Ryer for approval, "why can't Marcus come along with us?"

"Why, of course," exclaimed Mrs. Heise, disregarding her husband's vigorous nudges. "I guess we got lunch enough to go round, all right; don't you say so, Mrs. McTeague?"

Thus appealed to, Trina could only concur.

"Why, of course, Cousin Mark," she said; "of course, come along with us if you want to."

"Why, you bet I will," cried Marcus, enthusiastic in an instant. "Say, this is outa sight; it is, for a fact; a picnic—ah, sure—and we'll meet Selina at the station."

Just as the boat was passing Goat Island, the harness-maker proposed that the men of the party should go down to the bar on the lower deck and shake for the drinks. The idea had an immediate success.

"Have to see you on that," said Ryer.

"By damn, we'll have a drink! Yes, sir, we will, for a fact."

"Sure, sure, drinks, that's the word."

At the bar Heise and Ryer ordered cocktails, Marcus called for a "creme Yvette" in order to astonish the others. The dentist spoke for a glass of beer.

"Say, look here," suddenly exclaimed Heise as they took their glasses. "Look here, you fellahs," he had turned to Marcus and the dentist. "You two fellahs have had a grouch at each other for the last year or so; now what's the matter with your shaking hands and calling quits?"

McTeague was at once overcome with a great feeling of magnanimity. He put out his great hand.

"I got nothing against Marcus," he growled.

"Well, I don't care if I shake," admitted Marcus, a little shamefacedly, as their palms touched. "I guess that's all right."

"That's the idea," exclaimed Heise, delighted at his success. "Come on, boys, now let's drink." Their elbows crooked and they drank silently.

Their picnic that day was very jolly. Nothing had changed at Schuetzen Park since the day of that other memorable Sieppe picnic four years previous. After lunch the men took themselves off to the rifle range, while Selina, Trina, and the other two women put away the dishes. An hour later the men joined them in great spirits. Ryer had won the impromptu match which they had arranged, making quite a wonderful score, which included three clean bulls' eyes, while McTeague had not been able even to hit the target itself.

Their shooting match had awakened a spirit of rivalry in the men, and the rest of the afternoon was passed in athletic exercises between them. The women sat on the slope of the grass, their hats and gloves laid aside, watching the men as they strove together. Aroused by the little feminine cries of wonder and the clapping of their ungloved palms, these latter began to show off at once. They took off their coats and vests, even their neckties and collars, and worked themselves into a lather of perspiration for the sake of making an impression on their wives. They ran hundred-yard sprints on the cinder path and executed clumsy feats on the rings and on the parallel bars. They even found a huge round stone on the beach and "put the shot" for a while. As long as it was a question of agility, Marcus was easily the best of the four; but the dentist's enormous strength, his crude, untutored brute force, was a matter of wonder for the entire party. McTeague cracked English walnuts—taken from the lunch baskets—in the hollow of his arm, and tossed the round stone a full five feet beyond their best mark. Heise believed himself to be particularly strong in the wrists, but the dentist, using but one hand, twisted a cane out of Heise's two with a wrench that all but sprained the harnessmaker's arm. Then the dentist raised weights and chinned himself on the rings till they thought he would never tire.

His great success quite turned his head; he strutted back and forth in front of the women, his chest thrown out, and his great mouth perpetually expanded in a triumphant grin. As he felt his strength more and more, he began to abuse it; he domineered over the others, gripping suddenly at their arms till they squirmed with pain, and slapping Marcus on the back so that he gasped and gagged for breath. The childish vanity of the great fellow was as undisguised as that of a schoolboy. He began to tell of wonderful feats of strength he had accomplished when he was a young man. Why, at one time he had knocked down a half-grown heifer with a blow of his fist between the eyes, sure, and the heifer had just stiffened out and trembled all over and died without getting up.

McTeague told this story again, and yet again. All through the afternoon he could be overheard relating the wonder to any one who would listen, exaggerating the effect of his blow, inventing terrific details. Why, the heifer had just frothed at the mouth, and his eyes had rolled up—ah, sure, his eyes rolled up just like that—and the butcher had said his skull was all mashed in—just all mashed in, sure, that's the word—just as if from a sledge-hammer.

Notwithstanding his reconciliation with the dentist on the boat, Marcus's gorge rose within him at McTeague's boasting swagger. When McTeague had slapped him on the back, Marcus had retired to some little distance while he recovered his breath, and glared at the dentist fiercely as he strode up and down, glorying in the admiring glances of the women.

"Ah, one-horse dentist," he muttered between his teeth. "Ah, zinc-plugger, cow-killer, I'd like to show you once, you overgrown mucker, you—you—COW-KILLER!"

When he rejoined the group, he found them preparing for a wrestling bout.

"I tell you what," said Heise, "we'll have a tournament. Marcus and I will rastle, and Doc and Ryer, and then the winners will rastle each other."

The women clapped their hands excitedly. This would be exciting. Trina cried:

"Better let me hold your money, Mac, and your keys, so as you won't lose them out of your pockets." The men gave their valuables into the keeping of their wives and promptly set to work.

The dentist thrust Ryer down without even changing his grip; Marcus and the harness-maker struggled together for a few moments till Heise all at once slipped on a bit of turf and fell backwards. As they toppled over together, Marcus writhed himself from under his opponent, and, as they reached the ground, forced down first one shoulder and then the other.

"All right, all right," panted the harness-maker, goodnaturedly, "I'm down. It's up to you and Doc now," he added, as he got to his feet.

The match between McTeague and Marcus promised to be interesting. The dentist, of course, had an enormous advantage in point of strength, but Marcus prided himself on his wrestling, and knew something about strangle-holds and half-Nelsons. The men drew back to allow them a free space as they faced each other, while Trina and the other women rose to their feet in their excitement.

"I bet Mac will throw him, all the same," said Trina.

"All ready!" cried Ryer.

The dentist and Marcus stepped forward, eyeing each other cautiously. They circled around the impromptu ring. Marcus watching eagerly for an opening. He ground his teeth, telling himself he would throw McTeague if it killed him. Ah, he'd show him now. Suddenly the two men caught at each other; Marcus went to his knees. The dentist threw his vast bulk on his adversary's shoulders and, thrusting a huge palm against his face, pushed him backwards and downwards. It was out of the question to resist that enormous strength. Marcus wrenched himself over and fell face downward on the ground.

McTeague rose on the instant with a great laugh of exultation.

"You're down!" he exclaimed.

Marcus leaped to his feet.

"Down nothing," he vociferated, with clenched fists. "Down nothing, by damn! You got to throw me so's my shoulders touch."

McTeague was stalking about, swelling with pride.

"Hoh, you're down. I threw you. Didn't I throw him, Trina? Hoh, you can't rastle ME."

Marcus capered with rage.

"You didn't! you didn't! you didn't! and you can't! You got to give me another try."

The other men came crowding up. Everybody was talking at once.

"He's right."

"You didn't throw him."

"Both his shoulders at the same time."

Trina clapped and waved her hand at McTeague from where she stood on the little slope of lawn above the wrestlers. Marcus broke through the group, shaking all over with excitement and rage.

"I tell you that ain't the WAY to rastle. You've got to throw a man so's his shoulders touch. You got to give me another bout."

"That's straight," put in Heise, "both his shoulders down at the same time. Try it again. You and Schouler have another try."

McTeague was bewildered by so much simultaneous talk. He could not make out what it was all about. Could he have offended Marcus again?

"What? What? Huh? What is it?" he exclaimed in perplexity, looking from one to the other.

"Come on, you must rastle me again," shouted Marcus.

"Sure, sure," cried the dentist. "I'll rastle you again. I'll rastle everybody," he cried, suddenly struck with an idea. Trina looked on in some apprehension.

"Mark gets so mad," she said, half aloud.

"Yes," admitted Selina. "Mister Schouler's got an awful quick temper, but he ain't afraid of anything."

"All ready!" shouted Ryer.

This time Marcus was more careful. Twice, as McTeague rushed at him, he slipped cleverly away. But as the dentist came in a third time, with his head bowed, Marcus, raising himself to his full height, caught him with both arms around the neck. The dentist gripped at him and rent away the sleeve of his shirt. There was a great laugh.

"Keep your shirt on," cried Mrs. Ryer.

The two men were grappling at each other wildly. The party could hear them panting and grunting as they labored and struggled. Their boots tore up great clods of turf. Suddenly they came to the ground with a tremendous shock. But even as they were in the act of falling, Marcus, like a very eel, writhed in the dentist's clasp and fell upon his side. McTeague crashed down upon him like the collapse of a felled ox.

"Now, you gotta turn him on his back," shouted Heise to the dentist. "He ain't down if you don't."

With his huge salient chin digging into Marcus's shoulder, the dentist heaved and tugged. His face was flaming, his huge shock of yellow hair fell over his forehead, matted with sweat. Marcus began to yield despite his frantic efforts. One shoulder was down, now the other began to go; gradually, gradually it was forced over. The little audience held its breath in the suspense of the moment. Selina broke the silence, calling out shrilly:

"Ain't Doctor McTeague just that strong!"

Marcus heard it, and his fury came instantly to a head. Rage at his defeat at the hands of the dentist and before Selina's eyes, the hate he still bore his old-time "pal" and the impotent wrath of his own powerlessness were suddenly unleashed.

"God damn you! get off of me," he cried under his breath, spitting the words as a snake spits its venom. The little audience uttered a cry. With the oath Marcus had twisted his head and had bitten through the lobe of the dentist's ear. There was a sudden flash of bright-red blood.

Then followed a terrible scene. The brute that in McTeague lay so close to the surface leaped instantly to life, monstrous, not to be resisted. He sprang to his feet with a shrill and meaningless clamor, totally unlike the ordinary bass of his speaking tones. It was the hideous yelling of a hurt beast, the squealing of a wounded elephant. He framed no words; in the rush of high-pitched sound that issued from his wide-open mouth there was nothing articulate. It was something no longer human; it was rather an echo from the jungle.

Sluggish enough and slow to anger on ordinary occasions, McTeague when finally aroused became another man. His rage was a kind of obsession, an evil mania, the drunkenness of passion, the exalted and perverted fury of the Berserker, blind and deaf, a thing insensate.

As he rose he caught Marcus's wrist in both his hands. He did not strike, he did not know what he was doing. His only idea was to batter the life out of the man before him, to crush and annihilate him upon the instant. Gripping his enemy in his enormous hands, hard and knotted, and covered with a stiff fell of yellow hair—the hands of the old-time car-boy—he swung him wide, as a hammer-thrower swings his hammer. Marcus's feet flipped from the ground, he spun through the air about McTeague as helpless as a bundle of clothes. All at once there was a sharp snap, almost like the report of a small pistol. Then Marcus rolled over and over upon the ground as McTeague released his grip; his arm, the one the dentist had seized, bending suddenly, as though a third joint had formed between wrist and elbow. The arm was broken.

But by this time every one was crying out at once. Heise and Ryan ran in between the two men. Selina turned her head away. Trina was wringing her hands and crying in an agony of dread:

"Oh, stop them, stop them! Don't let them fight. Oh, it's too awful."

"Here, here, Doc, quit. Don't make a fool of yourself," cried Heise, clinging to the dentist. "That's enough now. LISTEN to me, will you?"

"Oh, Mac, Mac," cried Trina, running to her husband. "Mac, dear, listen; it's me, it's Trina, look at me, you——"

"Get hold of his other arm, will you, Ryer?" panted Heise. "Quick!"

"Mac, Mac," cried Trina, her arms about his neck.

"For God's sake, hold up, Doc, will you?" shouted the harness-maker. "You don't want to kill him, do you?"

Mrs. Ryer and Heise's lame wife were filling the air with their outcries. Selina was giggling with hysteria. Marcus, terrified, but too brave to run, had picked up a jagged stone with his left hand and stood on the defensive. His swollen right arm, from which the shirt sleeve had been torn, dangled at his side, the back of the hand twisted where the palm should have been. The shirt itself was a mass of grass stains and was spotted with the dentist's blood.

But McTeague, in the centre of the group that struggled to hold him, was nigh to madness. The side of his face, his neck, and all the shoulder and breast of his shirt were covered with blood. He had ceased to cry out, but kept muttering between his gripped jaws, as he labored to tear himself free of the retaining hands:

"Ah, I'll kill him! Ah, I'll kill him! I'll kill him! Damn you, Heise," he exclaimed suddenly, trying to strike the harness-maker, "let go of me, will you!"

Little by little they pacified him, or rather (for he paid but little attention to what was said to him) his bestial fury lapsed by degrees. He turned away and let fall his arms, drawing long breaths, and looking stupidly about him, now searching helplessly upon the ground, now gazing vaguely into the circle of faces about him. His ear bled as though it would never stop.

"Say, Doctor," asked Heise, "what's the best thing to do?"

"Huh?" answered McTeague. "What—what do you mean? What is it?"

"What'll we do to stop this bleeding here?"

McTeague did not answer, but looked intently at the blood-stained bosom of his shirt.

"Mac," cried Trina, her face close to his, "tell us something—the best thing we can do to stop your ear bleeding."

"Collodium," said the dentist.

"But we can't get to that right away; we—"

"There's some ice in our lunch basket," broke in Heise. "We brought it for the beer; and take the napkins and make a bandage."

"Ice," muttered the dentist, "sure, ice, that's the word."

Mrs. Heise and the Ryers were looking after Marcus's broken arm. Selina sat on the slope of the grass, gasping and sobbing. Trina tore the napkins into strips, and, crushing some of the ice, made a bandage for her husband's head.'

The party resolved itself into two groups; the Ryers and Mrs. Heise bending over Marcus, while the harness-maker and Trina came and went about McTeague, sitting on the ground, his shirt, a mere blur of red and white, detaching itself violently from the background of pale-green grass. Between the two groups was the torn and trampled bit of turf, the wrestling ring; the picnic baskets, together with empty beer bottles, broken egg-shells, and discarded sardine tins, were scattered here and there. In the middle of the improvised wrestling ring the sleeve of Marcus's shirt fluttered occasionally in the sea breeze.

Nobody was paying any attention to Selina. All at once she began to giggle hysterically again, then cried out with a peal of laughter:

"Oh, what a way for our picnic to end!"

CHAPTER 12

"Now, then, Maria," said Zerkow, his cracked, strained voice just rising above a whisper, hitching his chair closer to the table, "now, then, my girl, let's have it all over again. Tell us about the gold plate—the service. Begin with, 'There were over a hundred pieces and every one of them gold.'"

"I don't know what you're talking about, Zerkow," answered Maria. "There never was no gold plate, no gold service. I guess you must have dreamed it."

Maria and the red-headed Polish Jew had been married about a month after the McTeague's picnic which had ended in such lamentable fashion. Zerkow had taken Maria home to his wretched hovel in the alley back of the flat, and the flat had been obliged to get another maid of all work. Time passed, a month, six months, a whole year went by. At length Maria gave birth to a child, a wretched, sickly child, with not even strength enough nor wits enough to cry. At the time of its birth Maria was out of her mind, and continued in a state of dementia for nearly ten days. She recovered just in time to make the arrangements for the baby's burial. Neither Zerkow nor Maria was much affected by either the birth or the death of this little child. Zerkow had welcomed it with pronounced disfavor, since it had a mouth to be fed and wants to be provided for. Maria was out of her head so much of the time that she could scarcely remember how it looked when alive. The child was a mere incident in their lives, a thing that had come undesired and had gone unregretted. It had not even a name; a strange, hybrid little being, come and gone within a fortnight's time, yet combining in its puny little body the blood of the Hebrew, the Pole, and the Spaniard.

But the birth of this child had peculiar consequences. Maria came out of her dementia, and in a few days the household settled itself again to its sordid regime and Maria went about her duties as usual. Then one evening, about a week after the child's burial, Zerkow had asked Maria to tell him the story of the famous service of gold plate for the hundredth time.

Zerkow had come to believe in this story infallibly. He was immovably persuaded that at one time Maria or Maria's people had possessed these hundred golden dishes. In his perverted mind the hallucination had developed still further. Not only had that service of gold plate once existed, but it existed now, entire, intact; not a single burnished golden piece of it was missing. It was somewhere, somebody had it, locked away in that leather trunk with its quilted lining and round brass locks. It was to be searched for and secured, to be fought for, to be gained at all hazards. Maria must know where it was; by dint of questioning, Zerkow would surely get the information from her. Some day, if only he was persistent, he would hit upon the right combination of questions, the right suggestion that would disentangle Maria's confused recollections. Maria would tell him where the thing was kept, was concealed, was buried, and he would go to that place and secure it, and all that wonderful gold would be his forever and forever. This service of plate had come to be Zerkow's mania.

On this particular evening, about a week after the child's burial, in the wretched back room of the Junk shop, Zerkow had made Maria sit down to the table opposite him—the whiskey bottle and the red glass tumbler with its broken base between them—and had said:

"Now, then, Maria, tell us that story of the gold dishes again."

Maria stared at him, an expression of perplexity coming into her face.

"What gold dishes?" said she.

"The ones your people used to own in Central America. Come on, Maria, begin, begin." The Jew craned himself forward, his lean fingers clawing eagerly at his lips.

"What gold plate?" said Maria, frowning at him as she drank her whiskey. "What gold plate? I don' know what you're talking about, Zerkow."

Zerkow sat back in his chair, staring at her.

"Why, your people's gold dishes, what they used to eat off of. You've told me about it a hundred times."

"You're crazy, Zerkow," said Maria. "Push the bottle here, will you?"

"Come, now," insisted Zerkow, sweating with desire, "come, now, my girl, don't be a fool; let's have it, let's have it. Begin now, 'There were more'n a hundred pieces, and every one of 'em gold.' Oh, YOU know; come on, come on."

"I don't remember nothing of the kind," protested Maria, reaching for the bottle. Zerkow snatched it from her.

"You fool!" he wheezed, trying to raise his broken voice to a shout. "You fool! Don't you dare try an' cheat ME, or I'll DO for you. You know about the gold plate, and you know where it is." Suddenly he pitched his voice at the prolonged rasping shout with which he made his street cry. He rose to his feet, his long, prehensile fingers curled into fists. He was menacing, terrible in his rage. He leaned over Maria, his fists in her face.

"I believe you've got it!" he yelled. "I believe you've got it, an' are hiding it from me. Where is it, where is it? Is it here?" he rolled his eyes wildly about the room. "Hey? hey?" he went on, shaking Maria by the shoulders. "Where is it? Is it here? Tell me where it is. Tell me, or I'll do for you!"

"It ain't here," cried Maria, wrenching from him. "It ain't anywhere. What gold plate? What are you talking about? I don't remember nothing about no gold plate at all."

No, Maria did not remember. The trouble and turmoil of her mind consequent upon the birth of her child seemed to have readjusted her disordered ideas upon this point. Her mania had come to a crisis, which in subsiding had cleared her brain of its one illusion. She did not remember. Or it was possible that the gold plate she had once remembered had had some foundation in fact, that her recital of its splendors had been truth, sound and sane. It was possible that now her FORGETFULNESS of it was some form of brain trouble, a relic of the dementia of childbirth. At all events Maria did not remember; the idea of the gold plate had passed entirely out of her mind, and it was now Zerkow who labored under its hallucination. It was now Zerkow, the raker of the city's muck heap, the searcher after gold, that saw that wonderful service in the eye of his perverted mind. It was he who could now describe it in a language almost eloquent. Maria had been content merely to remember it; but Zerkow's avarice goaded him to a belief that it was still in existence, hid somewhere, perhaps in that very house, stowed away there by Maria. For it stood to reason, didn't it, that Maria could not have described it with such wonderful accuracy and such careful detail unless she had seen it recently—the day before, perhaps, or that very day, or that very hour, that very HOUR?

"Look out for yourself," he whispered, hoarsely, to his wife. "Look out for yourself, my girl. I'll hunt for it, and hunt for it, and hunt for it, and some day I'll find it—I will, you'll see—I'll find it, I'll find it; and if I don't, I'll find a way that'll make you tell me where it is. I'll make you speak—believe me, I will, I will, my girl—trust me for that."

And at night Maria would sometimes wake to find Zerkow gone from the bed, and would see him burrowing into some corner by the light of his dark-lantern and would hear him mumbling to himself: "There were more'n a hundred pieces, and every one of 'em gold—when the leather trunk was opened it fair dazzled your eyes—why, just that punchbowl was worth a fortune, I guess; solid, solid, heavy, rich, pure gold, nothun but gold, gold, heaps and heaps of it—what a glory! I'll find it yet, I'll find it. It's here somewheres, hid somewheres in this house."

At length his continued ill success began to exasperate him. One day he took his whip from his junk wagon and thrashed Maria with it, gasping the while, "Where is it, you beast? Where is it? Tell me where it is; I'll make you speak."

"I don' know, I don' know," cried Maria, dodging his blows. "I'd tell you, Zerkow, if I knew; but I don' know nothing about it. How can I tell you if I don' know?"

Then one evening matters reached a crisis. Marcus Schouler was in his room, the room in the flat just over McTeague's "Parlors" which he had always occupied. It was between eleven and twelve o'clock. The vast house was quiet; Polk Street outside was very still, except for the occasional whirr and trundle of a passing cable car and the persistent calling of ducks and geese in the deserted market directly opposite. Marcus was in his shirt sleeves, perspiring and swearing with exertion as he tried to get all his belongings into an absurdly inadequate trunk. The room was in great confusion. It looked as though Marcus was about to move. He stood in front of his trunk, his precious silk hat in its hat-box in his hand. He was raging at the perverseness of a pair of boots that refused to fit in his trunk, no matter how he arranged them.

"I've tried you SO, and I've tried you SO," he exclaimed fiercely, between his teeth, "and you won't go." He began to swear horribly, grabbing at the boots with his free hand. "Pretty soon I won't take you at all; I won't, for a fact."

He was interrupted by a rush of feet upon the back stairs and a clamorous pounding upon his door. He opened it to let in Maria Macapa, her hair dishevelled and her eyes starting with terror.

"Oh, MISTER Schouler," she gasped, "lock the door quick. Don't let him get me. He's got a knife, and he says sure he's going to do for me, if I don't tell him where it is."

"Who has? What has? Where is what?" shouted Marcus, flaming with excitement upon the instant. He opened the door and peered down the dark hall, both fists clenched, ready to fight—he did not know whom, and he did not know why.

"It's Zerkow," wailed Maria, pulling him back into the room and bolting the door, "and he's got a knife as long as THAT. Oh, my Lord, here he comes now! Ain't that him? Listen."

Zerkow was coming up the stairs, calling for Maria.

"Don't you let him get me, will you, Mister Schouler?" gasped Maria.

"I'll break him in two," shouted Marcus, livid with rage. "Think I'm afraid of his knife?"

"I know where you are," cried Zerkow, on the landing outside. "You're in Schouler's room. What are you doing in Schouler's room at this time of night? Come outa there; you oughta be ashamed. I'll do for you yet, my girl. Come outa there once, an' see if I don't."

"I'll do for you myself, you dirty Jew," shouted Marcus, unbolting the door and running out into the hall.

"I want my wife," exclaimed the Jew, backing down the stairs. "What's she mean by running away from me and going into your room?"

"Look out, he's got a knife!" cried Maria through the crack of the door.

"Ah, there you are. Come outa that, and come back home," exclaimed Zerkow.

"Get outa here yourself," cried Marcus, advancing on him angrily. "Get outa here."

"Maria's gota come too."

"Get outa here," vociferated Marcus, "an' put up that knife. I see it; you needn't try an' hide it behind your leg. Give it to me, anyhow," he shouted suddenly, and before Zerkow was aware, Marcus had wrenched it away. "Now, get outa here."

Zerkow backed away, peering and peeping over Marcus's shoulder.

"I want Maria."

"Get outa here. Get along out, or I'll PUT you out." The street door closed. The Jew was gone.

"Huh!" snorted Marcus, swelling with arrogance. "Huh! Think I'm afraid of his knife? I ain't afraid of ANYBODY," he shouted pointedly, for McTeague and his wife, roused by the clamor, were peering over the banisters from the landing above. "Not of anybody," repeated Marcus.

Maria came out into the hall.

"Is he gone? Is he sure gone?"

"What was the trouble?" inquired Marcus, suddenly.

"I woke up about an hour ago," Maria explained, "and Zerkow wasn't in bed; maybe he hadn't come to bed at all. He was down on his knees by the sink, and he'd pried up some boards off the floor and was digging there. He had his dark-lantern. He was digging with that knife, I guess, and all the time he kept mumbling to himself, 'More'n a hundred pieces, an' every one of 'em gold; more'n a hundred pieces, an' every one of 'em gold.' Then, all of a sudden, he caught sight of me. I was sitting up in bed, and he jumped up and came at me with his knife, an' he says, 'Where is it? Where is it? I know you got it hid somewhere. Where is it? Tell me or I'll knife you.' I kind of fooled him and kept him off till I got my wrapper on, an' then I run out. I didn't dare stay."

"Well, what did you tell him about your gold dishes for in the first place?" cried Marcus.

"I never told him," protested Maria, with the greatest energy. "I never told him; I never heard of any gold dishes. I don' know where he got the idea; he must be crazy."

By this time Trina and McTeague, Old Grannis, and little Miss Baker—all the lodgers on the upper floors of the flat—had gathered about Maria. Trina and the dentist, who had gone to bed, were partially dressed, and Trina's enormous mane of black hair was hanging in two thick braids far down her back. But, late as it was, Old Grannis and the retired dressmaker had still been up and about when Maria had aroused them.

"Why, Maria," said Trina, "you always used to tell us about your gold dishes. You said your folks used to have them."

"Never, never, never!" exclaimed Maria, vehemently. "You folks must all be crazy. I never HEARD of any gold dishes."

"Well," spoke up Miss Baker, "you're a queer girl, Maria; that's all I can say." She left the group and returned to her room. Old Grannis watched her go from the corner of his eye, and in a few moments followed her, leaving the group as unnoticed as he had joined it. By degrees the flat quieted down again. Trina and McTeague returned to their rooms.

"I guess I'll go back now," said Maria. "He's all right now. I ain't afraid of him so long as he ain't got his knife."

"Well, say," Marcus called to her as she went down stairs, "if he gets funny again, you just yell out; I'LL hear you. I won't let him hurt you."

Marcus went into his room again and resumed his wrangle with the refractory boots. His eye fell on Zerkow's knife, a long, keen-bladed hunting-knife, with a buckhorn handle. "I'll take you along with me," he exclaimed, suddenly. "I'll just need you where I'm going."

Meanwhile, old Miss Baker was making tea to calm her nerves after the excitement of Maria's incursion. This evening she went so far as to make tea for two, laying an extra place on the other side of her little tea-table, setting out a cup and saucer and one of the Gorham silver spoons. Close upon the other side of the partition Old Grannis bound uncut numbers of the "Nation."

"Do you know what I think, Mac?" said Trina, when the couple had returned to their rooms. "I think Marcus is going away."

"What? What?" muttered the dentist, very sleepy and stupid, "what you saying? What's that about Marcus?"

"I believe Marcus has been packing up, the last two or three days. I wonder if he's going away."

"Who's going away?" said McTeague, blinking at her.

"Oh, go to bed," said Trina, pushing him goodnaturedly. "Mac, you're the stupidest man I ever knew."

But it was true. Marcus was going away. Trina received a letter the next morning from her mother. The carpet-cleaning and upholstery business in which Mr. Sieppe had involved himself was going from bad to worse. Mr. Sieppe had even been obliged to put a mortgage upon their house. Mrs. Sieppe didn't know what was to become of them all. Her husband had even begun to talk of emigrating to New Zealand. Meanwhile, she informed Trina that Mr. Sieppe had finally come across a man with whom Marcus could "go in with on a ranch," a cattle ranch in the southeastern portion of the State. Her ideas were vague upon the subject, but she knew that Marcus was wildly enthusiastic at the prospect, and was expected down before the end of the month. In the meantime, could Trina send them fifty dollars?

"Marcus IS going away, after all, Mac," said Trina to her husband that day as he came out of his "Parlors" and sat down to the lunch of sausages, mashed potatoes, and chocolate in the sitting-room.

"Huh?" said the dentist, a little confused. "Who's going away? Schouler going away? Why's Schouler going away?"

Trina explained. "Oh!" growled McTeague, behind his thick mustache, "he can go far before I'LL stop him."

"And, say, Mac," continued Trina, pouring the chocolate, "what do you think? Mamma wants me—wants us to send her fifty dollars. She says they're hard up."

"Well," said the dentist, after a moment, "well, I guess we can send it, can't we?"

"Oh, that's easy to say," complained Trina, her little chin in the air, her small pale lips pursed. "I wonder if mamma thinks we're millionaires?"

"Trina, you're getting to be regular stingy," muttered McTeague. "You're getting worse and worse every day."

"But fifty dollars is fifty dollars, Mac. Just think how long it takes you to earn fifty dollars. Fifty dollars! That's two months of our interest."

"Well," said McTeague, easily, his mouth full of mashed potato, "you got a lot saved up."

Upon every reference to that little hoard in the brass match-safe and chamois-skin bag at the bottom of her trunk, Trina bridled on the instant.

"Don't TALK that way, Mac. 'A lot of money.' What do you call a lot of money? I don't believe I've got fifty dollars saved."

"Hoh!" exclaimed McTeague. "Hoh! I guess you got nearer a hundred AN' fifty. That's what I guess YOU got."

"I've NOT, I've NOT," declared Trina, "and you know I've not. I wish mamma hadn't asked me for any money. Why can't she be a little more economical? I manage all right. No, no, I can't possibly afford to send her fifty."

"Oh, pshaw! What WILL you do, then?" grumbled her husband.

"I'll send her twenty-five this month, and tell her I'll send the rest as soon as I can afford it."

"Trina, you're a regular little miser," said McTeague.

"I don't care," answered Trina, beginning to laugh. "I guess I am, but I can't help it, and it's a good fault."

Trina put off sending this money for a couple of weeks, and her mother made no mention of it in her next letter. "Oh, I guess if she wants it so bad," said Trina, "she'll speak about it again." So she again postponed the sending of it. Day by day she put it off. When her mother asked her for it a second time, it seemed harder than ever for Trina to part with even half the sum requested. She answered her mother, telling her that they were very hard up themselves for that month, but that she would send down the amount in a few weeks.

"I'll tell you what we'll do, Mac," she said to her husband, "you send half and I'll send half; we'll send twenty-five dollars altogether. Twelve and a half apiece. That's an idea. How will that do?"

"Sure, sure," McTeague had answered, giving her the money. Trina sent McTeague's twelve dollars, but never sent the twelve that was to be her share. One day the dentist happened to ask her about it.

"You sent that twenty-five to your mother, didn't you?" said he.

"Oh, long ago," answered Trina, without thinking.

In fact, Trina never allowed herself to think very much of this affair. And, in fact, another matter soon came to engross her attention.

One Sunday evening Trina and her husband were in their sitting-room together. It was dark, but the lamp had not been lit. McTeague had brought up some bottles of beer from the "Wein Stube" on the ground floor, where the branch post-office used to be. But they had not opened the beer. It was a warm evening in summer. Trina was sitting on McTeague's lap in the bay window, and had looped back the Nottingham curtains so the two could look out into the darkened street and watch the moon coming up over the glass roof of the huge public baths. On occasions they sat like this for an hour or so, "philandering," Trina cuddling herself down upon McTeague's enormous body, rubbing her cheek against the grain of his unshaven chin, kissing the bald spot on the top of his head, or putting her fingers into his ears and eyes. At times, a brusque access of passion would seize upon her, and, with a nervous little sigh, she would clasp his thick red neck in both her small arms and whisper in his ear:

"Do you love me, Mac, dear? Love me BIG, BIG? Sure, do you love me as much as you did when we were married?"

Puzzled, McTeague would answer: "Well, you know it, don't you, Trina?"

"But I want you to SAY so; say so always and always."

"Well, I do, of course I do."

"Say it, then."

"Well, then, I love you."

"But you don't say it of your own accord."

"Well, what—what—what—I don't understand," stammered the dentist, bewildered.

There was a knock on the door. Confused and embarrassed, as if they were not married, Trina scrambled off McTeague's lap, hastening to light the lamp, whispering, "Put on your coat, Mac, and smooth your hair," and making gestures for him to put the beer bottles out of sight. She opened the door and uttered an exclamation.

"Why, Cousin Mark!" she said. McTeague glared at him, struck speechless, confused beyond expression. Marcus Schouler, perfectly at his ease, stood in the doorway, smiling with great affability.

"Say," he remarked, "can I come in?"

Taken all aback, Trina could only answer:

"Why—I suppose so. Yes, of course—come in."

"Yes, yes, come in," exclaimed the dentist, suddenly, speaking without thought. "Have some beer?" he added, struck with an idea.

"No, thanks, Doctor," said Marcus, pleasantly.

McTeague and Trina were puzzled. What could it all mean? Did Marcus want to become reconciled to his enemy? "I know." Trina said to herself. "He's going away, and he wants to borrow some money. He won't get a penny, not a penny." She set her teeth together hard.

"Well," said Marcus, "how's business, Doctor?"

"Oh," said McTeague, uneasily, "oh, I don' know. I guess—I guess," he broke off in helpless embarrassment. They had all sat down by now. Marcus continued, holding his hat and his cane—the black wand of ebony with the gold top presented to him by the "Improvement Club."

"Ah!" said he, wagging his head and looking about the sitting-room, "you people have got the best fixed rooms in the whole flat. Yes, sir; you have, for a fact." He glanced from the lithograph framed in gilt and red plush—the two little girls at their prayers—to the "I'm Grandpa" and "I'm Grandma" pictures, noted the clean white matting and the gay worsted tidies over the chair backs, and appeared to contemplate in ecstasy the framed photograph of McTeague and Trina in their wedding finery.

"Well, you two are pretty happy together, ain't you?" said he, smiling good-humoredly.

"Oh, we don't complain," answered Trina.

"Plenty of money, lots to do, everything fine, hey?"

"We've got lots to do," returned Trina, thinking to head him off, "but we've not got lots of money."

But evidently Marcus wanted no money.

"Well, Cousin Trina," he said, rubbing his knee, "I'm going away."

"Yes, mamma wrote me; you're going on a ranch."

"I'm going in ranching with an English duck," corrected Marcus. "Mr. Sieppe has fixed things. We'll see if we can't raise some cattle. I know a lot about horses, and he's ranched some before—this English duck. And then I'm going to keep my eye open for a political chance down there. I got some introductions from the President of the Improvement Club. I'll work things somehow, oh, sure."

"How long you going to be gone?" asked Trina.

Marcus stared.

"Why, I ain't EVER coming back," he vociferated. "I'm going tomorrow, and I'm going for good. I come to say good-by."

Marcus stayed for upwards of an hour that evening. He talked on easily and agreeably, addressing himself as much to McTeague as to Trina. At last he rose.

"Well, good-by, Doc."

"Good-by, Marcus," returned McTeague. The two shook hands.

"Guess we won't ever see each other again," continued Marcus. "But good luck to you, Doc. Hope some day you'll have the patients standing in line on the stairs."

"Huh! I guess so, I guess so," said the dentist.

"Good-by, Cousin Trina."

"Good-by, Marcus," answered Trina. "You be sure to remember me to mamma, and papa, and everybody. I'm going to make two great big sets of Noah's ark animals for the twins on their next birthday; August is too old for toys. But you can tell the twins that I'll make them some great big animals. Good-by, success to you, Marcus."

"Good-by, good-by. Good luck to you both."

"Good-by, Cousin Mark."

"Good-by, Marcus."

He was gone.

CHAPTER 13

One morning about a week after Marcus had left for the southern part of the State, McTeague found an oblong letter thrust through the letter-drop of the door of his "Parlors." The address was typewritten. He opened it. The letter had been sent from the City Hall and was stamped in one corner with the seal of the State of California, very official; the form and file numbers superscribed.

McTeague had been making fillings when this letter arrived. He was in his "Parlors," pottering over his movable rack underneath the bird cage in the bay window. He was making "blocks" to be used in large proximal cavities and "cylinders" for commencing fillings. He heard the postman's step in the hall and saw the envelopes begin to shuttle themselves through the slit of his letter-drop. Then came the fat oblong envelope, with its official seal, that dropped flatwise to the floor with a sodden, dull impact.

The dentist put down the broach and scissors and gathered up his mail. There were four letters altogether. One was for Trina, in Selina's "elegant" handwriting; another was an advertisement of a new kind of operating chair for dentists; the third was a card from a milliner on the next block, announcing an opening; and the fourth, contained in the fat oblong envelope, was a printed form with blanks left for names and dates, and addressed to McTeague, from an office in the City Hall. McTeague read it through laboriously. "I don' know, I don' know," he muttered, looking stupidly at the rifle manufacturer's calendar. Then he heard Trina, from the kitchen, singing as she made a clattering noise with the breakfast dishes. "I guess I'll ask Trina about it," he muttered.

He went through the suite, by the sitting-room, where the sun was pouring in through the looped backed Nottingham curtains upon the clean white matting and the varnished surface of the melodeon, passed on through the bedroom, with its framed lithographs of round-cheeked English babies and alert fox terriers, and came out into the brick-paved kitchen. The kitchen was clean as a new whistle; the freshly blackened cook stove glowed like a negro's hide; the tins and porcelain-lined stew-pans might have been of silver and of ivory. Trina was in the centre of the room, wiping off, with a damp sponge, the oilcloth table-cover, on which they had breakfasted.

Never had she looked so pretty. Early though it was, her enormous tiara of swarthy hair was neatly combed and coiled, not a pin was so much as loose. She wore a blue calico skirt with a white figure, and a belt of imitation alligator skin clasped around her small, firmly-corseted waist; her shirt waist was of pink linen, so new and crisp that it crackled with every movement, while around the collar, tied in a neat knot, was one of McTeague's lawn ties which she had appropriated. Her sleeves were carefully rolled up almost to her shoulders, and nothing could have been more delicious than the sight of her small round arms, white as milk, moving back and forth as she sponged the table-cover, a faint touch of pink coming and going at the elbows as they bent and straightened. She looked up quickly as her husband entered, her narrow eyes alight, her adorable little chin in the air; her lips rounded and opened with the last words of her song, so that one could catch a glint of gold in the fillings of her upper teeth.

The whole scene—the clean kitchen and its clean brick floor; the smell of coffee that lingered in the air; Trina herself, fresh as if from a bath, and singing at her work; the morning sun, striking obliquely through the white muslin half-curtain of the window and spanning the little kitchen with a bridge of golden mist—gave off, as it were, a note of gayety that was not to be resisted. Through the opened top of the window came the noises of Polk Street, already long awake. One heard the chanting of street cries, the shrill calling of children on their way to school, the merry rattle of a butcher's cart, the brisk noise of hammering, or the occasional prolonged roll of a cable car trundling heavily past, with a vibrant whirring of its jostled glass and the joyous clanging of its bells.

"What is it, Mac, dear?" said Trina.

McTeague shut the door behind him with his heel and handed her the letter. Trina read it through. Then suddenly her small hand gripped tightly upon the sponge, so that the water started from it and dripped in a little pattering deluge upon the bricks.

The letter—or rather printed notice—informed McTeague that he had never received a diploma from a dental college, and that in consequence he was forbidden to practise his profession any longer. A legal extract bearing upon the case was attached in small type.

"Why, what's all this?" said Trina, calmly, without thought as yet.

"I don' know, I don' know," answered her husband.

"You can't practise any longer," continued Trina,—"'is herewith prohibited and enjoined from further continuing——'" She re-read the extract, her forehead lifting and puckering. She put the sponge carefully away in its wire rack over the sink, and drew up a chair to the table, spreading out the notice before her. "Sit down," she said to McTeague. "Draw up to the table here, Mac, and let's see what this is."

"I got it this morning," murmured the dentist. "It just now came. I was making some fillings—there, in the 'Parlors,' in the window—and the postman shoved it through the door. I thought it was a number of the 'American System of Dentistry' at first, and when I'd opened it and looked at it I thought I'd better——"

"Say, Mac," interrupted Trina, looking up from the notice, "DIDN'T you ever go to a dental college?"

"Huh? What? What?" exclaimed McTeague.

"How did you learn to be a dentist? Did you go to a college?"

"I went along with a fellow who came to the mine once. My mother sent me. We used to go from one camp to another. I sharpened his excavators for him, and put up his notices in the towns—stuck them up in the post-offices and on the doors of the Odd Fellows' halls. He had a wagon."

"But didn't you never go to a college?"

"Huh? What? College? No, I never went. I learned from the fellow."

Trina rolled down her sleeves. She was a little paler than usual. She fastened the buttons into the cuffs and said:

"But do you know you can't practise unless you're graduated from a college? You haven't the right to call yourself, 'doctor.'"

McTeague stared a moment; then:

"Why, I've been practising ten years. More—nearly twelve."

"But it's the law."

"What's the law?"

"That you can't practise, or call yourself doctor, unless you've got a diploma."

"What's that—a diploma?"

"I don't know exactly. It's a kind of paper that—that—oh, Mac, we're ruined." Trina's voice rose to a cry.

"What do you mean, Trina? Ain't I a dentist? Ain't I a doctor? Look at my sign, and the gold tooth you gave me. Why, I've been practising nearly twelve years."

Trina shut her lips tightly, cleared her throat, and pretended to resettle a hair-pin at the back of her head.

"I guess it isn't as bad as that," she said, very quietly. "Let's read this again. 'Herewith prohibited and enjoined from further continuing——'" She read to the end.

"Why, it isn't possible," she cried. "They can't mean—oh, Mac, I do believe—pshaw!" she exclaimed, her pale face flushing. "They don't know how good a dentist you are. What difference does a diploma make, if you're a first-class dentist? I guess that's all right. Mac, didn't you ever go to a dental college?"

"No," answered McTeague, doggedly. "What was the good? I learned how to operate; wa'n't that enough?"

"Hark," said Trina, suddenly. "Wasn't that the bell of your office?" They had both heard the jangling of the bell that McTeague had hung over the door of his "Parlors." The dentist looked at the kitchen clock.

"That's Vanovitch," said he. "He's a plumber round on Sutter Street. He's got an appointment with me to have a bicuspid pulled. I got to go back to work." He rose.

"But you can't," cried Trina, the back of her hand upon her lips, her eyes brimming. "Mac, don't you see? Can't you understand? You've got to stop. Oh, it's dreadful! Listen." She hurried around the table to him and caught his arm in both her hands.

"Huh?" growled McTeague, looking at her with a puzzled frown.

"They'll arrest you. You'll go to prison. You can't work—can't work any more. We're ruined."

Vanovitch was pounding on the door of the sitting-room.

"He'll be gone in a minute," exclaimed McTeague.

"Well, let him go. Tell him to go; tell him to come again."

"Why, he's got an APPOINTMENT with me," exclaimed McTeague, his hand upon the door.

Trina caught him back. "But, Mac, you ain't a dentist any longer; you ain't a doctor. You haven't the right to work. You never went to a dental college."

"Well, suppose I never went to a college, ain't I a dentist just the same? Listen, he's pounding there again. No, I'm going, sure."

"Well, of course, go," said Trina, with sudden reaction. "It ain't possible they'll make you stop. If you're a good dentist, that's all that's wanted. Go on, Mac; hurry, before he goes."

McTeague went out, closing the door. Trina stood for a moment looking intently at the bricks at her feet. Then she returned to the table, and sat down again before the notice, and, resting her head in both her fists, read it yet another time. Suddenly the conviction seized upon her that it was all true. McTeague would be obliged to stop work, no matter how good a dentist he was. But why had the authorities at the City Hall waited this long before serving the notice? All at once Trina snapped her fingers, with a quick flash of intelligence.

"It's Marcus that's done it," she cried.

It was like a clap of thunder. McTeague was stunned, stupefied. He said nothing. Never in his life had he been so taciturn. At times he did not seem to hear Trina when she spoke to him, and often she had to shake him by the shoulder to arouse his attention. He would sit apart in his "Parlors," turning the notice about in his enormous clumsy fingers, reading it stupidly over and over again. He couldn't understand. What had a clerk at the City Hall to do with him? Why couldn't they let him alone?

"Oh, what's to become of us NOW?" wailed Trina. "What's to become of us now? We're paupers, beggars—and all so sudden." And once, in a quick, inexplicable fury, totally unlike anything that McTeague had noticed in her before, she had started up, with fists and teeth shut tight, and had cried, "Oh, if you'd only KILLED Marcus Schouler that time he fought you!"

McTeague had continued his work, acting from sheer force of habit; his sluggish, deliberate nature, methodical, obstinate, refusing to adapt itself to the new conditions.

"Maybe Marcus was only trying to scare us," Trina had said. "How are they going to know whether you're practising or not?"

"I got a mould to make to-morrow," McTeague said, "and Vanovitch, that plumber round on Sutter Street, he's coming again at three."

"Well, you go right ahead," Trina told him, decisively; "you go right ahead and make the mould, and pull every tooth in Vanovitch's head if you want to. Who's going to know? Maybe they just sent that notice as a matter of form. Maybe Marcus got that paper and filled it in himself."

The two would lie awake all night long, staring up into the dark, talking, talking, talking.

"Haven't you got any right to practise if you've not been to a dental college, Mac? Didn't you ever go?" Trina would ask again and again.

"No, no," answered the dentist, "I never went. I learnt from the fellow I was apprenticed to. I don' know anything about a dental college. Ain't I got a right to do as I like?" he suddenly exclaimed.

"If you know your profession, isn't that enough?" cried Trina.

"Sure, sure," growled McTeague. "I ain't going to stop for them."

"You go right on," Trina said, "and I bet you won't hear another word about it."

"Suppose I go round to the City Hall and see them," hazarded McTeague.

"No, no, don't you do it, Mac," exclaimed Trina. "Because, if Marcus has done this just to scare you, they won't know anything about it there at the City Hall; but they'll begin to ask you questions, and find out that you never HAD graduated from a dental college, and you'd be just as bad off as ever."

"Well, I ain't going to quit for just a piece of paper," declared the dentist. The phrase stuck to him. All day long he went about their rooms or continued at his work in the "Parlors," growling behind his thick mustache: "I ain't going to quit for just a piece of paper. No, I ain't going to quit for just a piece of paper. Sure not."

The days passed, a week went by, McTeague continued his work as usual. They heard no more from the City Hall, but the suspense of the situation was harrowing. Trina was actually sick with it. The terror of the thing was ever at their elbows, going to bed with them, sitting down with them at breakfast in the kitchen, keeping them company all through the day. Trina dared not think of what would be their fate if the income derived from McTeague's practice was suddenly taken from them. Then they would have to fall back on the interest of her lottery money and the pittance she derived from the manufacture of the Noah's ark animals, a little over thirty dollars a month. No, no, it was not to be thought of. It could not be that their means of livelihood was to be thus stricken from them.

A fortnight went by. "I guess we're all right, Mac," Trina allowed herself to say. "It looks as though we were all right. How are they going to tell whether you're practising or not?"

That day a second and much more peremptory notice was served upon McTeague by an official in person. Then suddenly Trina was seized with a panic terror, unreasoned, instinctive. If McTeague persisted they would both be sent to a prison, she was sure of it; a place where people were chained to the wall, in the dark, and fed on bread and water.

"Oh, Mac, you've got to quit," she wailed. "You can't go on. They can make you stop. Oh, why didn't you go to a dental college? Why didn't you find out that you had to have a college degree? And now we're paupers, beggars. We've got to leave here—leave this flat where I've been—where WE'VE been so happy, and sell all the pretty things; sell the pictures and the melodeon, and—Oh, it's too dreadful!"

"Huh? Huh? What? What?" exclaimed the dentist, bewildered. "I ain't going to quit for just a piece of paper. Let them put me out. I'll show them. They—they can't make small of me."

"Oh, that's all very fine to talk that way, but you'll have to quit."

"Well, we ain't paupers," McTeague suddenly exclaimed, an idea entering his mind. "We've got our money yet. You've got your five thousand dollars and the money you've been saving up. People ain't paupers when they've got over five thousand dollars."

"What do you mean, Mac?" cried Trina, apprehensively.

"Well, we can live on THAT money until—until—until—" he broke off with an uncertain movement of his shoulders, looking about him stupidly.

"Until WHEN?" cried Trina. "There ain't ever going to be any 'until.' We've got the INTEREST of that five thousand and we've got what Uncle Oelbermann gives me, a little over thirty dollars a month, and that's all we've got. You'll have to find something else to do."

"What will I find to do?"

What, indeed? McTeague was over thirty now, sluggish and slow-witted at best. What new trade could he learn at this age?

Little by little Trina made the dentist understand the calamity that had befallen them, and McTeague at last began cancelling his appointments. Trina gave it out that he was sick.

"Not a soul need know what's happened to us," she said to her husband.

But it was only by slow degrees that McTeague abandoned his profession. Every morning after breakfast he would go into his "Parlors" as usual and potter about his instruments, his dental engine, and his washstand in the corner behind his screen where he made his moulds. Now he would sharpen a "hoe" excavator, now he would busy himself for a whole hour making "mats" and "cylinders." Then he would look over his slate where he kept a record of his appointments.

One day Trina softly opened the door of the "Parlors" and came in from the sitting-room. She had not heard McTeague moving about for some time and had begun to wonder what he was doing. She came in, quietly shutting the door behind her.

McTeague had tidied the room with the greatest care. The volumes of the "Practical Dentist" and the "American System of Dentistry" were piled upon the marble-top centre-table in rectangular blocks. The few chairs were drawn up against the wall under the steel engraving of "Lorenzo de' Medici" with more than usual precision. The dental engine and the nickelled trimmings of the operating chair had been furbished till they shone, while on the movable rack in the bay window McTeague had arranged his instruments with the greatest neatness and regularity. "Hoe" excavators, pluggers, forceps, pliers, corundum disks and burrs, even the boxwood mallet that Trina was never to use again, all were laid out and ready for immediate use.

McTeague himself sat in his operating chair, looking stupidly out of the windows, across the roofs opposite, with an unseeing gaze, his red hands lying idly in his lap. Trina came up to him. There was something in his eyes that made her put both arms around his neck and lay his huge head with its coarse blond hair upon her shoulder.

"I—I got everything fixed," he said. "I got everything fixed an' ready. See, everything ready an' waiting, an'—an'—an' nobody comes, an' nobody's ever going to come any more. Oh, Trina!" He put his arms about her and drew her down closer to him.

"Never mind, dear; never mind," cried Trina, through her tears. "It'll all come right in the end, and we'll be poor together if we have to. You can sure find something else to do. We'll start in again."

"Look at the slate there," said McTeague, pulling away from her and reaching down the slate on which he kept a record of his appointments. "Look at them. There's Vanovitch at two on Wednesday, and Loughhead's wife Thursday morning, and Heise's little girl Thursday afternoon at one-thirty; Mrs. Watson on Friday, and Vanovitch again Saturday morning early—at seven. That's what I was to have had, and they ain't going to come. They ain't ever going to come any more."

Trina took the little slate from him and looked at it ruefully.

"Rub them out," she said, her voice trembling; "rub it all out;" and as she spoke her eyes brimmed again, and a great tear dropped on the slate.

"That's it," she said; "that's the way to rub it out, by me crying on it." Then she passed her fingers over the tear-blurred writing and washed the slate clean. "All gone, all gone," she said.

"All gone," echoed the dentist. There was a silence. Then McTeague heaved himself up to his full six feet two, his face purpling, his enormous mallet-like fists raised over his head. His massive jaw protruded more than ever, while his teeth clicked and grated together; then he growled:

"If ever I meet Marcus Schouler—" he broke off abruptly, the white of his eyes growing suddenly pink.

"Oh, if ever you DO," exclaimed Trina, catching her breath.

CHAPTER 14

"Well, what do you think?" said Trina.

She and McTeague stood in a tiny room at the back of the flat and on its very top floor. The room was whitewashed. It contained a bed, three cane-seated chairs, and a wooden washstand with its washbowl and pitcher. From its single uncurtained window one looked down into the flat's dirty back yard and upon the roofs of the hovels that bordered the alley in the rear. There was a rag carpet on the floor. In place of a closet some dozen wooden pegs were affixed to the wall over the washstand. There was a smell of cheap soap and of ancient hair-oil in the air.

"That's a single bed," said Trina, "but the landlady says she'll put in a double one for us. You see——"

"I ain't going to live here," growled McTeague.

"Well, you've got to live somewhere," said Trina, impatiently. "We've looked Polk Street over, and this is the only thing we can afford."

"Afford, afford," muttered the dentist. "You with your five thousand dollars, and the two or three hundred you got saved up, talking about 'afford.' You make me sick."

"Now, Mac," exclaimed Trina, deliberately, sitting down in one of the cane-seated chairs; "now, Mac, let's have this thing——"

"Well, I don't figure on living in one room," growled the dentist, sullenly. "Let's live decently until we can get a fresh start. We've got the money."

"Who's got the money?"

"WE'VE got it."

"We!"

"Well, it's all in the family. What's yours is mine, and what's mine is yours, ain't it?"

"No, it's not; no, it's not," cried Trina, vehemently. "It's all mine, mine. There's not a penny of it belongs to anybody else. I don't like to have to talk this way to you, but you just make me. We're not going to touch a penny of my five thousand nor a penny of that little money I managed to save—that seventy-five."

"That TWO hundred, you mean."

"That SEVENTY-FIVE. We're just going to live on the interest of that and on what I earn from Uncle Oelbermann—on just that thirty-one or two dollars."

"Huh! Think I'm going to do that, an' live in such a room as this?"

Trina folded her arms and looked him squarely in the face.

"Well, what ARE you going to do, then?"

"Huh?"

"I say, what ARE you going to do? You can go on and find something to do and earn some more money, and THEN we'll talk."

"Well, I ain't going to live here."

"Oh, very well, suit yourself. I'M going to live here."

"You'll live where I TELL you," the dentist suddenly cried, exasperated at the mincing tone she affected.

"Then YOU'LL pay the rent," exclaimed Trina, quite as angry as he.

"Are you my boss, I'd like to know? Who's the boss, you or I?"

"Who's got the MONEY, I'd like to know?" cried Trina, flushing to her pale lips. "Answer me that, McTeague, who's got the money?"

"You make me sick, you and your money. Why, you're a miser. I never saw anything like it. When I was practising, I never thought of my fees as my own; we lumped everything in together."

"Exactly; and I'M doing the working now. I'm working for Uncle Oelbermann, and you're not lumping in ANYTHING now. I'm doing it all. Do you know what I'm doing, McTeague? I'm supporting you."

"Ah, shut up; you make me sick."

"You got no RIGHT to talk to me that way. I won't let you. I—I won't have it." She caught her breath. Tears were in her eyes.

"Oh, live where you like, then," said McTeague, sullenly.

"Well, shall we take this room then?"

"All right, we'll take it. But why can't you take a little of your money an'—an'—sort of fix it up?"

"Not a penny, not a single penny."

"Oh, I don't care WHAT you do." And for the rest of the day the dentist and his wife did not speak.

This was not the only quarrel they had during these days when they were occupied in moving from their suite and in looking for new quarters. Every hour the question of money came up. Trina had become more niggardly than ever since the loss of McTeague's practice. It was not mere economy with her now. It was a panic terror lest a fraction of a cent of her little savings should be touched; a passionate eagerness to continue to save in spite of all that had happened. Trina could have easily afforded better quarters than the single whitewashed room at the top of the flat, but she made McTeague believe that it was impossible.

"I can still save a little," she said to herself, after the room had been engaged; "perhaps almost as much as ever. I'll have three hundred dollars pretty soon, and Mac thinks it's only two hundred. It's almost two hundred and fifty; and I'll get a good deal out of the sale."

But this sale was a long agony. It lasted a week. Everything went—everything but the few big pieces that went with the suite, and that belonged to the photographer. The melodeon, the chairs, the black walnut table before which they were married, the extension table in the sitting-room, the kitchen table with its oilcloth cover, the framed lithographs from the English illustrated papers, the very carpets on the floors. But Trina's heart nearly broke when the kitchen utensils and furnishings began to go. Every pot, every stewpan, every knife and fork, was an old friend. How she had worked over them! How clean she had kept them! What a pleasure it had been to invade that little brick-paved kitchen every morning, and to wash up and put to rights after breakfast, turning on the hot water at the sink, raking down the ashes in the cook-stove, going and coming over the warm bricks, her head in the air, singing at her work, proud in the sense of her proprietorship and her independence! How happy had she been the day after her marriage when she had first entered that kitchen and knew that it was all her own! And how well she remembered her raids upon the bargain counters in the house-furnishing departments of the great downtown stores! And now it was all to go. Some one else would have it all, while she was relegated to cheap restaurants and meals cooked by hired servants. Night after night she sobbed herself to sleep at the thought of her past happiness and her present wretchedness. However, she was not alone in her unhappiness.

"Anyhow, I'm going to keep the steel engraving an' the stone pug dog," declared the dentist, his fist clenching. When it had come to the sale of his office effects McTeague had rebelled with the instinctive obstinacy of a boy, shutting his eyes and ears. Only little by little did Trina induce him to part with his office furniture. He fought over every article, over the little iron stove, the bed-lounge, the marble-topped centre table, the whatnot in the corner, the bound volumes of "Allen's Practical Dentist," the rifle manufacturer's calendar, and the prim, military chairs. A veritable scene took place between him and his wife before he could bring himself to part with the steel engraving of "Lorenzo de' Medici and His Court" and the stone pug dog with its goggle eyes.

"Why," he would cry, "I've had 'em ever since—ever since I BEGAN; long before I knew you, Trina. That steel engraving I bought in Sacramento one day when it was raining. I saw it in the window of a second-hand store, and a fellow GAVE me that stone pug dog. He was a druggist. It was in Sacramento too. We traded. I gave him a shaving-mug and a razor, and he gave me the pug dog."

There were, however, two of his belongings that even Trina could not induce him to part with.

"And your concertina, Mac," she prompted, as they were making out the list for the second-hand dealer. "The concertina, and—oh, yes, the canary and the bird cage."

"No."

"Mac, you MUST be reasonable. The concertina would bring quite a sum, and the bird cage is as good as new. I'll sell the canary to the bird-store man on Kearney Street."

"No."

"If you're going to make objections to every single thing, we might as well quit. Come, now, Mac, the concertina and the bird cage. We'll put them in Lot D."

"No."

"You'll have to come to it sooner or later. I'M giving up everything. I'm going to put them down, see."

"No."

And she could get no further than that. The dentist did not lose his temper, as in the case of the steel engraving or the stone pug dog; he simply opposed her entreaties and persuasions with a passive, inert obstinacy that nothing could move. In the end Trina was obliged to submit. McTeague kept his concertina and his canary, even going so far as to put them both away in the bedroom, attaching to them tags on which he had scrawled in immense round letters, "Not for Sale."

One evening during that same week the dentist and his wife were in the dismantled sitting-room. The room presented the appearance of a wreck. The Nottingham lace curtains were down. The extension table was heaped high with dishes, with tea and coffee pots, and with baskets of spoons and knives and forks. The melodeon was hauled out into the middle of the floor, and covered with a sheet marked "Lot A," the pictures were in a pile in a corner, the chenille portieres were folded on top of the black walnut table. The room was desolate, lamentable. Trina was going over the inventory; McTeague, in his shirt sleeves, was smoking his pipe, looking stupidly out of the window. All at once there was a brisk rapping at the door.

"Come in," called Trina, apprehensively. Now-a-days at every unexpected visit she anticipated a fresh calamity. The door opened to let in a young man wearing a checked suit, a gay cravat, and a marvellously figured waistcoat. Trina and McTeague recognized him at once. It was the Other Dentist, the debonair fellow whose clients were the barbers and the young women of the candy stores and soda-water fountains, the poser, the wearer of waistcoats, who bet money on greyhound races.

"How'do?" said this one, bowing gracefully to the McTeagues as they stared at him distrustfully.

"How'do? They tell me, Doctor, that you are going out of the profession."

McTeague muttered indistinctly behind his mustache and glowered at him.

"Well, say," continued the other, cheerily, "I'd like to talk business with you. That sign of yours, that big golden tooth that you got outside of your window, I don't suppose you'll have any further use for it. Maybe I'd buy it if we could agree on terms."

Trina shot a glance at her husband. McTeague began to glower again.

"What do you say?" said the Other Dentist.

"I guess not," growled McTeague

"What do you say to ten dollars?"

"Ten dollars!" cried Trina, her chin in the air.

"Well, what figure DO you put on it?"

Trina was about to answer when she was interrupted by McTeague.

"You go out of here."

"Hey? What?"

"You go out of here."

The other retreated toward the door.

"You can't make small of me. Go out of here."

McTeague came forward a step, his great red fist clenching. The young man fled. But half way down the stairs he paused long enough to call back:

"You don't want to trade anything for a diploma, do you?"

McTeague and his wife exchanged looks.

"How did he know?" exclaimed Trina, sharply. They had invented and spread the fiction that McTeague was merely retiring from business, without assigning any reason. But evidently every one knew the real cause. The humiliation was complete now. Old Miss Baker confirmed their suspicions on this point the next day. The little retired dressmaker came down and wept with Trina over her misfortune, and did what she could to encourage her. But she too knew that McTeague had been forbidden by the authorities from practising. Marcus had evidently left them no loophole of escape.

"It's just like cutting off your husband's hands, my dear," said Miss Baker. "And you two were so happy. When I first saw you together I said, 'What a pair!'"

Old Grannis also called during this period of the breaking up of the McTeague household.

"Dreadful, dreadful," murmured the old Englishman, his hand going tremulously to his chin. "It seems unjust; it does. But Mr. Schouler could not have set them on to do it. I can't quite believe it of him."

"Of Marcus!" cried Trina. "Hoh! Why, he threw his knife at Mac one time, and another time he bit him, actually bit him with his teeth, while they were wrestling just for fun. Marcus would do anything to injure Mac."

"Dear, dear," returned Old Grannis, genuinely pained. "I had always believed Schouler to be such a good fellow."

"That's because you're so good yourself, Mr. Grannis," responded Trina.

"I tell you what, Doc," declared Heise the harness-maker, shaking his finger impressively at the dentist, "you must fight it; you must appeal to the courts; you've been practising too long to be debarred now. The statute of limitations, you know."

"No, no," Trina had exclaimed, when the dentist had repeated this advice to her. "No, no, don't go near the law courts. I know them. The lawyers take all your money, and you lose your case. We're bad off as it is, without lawing about it."

Then at last came the sale. McTeague and Trina, whom Miss Baker had invited to her room for that day, sat there side by side, holding each other's hands, listening nervously to the turmoil that rose to them from the direction of their suite. From nine o'clock till dark the crowds came and went. All Polk Street seemed to have invaded the suite, lured on by the red flag that waved from the front windows. It was a fete, a veritable holiday, for the whole neighborhood. People with no thought of buying presented themselves. Young women—the candy-store girls and florist's apprentices—came to see the fun, walking arm in arm from room to room, making jokes about the pretty lithographs and mimicking the picture of the two little girls saying their prayers.

"Look here," they would cry, "look here what she used for curtains— NOTTINGHAM lace, actually! Whoever thinks of buying Nottingham lace now-a-days? Say, don't that JAR you?"

"And a melodeon," another one would exclaim, lifting the sheet. "A melodeon, when you can rent a piano for a dollar a week; and say, I really believe they used to eat in the kitchen."

"Dollarn-half, dollarn-half, dollarn-half, give me two," intoned the auctioneer from the second-hand store. By noon the crowd became a jam. Wagons backed up to the curb outside and departed heavily laden. In all directions people could be seen going away from the house, carrying small articles of furniture—a clock, a water pitcher, a towel rack. Every now and then old Miss Baker, who had gone below to see how things were progressing, returned with reports of the foray.

"Mrs. Heise bought the chenille portieres. Mister Ryer made a bid for your bed, but a man in a gray coat bid over him. It was knocked down for three dollars and a half. The German shoe-maker on the next block bought the stone pug dog. I saw our postman going away with a lot of the pictures. Zerkow has come, on my word! the rags-bottles-sacks man; he's buying lots; he bought all Doctor McTeague's gold tape and some of the instruments. Maria's there too. That dentist on the corner took the dental engine, and wanted to get the sign, the big gold tooth," and so on and so on. Cruelest of all, however, at least to Trina, was when Miss Baker herself began to buy, unable to resist a bargain. The last time she came up she carried a bundle of the gay tidies that used to hang over the chair backs.

"He offered them, three for a nickel," she explained to Trina, "and I thought I'd spend just a quarter. You don't mind, now, do you, Mrs. McTeague?"

"Why, no, of course not, Miss Baker," answered Trina, bravely.

"They'll look very pretty on some of my chairs," went on the little old dressmaker, innocently. "See." She spread one of them on a chair back for inspection. Trina's chin quivered.

"Oh, VERY pretty," she answered.

At length that dreadful day was over. The crowd dispersed. Even the auctioneer went at last, and as he closed the door with a bang, the reverberation that went through the suite gave evidence of its emptiness.

"Come," said Trina to the dentist, "let's go down and look—take a last look."

They went out of Miss Baker's room and descended to the floor below. On the stairs, however, they were met by Old Grannis. In his hands he carried a little package. Was it possible that he too had taken advantage of their misfortunes to join in the raid upon the suite?

"I went in," he began, timidly, "for—for a few moments. This"—he indicated the little package he carried—"this was put up. It was of no value but to you. I—I ventured to bid it in. I thought perhaps"—his hand went to his chin, "that you wouldn't mind; that—in fact, I bought it for you—as a present. Will you take it?" He handed the package to Trina and hurried on. Trina tore off the wrappings.

It was the framed photograph of McTeague and his wife in their wedding finery, the one that had been taken immediately after the marriage. It represented Trina sitting very erect in a rep armchair, holding her wedding bouquet straight before her, McTeague standing at her side, his left foot forward, one hand upon her shoulder, and the other thrust into the breast of his "Prince Albert" coat, in the attitude of a statue of a Secretary of State.

"Oh, it WAS good of him, it WAS good of him," cried Trina, her eyes filling again. "I had forgotten to put it away. Of course it was not for sale."

They went on down the stairs, and arriving at the door of the sitting-room, opened it and looked in. It was late in the afternoon, and there was just light enough for the dentist and his wife to see the results of that day of sale. Nothing was left, not even the carpet. It was a pillage, a devastation, the barrenness of a field after the passage of a swarm of locusts. The room had been picked and stripped till only the bare walls and floor remained. Here where they had been married, where the wedding supper had taken place, where Trina had bade farewell to her father and mother, here where she had spent those first few hard months of her married life, where afterward she had grown to be happy and contented, where she had passed the long hours of the afternoon at her work of whittling, and where she and her husband had spent so many evenings looking out of the window before the lamp was lit—here in what had been her home, nothing was left but echoes and the emptiness of complete desolation. Only one thing remained. On the wall between the windows, in its oval glass frame, preserved by some unknown and fearful process, a melancholy relic of a vanished happiness, unsold, neglected, and forgotten, a thing that nobody wanted, hung Trina's wedding bouquet.

CHAPTER 15

Then the grind began. It would have been easier for the McTeagues to have faced their misfortunes had they befallen them immediately after their marriage, when their love for each other was fresh and fine, and when they could have found a certain happiness in helping each other and sharing each other's privations. Trina, no doubt, loved her husband more than ever, in the sense that she felt she belonged to him. But McTeague's affection for his wife was dwindling a little every day—HAD been dwindling for a long time, in fact. He had become used to her by now. She was part of the order of the things with which he found himself surrounded. He saw nothing extraordinary about her; it was no longer a pleasure for him to kiss her and take her in his arms; she was merely his wife. He did not dislike her; he did not love her. She was his wife, that was all. But he sadly missed and regretted all those little animal comforts which in the old prosperous life Trina had managed to find for him. He missed the cabbage soups and steaming chocolate that Trina had taught him to like; he missed his good tobacco that Trina had educated him to prefer; he missed the Sunday afternoon walks that she had caused him to substitute in place of his nap in the operating chair; and he missed the bottled beer that she had induced him to drink in place of the steam beer from Frenna's. In the end he grew morose and sulky, and sometimes neglected to answer his wife when she spoke to him. Besides this, Trina's avarice was a perpetual annoyance to him. Oftentimes when a considerable alleviation of this unhappiness could have been obtained at the expense of a nickel or a dime, Trina refused the money with a pettishness that was exasperating.

"No, no," she would exclaim. "To ride to the park Sunday afternoon, that means ten cents, and I can't afford it."

"Let's walk there, then."

"I've got to work."

"But you've worked morning and afternoon every day this week."

"I don't care, I've got to work."

There had been a time when Trina had hated the idea of McTeague drinking steam beer as common and vulgar.

"Say, let's have a bottle of beer to-night. We haven't had a drop of beer in three weeks."

"We can't afford it. It's fifteen cents a bottle."

"But I haven't had a swallow of beer in three weeks."

"Drink STEAM beer, then. You've got a nickel. I gave you a quarter day before yesterday."

"But I don't like steam beer now."

It was so with everything. Unfortunately, Trina had cultivated tastes in McTeague which now could not be gratified. He had come to be very proud of his silk hat and "Prince Albert" coat, and liked to wear them on Sundays. Trina had made him sell both. He preferred "Yale mixture" in his pipe; Trina had made him come down to "Mastiff," a five-cent tobacco with which he was once contented, but now abhorred. He liked to wear clean cuffs; Trina allowed him a fresh pair on Sundays only. At first these deprivations angered McTeague. Then, all of a sudden, he slipped back into the old habits (that had been his before he knew Trina) with an ease that was surprising. Sundays he dined at the car conductors' coffee-joint once more, and spent the afternoon lying full length upon the bed, crop-full, stupid, warm, smoking his huge pipe, drinking his steam beer, and playing his six mournful tunes upon his concertina, dozing off to sleep towards four o'clock.

The sale of their furniture had, after paying the rent and outstanding bills, netted about a hundred and thirty dollars. Trina believed that the auctioneer from the second-hand store had swindled and cheated them and had made a great outcry to no effect. But she had arranged the affair with the auctioneer herself, and offset her disappointment in the matter of the sale by deceiving her husband as to the real amount of the returns. It was easy to lie to McTeague, who took everything for granted; and since the occasion of her trickery with the money that was to have been sent to her mother, Trina had found falsehood easier than ever.

"Seventy dollars is all the auctioneer gave me," she told her husband; "and after paying the balance due on the rent, and the grocer's bill, there's only fifty left."

"Only fifty?" murmured McTeague, wagging his head, "only fifty? Think of that."

"Only fifty," declared Trina. Afterwards she said to herself with a certain admiration for her cleverness:

"Couldn't save sixty dollars much easier than that," and she had added the hundred and thirty to the little hoard in the chamois-skin bag and brass match-box in the bottom of her trunk.

In these first months of their misfortunes the routine of the McTeagues was as follows: They rose at seven and breakfasted in their room, Trina cooking the very meagre meal on an oil stove. Immediately after breakfast Trina sat down to her work of whittling the Noah's ark animals, and McTeague took himself off to walk down town. He had by the greatest good luck secured a position with a manufacturer of surgical instruments, where his manual dexterity in the making of excavators, pluggers, and other dental contrivances stood him in fairly good stead. He lunched at a sailor's boarding-house near the water front, and in the afternoon worked till six. He was home at six-thirty, and he and Trina had supper together in the "ladies' dining parlor," an adjunct of the car conductors' coffee-joint. Trina, meanwhile, had worked at her whittling all day long, with but half an hour's interval for lunch, which she herself prepared upon the oil stove. In the evening they were both so tired that they were in no mood for conversation, and went to bed early, worn out, harried, nervous, and cross.

Trina was not quite so scrupulously tidy now as in the old days. At one time while whittling the Noah's ark animals she had worn gloves. She never wore them now. She still took pride in neatly combing and coiling her wonderful black hair, but as the days passed she found it more and more comfortable to work in her blue flannel wrapper. Whittlings and chips accumulated under the window where she did her work, and she was at no great pains to clear the air of the room vitiated by the fumes of the oil stove and heavy with the smell of cooking. It was not gay, that life. The room itself was not gay. The huge double bed sprawled over nearly a fourth of the available space; the angles of Trina's trunk and the washstand projected into the room from the walls, and barked shins and scraped elbows. Streaks and spots of the "non-poisonous" paint that Trina used were upon the walls and wood-work. However, in one corner of the room, next the window, monstrous, distorted, brilliant, shining with a light of its own, stood the dentist's sign, the enormous golden tooth, the tooth of a Brobdingnag.

One afternoon in September, about four months after the McTeagues had left their suite, Trina was at her work by the window. She had whittled some half-dozen sets of animals, and was now busy painting them and making the arks. Little pots of "non-poisonous" paint stood at her elbow on the table, together with a box of labels that read, "Made in France." Her huge clasp-knife was stuck into the under side of the table. She was now occupied solely with the brushes and the glue pot. She turned the little figures in her fingers with a wonderful lightness and deftness, painting the chickens

Naples yellow, the elephants blue gray, the horses Vandyke brown, adding a dot of Chinese white for the eyes and sticking in the ears and tail with a drop of glue. The animals once done, she put together and painted the arks, some dozen of them, all windows and no doors, each one opening only by a lid which was half the roof. She had all the work she could handle these days, for, from this time till a week before Christmas, Uncle Oelbermann could take as many "Noah's ark sets" as she could make.

Suddenly Trina paused in her work, looking expectantly toward the door. McTeague came in.

"Why, Mac," exclaimed Trina. "It's only three o'clock. What are you home so early for? Have they discharged you?"

"They've fired me," said McTeague, sitting down on the bed.

"Fired you! What for?"

"I don' know. Said the times were getting hard an' they had to let me go."

Trina let her paint-stained hands fall into her lap.

"OH!" she cried. "If we don't have the HARDEST luck of any two people I ever heard of. What can you do now? Is there another place like that where they make surgical instruments?"

"Huh? No, I don' know. There's three more."

"Well, you must try them right away. Go down there right now."

"Huh? Right now? No, I'm tired. I'll go down in the morning."

"Mac," cried Trina, in alarm, "what are you thinking of? You talk as though we were millionaires. You must go down this minute. You're losing money every second you sit there." She goaded the huge fellow to his feet again, thrust his hat into his hands, and pushed him out of the door, he obeying the while, docile and obedient as a big cart horse. He was on the stairs when she came running after him.

"Mac, they paid you off, didn't they, when they discharged you?"

"Yes."

"Then you must have some money. Give it to me."

The dentist heaved a shoulder uneasily.

"No, I don' want to."

"I've got to have that money. There's no more oil for the stove, and I must buy some more meal tickets to-night."